J R Giuliano is an octogenarian brother, husband of Audrey for 66 years, father of three daughters and a son, grandfather of nine ladies and five gentlemen, great grandfather of thirteen great grandsons, and seven great granddaughters. He's a friend, a curious entrepreneur, adventurer, watcher of sports, who enjoys reading, writing, nature, the outdoors, fishing in fresh water and the deep sea. He likes Italian food and enjoys cooking it, especially for groups of his large family. And, to travel anywhere learning about people, places, culture and food.

Dedicated to the people who gave me the most precious gifts of life and family.

Gerardo and Pellegrína (Santoro) Giuliano and to Audrey
(Holly-Smith) Giuliano.

JR Giuliano

THE ROCK IN OUR STORY

AUSTIN MACAULEY PUBLISHERS™

LONDON • CAMBRIDGE • NEW YORK • SHARJAH

Ordering Information
Quantity sales: Special discounts are available on quantity purchases by corporations, associations, and others. For details, contact the publisher at the address below.

Publisher's Cataloging-in-Publication data
Giuliano, JR
The Rock in Our Story

ISBN 9781685626259 (Paperback)
ISBN 9781685626266 (Hardback)
ISBN 9781685626280 (ePub e-book)
ISBN 9781685626273 (Audiobook)

Library of Congress Control Number: 2022923972

www.austinmacauley.com/us

First Published 2023
Austin Macauley Publishers LLC
40 Wall Street, 33rd Floor, Suite 3302
New York, NY 10005
USA

mail-usa@austinmacauley.com
+1 (646) 5125767

My parents rode in 'steerage' on the boat that left the Port of Naples on April 22 and arrived sixteen days later in 'Filadelfia' on May 6, 1921. They got married and settled in a small-town northwest of Philadelphia. There, Italian immigrants were directed to an area bordered by railroad tracks and a dead-end street, and that area became known as "Little Italy." I grew up with my parents, two brothers and two sisters among a half dozen Zias and Zios, scores of cousins, and hundreds of extended family and friends in that neighbourhood. Without that – nothing. So, thanks to my parents and siblings for their courage, hearts, spirit, and guidance. Thanks to my extended family, friends, and the old neighbourhood for the grit, experiences, and stories. And thanks to people I met along the route to adulthood – a few of them threads woven into the story I tell.

This represents at least ten rewrites and twice as many revisions – it's my first book. I didn't produce it by myself. Not by a long shot. Countless people were involved in this project long before I knew it would become a project or believed it could become a reality. Where to begin to acknowledge all of them! First, Audrey – mother of our four children, Terri, Karen, Audrey, and Jerry – grandmother to their fourteen children, and great grandmother to the twenty children that followed. She has been my rock for sixty-six years, my girlfriend for three years before that, and my best friend for six and a half decades. I can't repay or thank her enough for everything besides having accepted all the strange book characters that came to occupy our space and live with us rent-free throughout my writing journey. Thank you, Audrey.

For years, our daughter Terri told me a book existed in me. On birthdays, she gave me beautiful blank diaries, hoping, I suspected, that I would scribble something in them. I could have done better there. Then, one year she gave me a six-week course on how to write essays. I wrote a few of and she posted them on her blog. She never stopped reassuring me that I was capable. She read the first and last versions with enough of the right balance of criticism and enthusiasm for my work to convince me to try. Thank you, Terri.

Our granddaughter, Natalie, gifted me one Christmas with a challenge to write a memoir. She provided a list of questions that I answered in an unstructured, incorrectly punctuated, grammatically questionable manner. A dozen books were published. One copy sits in my closet as a silent reminder of why I never wrote a book before.

Thanks, and gratitude for William Greenleaf – the literary agent who read the original eighty-thousand words and responded the first time with thirty pages of notes and tips on the correct way to write a novel. The second time he read it, he underscored the importance of point of view, provided plenty of 'how to' guidance, and the encouragement to keep writing. Thank you, Bill.

When our granddaughter, Nicole, learned I was in the book-writing process, her unbridled excitement and eagerness towards it provided the catalyst that inspired me to see the project to the end. Thank you, Nicole. Our Grandson, Michael, an extraordinarily insatiable reader since he was a four-year-old, made notes on the margins of my almost final revision. "After you've clearly shown a scene, there's no reason to explain it at the end of the chapter. Instead, trust your reader to grasp the picture you've painted." He also redirected the ending to one more, I hope, satisfying conclusion. For your time and most valuable insight, many thanks, Michael. Michael's wife, Caroline LaBranti-Giuliano, photographer extraordinaire, designed and illustrated the cover for the fifth revision of my ninth rewrite. And this one, too. So, thank you, Caroline, for your motivating cheers from the side-lines and for your creative artistic talent demonstrated on the cover.

To my grandson, Marc, whose bright mind and generous gift of his time, created a Web Page, and guided me along the right path through social media. Thank you, Marc!

My thanks and gratitude extend to all the folks at Austin McCauley without whom this book might have remained thousands of words on stacks of paper in a tired-looking manuscript. From start to finish – everyone who touched this project made it better. I hope you find their work as praiseworthy as I have.

My occasional rookie fits of impatience landed mostly in the "in-boxes" of Jessica Bosak and Valerie Rose. Neither of them could have been more gracious, kind or understanding. Thank you, ladies, and Thank you all at Austin McCauley for breathing life into my dream.

Last, and nowhere near the least:
Dear Readers, please accept my heartfelt thanks for your investment in my book. No one can ever replace the time you spent reading it. I hope you found it worthwhile.

Introduction
Teenage Girl

I wished someone had told me, but no one did. Ever. My parents were too strict. They only let me out of the house to go to the market or to the river to wash clothes. So I didn't know what was happening when my body started to feel different. I was twelve years old—the oldest girl in my classroom. I was scared. Scared of what I saw and too afraid to ask anyone about it. None of the other girls I knew said anything strange was happening to them. Our teachers didn't talk about it. My parents didn't talk about it. Then I got lumps on my chest. I was embarrassed to be the only girl in class that had bumps on her chest. After that, I was shy—I tried to hide them. Whenever my mother and father were fighting, they said they would have been better off if I was never born. I cried myself to sleep when they said that.

I was almost fifteen when a boy I had seen in the neighborhood asked me what my name was. He said I was pretty. When he said that, I felt my body shiver, my face felt hot, and both my arms got goosebumps. He was eighteen. His name was Alessandro. I tried to see him from my window, and if no one was home, I went outside and stood there, hoping he would notice me. He was always nice to me.

One night, about six months after I first met Alessandro, I saw him outside my window after my parents went to bed. When he saw me, he waved for me to come outside. He touched my face and just stared into my eyes. I was shaking so much I couldn't stop. He put his arms around me, and I felt so warm and safe there. He laid down on the grass and asked me to come to lay with him. I wished someone would have warned me. Maybe then my life could have been worthwhile.

Chapter One
Sister Verona

Wars, lousy government, crime, corruption, and earthquakes impoverished the region I lived in, but I needed nothing in the world or wanted as a child or young adult. I was among the privileged, wealthy living in a valley town east of Naples in Southern Italy. My father was an extremely successful businessman who started his company when he was just a boy selling small local marble pieces he found as souvenirs for tourists. Before he was twenty years old, the demand for his souvenirs was so great he was encouraged to buy large quantities of marble directly from excavators to maximize his profits. Growing up, I was happy, proud, and filled with joy for all the things we could do and see in the world due to my father's success.

One Sunday morning, our family visited the Duomo of Milan—the fifth largest cathedral in the world, built in the city's center. Sculptors carved more than two thousand statues on the façade and four thousand more on the inside. When we entered, my father pointed to a sundial on the floor. He showed me the sunlight streaming in from a hole high in the wall providing a shadow beyond the dial to indicate the time. He said an astronomist placed it there in seventeen-sixty-eight and that it was so precise that people set their clocks and watches by it.

I stood mesmerized by the light shining through stained glass windows and the forty massive white marble columns that dwarfed me at its base and ended in arches eighty feet above me. Everything that touched my eyes took my breath away. Then I heard the bells—Gong. Gong. Gong. Eleven times—Mass was about to begin.

I sat with my family in one pew near the front of the main altar. We stood to watch the procession—at least a dozen altar boys followed by five priests slowly walked the aisle toward us. I smelled the incense—the ancient tradition used to purify any object touched by its smoke. The sights, sounds, and smells captivated me, and the nuns singing Gregorian Chant hypnotized me into self-examination. Then, I decided to dedicate my life to becoming a teaching nun and serving those less fortunate than I. Indeed, I was most grateful for my parents and all that was made possible for me through their sacrifices and hard work, but I felt it was my time to help others. I thought doing missionary or that type of work would enable me to carry out my intentions. When we got back home, I discussed my thoughts with my father.

"Papa, I want to become a missionary."

"A Missionary, huh?"

"Yes, Papa. I want to help people. There are so many poor and uneducated people I can help."

"You don't have to be a missionary to teach people or help them. You know that some missionaries go to distant, remote places. It won't be easy, maybe even impossible, for you to come home if you get homesick."

"I'm a big girl, Papa. If I go someplace far, I'm sure I'll get homesick—I'll miss all my family, but you've always said we must help people in need. No one in our family, at my school, or where we live is needy."

"But there are additional things you can do to help others—you can be a teacher or a nurse—you don't have to be a missionary, living in a faraway place, off in some remote jungle."

"Do all missionaries get sent to remote jungles?"

"Of course not, but they get assigned to places most in need of help."

"Then, maybe I'll get assigned to someplace in Italy."

"Maybe—that's the keyword. But, maybe not, is more likely."

"Papa, I've been thinking about this for a long time. It's what I want to do."

"Are you sure?"

"Yes, Papa, I'm very sure."

"I want you to follow your dream and do what your heart and conscience tell you. How about this? Let's go to the Convent in La Valle and talk with Mother Superior. Find out what you'd have to do and how to do it. If you agree with what she says, then I will stand behind your decision."

I jumped into his arms, hugged him, and spread my kissy thanks all over his face. He didn't seem to mind that a bit. I knew he wasn't enamored of my idea, but I was sure he'd never stand in my way if he believed in my mission.

He always said, "Parents should provide their children with wings to soar above the crowd and to fly where they must. We must also give them anchors to keep them attached to their home and secured in the values they learned there". I loved my father dearly and treasured his wisdom and advice.

Mother Superior agreed to meet with my parents to discuss my life in a missionary role. She was a little surprised to see my whole family show up at the door.

"I wasn't expecting to meet your entire family, Signore Verona—Signora—but I'm happy to meet you all. It shows me that all of you are interested in Maria's future."

"Yes, Reverend Mother, we are a family that cares deeply about each other."

"I can tell that by your actions."

"Maria would like to be a missionary—she feels strongly about dedicating her life to the service of others."

"Is this true, Maria?"

"Yes, Reverend Mother. I've read a lot about missionaries and the work they do. I think I can do that kind of work."

"I think your family has been very fortunate—well educated, well-traveled, and financially secure. That's very different from most of the population."

"Yes, Reverend Mother. My father's hard work and business have afforded us that luxury, and we have all benefitted from my mother's tireless support of his ethic and values, as well as her guiding us children personally, socially, academically, and spiritually."

"Well, that's quite a testimony of their excellent work, and it speaks well of your maturity and sophistication, young lady."

"Thank you."

"My question, though, is how do you suppose you can trade all that you have in exchange for a life without it?"

"I don't think I can truthfully answer that question. I don't know what I might believe in the future. But now, I think others can benefit from my life's experiences."

Reverend Mother turned to my parents. "Indeed, any organization, especially those doing missionary work, would welcome your child with open arms." I blushed when she said that and looked up at my father to see his reaction. Having seen the same look and smirk at home, when one of us kids got a little too self-assured, his eyes said, "Careful young lady (or man to my brothers), don't let your head outgrow your hat."

"Reverend Mother—would it be an imposition to ask to meet with you again in two weeks? There's a lot to think about and discuss with Maria and among the family. By then, we should have a more precise understanding of how to move forward."

"Of course. If you come back in two weeks, I will also have a much better idea of how I can help.'

During the two weeks between our visits to the Convent, my father asked me the same question fifty times. "Are you sure? Are you sure? Are you sure?" Although I assured him that I was every time he asked—I started to wonder if I did have what it took to go anywhere in the world if I were assigned to do so.

Chapter Two
Sister Verona
A Teenage Girl, Maria Della Notte

Mother Superior greeted us at the door with open, welcoming arms, then led us into the dining hall. Mealtime was hours away, and the dining hall had the chairs and space to accommodate my family. Mother Superior was not as surprised as the first time our whole gang showed up. After a few minutes of exchanging greetings and pleasantries, Mother Superior stood excusing herself to my sisters. She said, "If you all don't mind sitting here for fifteen minutes, I'd like to show your parents around."

With that, she turned and started walking with my father, mother, and me behind her. While she pointed out parts of the building, she paused to show us teachers, teaching while students sat quietly, listening. Then she took us outside to see children playing—boys with boys and girls with girls. She explained the duties and responsibilities of the children and her staff, and her own. She appeared heartbroken to say, "Sisters of Mercy is overcrowded, and very few young nuns are available to help."

Before we reached the dining hall, she stopped, faced both my parents, and said, "You must be very proud of Maria. When she saw the children, the look in her eyes spoke volumes of her love and compassion for them. But, unfortunately, none of the children volunteered to be here—some have been battered and abused—others abandoned and too young to fend for themselves. Maria, I know you want to be a missionary, so forgive me for even asking— would you consider becoming a nun and working with us, here?"

I wanted to scream, yes, but I looked at my father to gauge his reaction. He looked pleased, and I wasn't the least bit surprised. Working at the Convent presented an opportunity to satisfy my wish to serve and my father's hope to have me stay in my own country.

"When would you need me to start, Mother?"

"Sooner than immediately, if I had my way."

"What will she need, Reverend Mother?" my father asked.

"Nothing. We will teach Maria what she needs to know to become a nun. She will have some responsibilities and duties to perform while she is in training. We make our own clothing and food. The sharecroppers who raise the animals and tend the orchards and gardens surrounding the property provide our cooking needs. If she wants to bring anything, I would suggest bringing her favorite books."

It was not easy for me to say goodbye to my family, and bidding farewell to me was not my father's happiest moment either. Each in their turn, my brothers, sisters, and mother hugged me, wished me well, and kissed me goodbye that day in the vestibule at Sisters of Mercy. My father was last in line. His eyes were as moist as my throat was dry. He hugged me tightly and whispered, " God bless you, Maria. Fly as high as your heart will take you. I love you. Arrivederci."

My transition away from family and fortune into a life of minimalism and service was less complicated than I thought. My mother taught me to find comfort in everyday household chores like laundering, cooking, sewing, crocheting, and knitting. Despite our ability to buy whatever we needed or have someone else do it or make it for us, she always said, "You never know what the future will bring—it's a good idea to be self-sufficient."

My mother's guidance in those matters helped me adjust to leaving our high-energy family always on the go to a simpler, regimented communal life. The Reverend Mother was pleased with my established talents and eagerness to help lighten her burden. Not having to teach me housekeeping things, she more quickly guided me to my religious and teaching requirements and goals and set me free to accomplish them.

I was happy with my decision to join Mother Superior. Perhaps others would be bored with the daily routine's sameness—there was a time to wake up, say morning prayers, attend mass, teach, satisfy the children's physical, mental, and spiritual needs—and satisfy our own, but I was never bored. I loved the children and the challenges of having them learn new things. My goal was to teach—not only to fulfill my desire to teach but also to capture my students' imaginations, inspire them, and have them learn because that's what they needed. It was heart-wrenching to see children come—not knowing who left them here or why, and I never got used to seeing them go.

However, attaching to the children was much easier for me than detaching from them. Few of our resident children were adopted or reclaimed by parents or relatives when situations improved sufficiently to have them back. More often than not, especially the boys, went out on their own when they reached their sixteenth birthdays. Even after eight years, no child ever left the Convent without having my tears following them.

Thursday, 27 September 1923
Around Midnight East Village,
La Valle, Southern Italy

"Get out!

"But—"

"Get out now!"

"Where's momma?"

"She has nothing to say to you."

"I want to talk to momma."

"Can't you hear your father? You, and that lazy good for nothing Alessandro you hang around with."

"Momma. I love him."

"Love. What do you know about love? You thought that so-called boyfriend loved you? You're not even old enough to have a boyfriend."

"You just turned seventeen when you married, papa."

Slap! "We're dirt farmers in this godforsaken place, working like dogs to keep food on the table. And you. You act like you're some queen or something like we don't need you to help out around here. We tried to teach you how to grow up—be responsible—- but you have no respect for anyone but yourself. You're an ungrateful, selfish little brat. Get out. And don't come back."

Slap!

I bit my lip at the sound of her palm striking my cheek. The blood I tasted dripped across my tongue and stopped at the swallow in my parched throat. My face felt the sting of a hundred bees picking at the fire burning on my face. My mother's slap hurt, but the pain of being disowned felt so much worse.

"Why are you waiting? Take what's yours and get out of here. Now!"

I tried to swallow, but the taste of salty tears and drying blood made me gag. I had to get out. I was afraid to stay and even more afraid to leave. I had nowhere to go and no one to help get me there. So, I dressed quickly, and, in my haste, I slipped barefoot into my brother's work shoes, picked up my baby and all that mattered, and stormed out the door.

Groping through the darkness, I passed barely visible cows, goats, and chickens before reaching grain fields and apple orchards. I knew there was a convent somewhere, but I had to make it through the woods in front of me to get there. I moved as quickly as I could, but the oversized shoes, and the bundle I was carrying, slowed me. My heart pounded at the sound of every twig I stepped on, sending animals scurrying and birds squawking—all of it adding more fear to my already trembling body. My mouth was so dry I couldn't produce a drop of spit to dampen my parched throat.

I don't know how much time passed while I was tripping on stumps, slogging through wet gullies, and bending around trees thinking I was traveling in a straight line—it seemed like hours until I arrived at the very rock I touched soon after I entered the woods. I strolled around the rock, looking in all directions for a way forward. Then, when I got three-quarters around, I saw the light in the distance and aimed for it. There were hills along the way, and sometimes, I had to make adjustments at the bottom. When the light disappeared, I backed up to where I could see the glow, then lined up a series of trees to follow straight down the hill and up the next hill when I could see the light again.

I was exhausted, cold, and sweaty. The light glowed brighter as the night grew darker. At last, I could see a stone building—the Convent—gray and cold looking, not at all inviting. A black, iron fence with a gate opened to a cobblestone path leading to the front door. I tip-toed my way toward a large, gray rock, and crouched behind it, then scanned the area for signs of anyone who might try to stop me from reaching the gate. Seeing no one, I strolled, quietly, to the gate and placed my bundle on the grass beneath a sign: Sisters of Mercy. Convent. School.

I rested my nose against my baby's cheek, folded my swaddled infant into my arms, and with my palms touching and fingers pointed skyward—I prayed.

"Dear God, please forgive me. I have sinned against the laws of purity, and I am so very, very sorry. My sin has embarrassed me. I have shamed my parents. The villagers are shunning me, and the only man I have ever loved—the father of my child—has abandoned me. I failed in my obligations to everyone, but please, Lord, please don't punish my innocent baby for my sins. Please be with her in her times of need. Please give her a healthy body and an active mind. Give her strength to overcome life's hardships and temptations—whatever they may be. Please help her be kind—to find goodness in herself and goodness in the world—and be happy. Lord, grant her love and guide her only toward those who will love her in return. Thank you, Lord. Amen."

I kissed my baby's cheeks, her lips, the top of her head, and, through the blanket, I kissed her arms, her legs, and her feet. Then, conceived in love beyond my imagination, I slowly and gently placed my newborn baby on the grass in front of the gate. I stood up, turned, and without a backward glance, I stumbled my way back under cover of trees, dropping my tears into the blackness.

The Same Day, 5 a.m.
Front Gate, Sisters of Mercy

I loved getting outside as soon as possible to feed the birds and watch the rabbits and squirrels as they scrounged for the bread I dropped, especially in the autumn. I woke early, expecting the day to unwind the same as always. As always, the air was fresh and clean this day, inviting all the sweet fragrances that sprung from our herb garden, the fig and apple orchards, the vegetable gardens, the fields of wildflowers, and the vineyards that shared the valley with us. Dewdrops on leaves that glistened in the sun—all simple things—free for the taking.

Of course, I missed my family, but I treasured nothing more than the sounds of life. Birds chirped, little animals scampered—it was a slice of heaven for me. I loved the sweet fragrances of flowers on the wind, and homemade bread baking in the oven, to see sunrises, sunsets, rainbows, and feel warm summer rain on my lips—the sense of life all around me makes me happy. I couldn't wait to get outside.

I put an ample supply of bread pieces in my apron and skipped my way to the front door singing and humming merrily on my way. I heard a muffled unfamiliar sound coming from someplace near the front gate and strolled toward the noise sending the birds into the air and the rabbits and squirrels scampering away. I gulped at the sight of a tiny face staring up at me, gasping for breath and wordlessly pleading for me to take her into my arms. My heart sank at the thought of this poor child left alone and the helpless, hopeless person who left it—perhaps to die.

I knelt, picked up the child, and held her close against my chest. When she quieted, I opened the swaddle and found a slightly damp white cloth covering her bottom. Judging from that, I assumed she hadn't been there for more than a few hours. There was nothing on or near her to suggest where she came from, who left her, or why. Clutching her tightly, I ran back inside to present her to Mother Superior. I had no idea how my life would change after that. The excitement in my calling voice pushed through the early morning light and into the Convent.

"Vieni presto Madre! Come quickly, Mother—I found this beautiful baby girl lying on the grass in front of the gate."

Mother Superior approached me and crossed herself: "In the name of the Father, and the Son, and of the Holy Spirit, Amen. How can we keep another child in this overcrowded, understaffed, underfunded place?" she muttered Then, steeling herself against all negative thoughts about the complex challenges ahead, she looked sadly at the baby cradled in my arms.

"Bring her inside," ordered Mother Superior, "Bathe her—see if she will take from the Wet Nurse—otherwise, feed her with a bottle."

"Si Madre," I replied.

"This child is not more than two days old. Have you found any papers or instructions with her? Names? Anything?"

"No, Madre."

"As soon as you have her settled, please file the necessary papers required to document this."

"Si Madre. What shall I use for her name and birth date?"

"She came to us in the night, and you found her. We shall name her Maria Della Notte. Use 25 September 1923 for her birthdate. I want you to take full responsibility for her—as if you were her real mother."

"Si Madre—Grazie," I said nervously, then hurried away to help Baby Maria Della Notte begin her new life.

Chapter Three
Maria Della Notte
Teaching Me

There's not much I can say about my thoughts and feelings before I was four or five years old. I didn't know I was an orphan. I didn't even know what an orphan was. I lived in a place where other boys and girls lived. That's not different than any newborn arriving at a home with brothers and sisters already living there. The nuns were like parents. They satisfied our physical needs and nurtured us in other ways to help us get along in the world. While I was there, children of various young ages came and left the orphanage. I didn't know why that was, and no one said. The older children didn't talk much about where they came from, why, or how they arrived. No one claimed to be an orphan, and no one said we were, and I never thought to ask. If some of the older kids experienced lives with parents and siblings, I never knew it—they didn't talk about that.

Although there were not a lot of outsiders traipsing through our building, there were a few. Besides the eight nuns, a priest lived in a small addition attached to the Convent. The Pastor of the village parish, and a few farmhands, came by weekly. The Pastor came to get news about operations, offer advice, suggestions, and provide whatever money, food, or assistance he received through his parishioners. The farmhands delivered the fruit, produce, and by-products like milk, cheese, and meats, from the animals they raised. Occasionally, Signore Lucci, the man who owned the land surrounding us, came by for reasons not always clear to me, but Mother Superior was always pleased to greet him. I remember a few times he came with a child who stayed after he left. Those times, Signore Federico Lucci and the Mother Superior chatted in the vestibule, or her office, in tones too low for anyone to hear.

My formal education began when I turned five years old. At that point, I had to forfeit my freewheeling spirit to make way for the rules and the strict discipline enforced in my new learning environment. I learned religion, math, reading, writing, and, eventually, all the things I would need to know to become a nun or a mother. There were no other choices for me, in that place, at that time. I was an intelligent, happy child who liked every subject presented to me. I loved to learn new things and enjoyed every minute Sister Verona spent teaching me.

Often, after the school day ended, and during summers, we strolled hand in hand along the dirt path that wound its way through fields of wildflowers. She always picked a few and identified them for me. "This one is Jasmine—that one is called Aster—the purple one is Periwinkle. This blue one, and the white one with pink inside, are both Cornflower." She explained Tarasco (dandelion)—Fungi (mushrooms)—Cicoria (chicory, and an assortment of spices and herbs which, she told me, "are safe, and very good to eat."

Sometimes, we finished our strolls in the orchards where peach, pear, apple, and fig trees were spread across ten acres of fertile land on rolling hills. There were twelve more acres planted at orchards end—row after row of grapevines, with clusters of purple, plump, sweet, and very juicy, grapes hanging from wires that stretched across a long distance the length of a soccer field. First, sister Verona taught me about the nutritional benefits of fruits and vegetables—and figs and grapes. Later, she explained how factories made jellies, jams, and select wines for the exquisite tastes of people worldwide. Then, as the sun crawled its way down on the backsides of faraway mountain tops, Sister Verona called my attention to the long shadows cast across such a beautiful landscape. She always spoke lovingly about our land, our valley, and our country. But, Sister Verona also sparked my interest in a world beyond LaValle. Whatever she taught, I was eager to learn.

"Please, Sister," I begged, "please tell me about other, faraway, places—about the people who live there."

She was always happy to show me pictures, read stories to me, tell me about the places she'd been and the people she'd met. My eyes wandered into their dreamy look whenever Sister Verona spoke of ancient Roman times—Soldiers on Chariots—the Colosseum—Vatican—Sistine Chapel, and the years Michelangelo spent, on his back, painting his masterpiece on its famous, frescoed ceiling. She told me about Firenze and its importance to the world—

mainly, from the fourteenth to the sixteenth centuries—she talked about the Medici families and nobilities that shaped the country—and the world.

She told me about the time her parents took her to Austria when she was a child. I was puzzled hearing about the trains, buses, and boats that took Sister Verona from place to place—I had never seen or ridden on any of those things. But Sister Verona disregarded my bewildered looks and told me stories about the beautiful city of Salzburg and Mozart.

"He played piano, and composed music, *himself*, when he was your age," she said.

I didn't hesitate to ask, "Will you please teach me how to play the piano—please, Sister—please?"

"Yes, Principessa—I will teach you how to play the piano."

And so she did.

Black and white. Those are the colors that come to mind when I conjure my earliest memories of life in the orphanage. Nuns wear those colors and Habits to symbolize their dedication to God's service and simplicity. Black and white. Simple—just like the rules and regulations that governed our existence. There were no gray areas when it came to expectations, duties, responsibilities, or accountability. We did what we were told. Clanging pots and scurrying are also images of my early life. The nuns were always busy doing something, and they made sure we were never left to laze around.

"Idle hands are the devil's workshop."

There was no way any of us kids were going to enter the devil's workshop. That was a scary thought. Whatever free time we had, was after our scheduled chores cleaning the mealtime messes, doing our homework, scrubbing the floors, washing windows, polishing doorknobs, making the beds, emptying the trash, etc.

I can still feel the warmth of dying embers and gray ashes and smell it mixed with bread baking in clay pots over an open fire. And when I close my eyes, I can see the dark wood on the floors, stairs, railings, and halfway up to the ceiling, and the bunk beds lined up one atop another foot to foot against walls on both sides. I see a large round stained glass window, too high to reach, filtering sun and moon creating rays of dim yellow light coming to rest upon the hallway floor and the oversized sinks, and the bell in the bell tower, and the dank cellar through its musty smell. My early childhood memories are alive in those sights and smells.

Sister Verona was my best friend. Feeling folded in her arms and wrapped in her love has never left me. Maybe that bond started with our first meeting when she picked me up from the grass—a bond she strengthened by all the love and care she gave me for as long as I can remember. I didn't realize it then, but I know I learned something every time I was in her presence. She never preached, and she never stopped teaching me something. Her voice was soft and soothing—never harsh and demanding. Her face was like that, too—small, quiet, and smooth with no trace of lines or wrinkles.

Sister Verona was pretty, and her kindness made her more so. Her nose was straight, lips full, cheekbones high, and her eyes were wide-set, chestnut was "the color of my hair," she told me. I didn't know the color of her hair because her headpiece covered it. She called me Principessa—Little Princess. I felt special when she called me that.

I must have been four or five years old when she began teaching me how to bake. The thing I remember most about that was the mess I made of myself.

"Will you help me make the bread today, Principessa?"

"I don't know how."

"It's easy—I'll show you. We'll need some flour, salt, warm water, and yeast."

She placed a chair in front of the cabinets holding the flour, yeast, and salt and asked me to get them and take them to the table. Meanwhile, she got the mixing bowl, warmed some water, and placed a giant board on the table where we would make the dough.

"First, we have to dust the board with some flour—you can do that."

"How much flour do I need?"

"Just put some in the cup of your hand, and spread it on top of the board."

I tried to do as she instructed, but I left traces of flour past the edges of the board, on the floor, and my floured handprints streaked across the top of my blouse. I don't think she noticed because she didn't mention it.

"OK. Good. Hold your hands together and make a cup. I'm going to fill your hands with flour, and you can drop it into the bowl."

I tried harder not to spill any flour, but I stretched my arms straight to reach the center of the bowl, and a little flour dropped from the backside of my cupped hands. Sister Verona didn't notice that, either. She handed me a wooden spoon after she let me add the salt and yeast and asked me to start stirring it together.

"Well done! Now we'll add the water and stir some more."

She couldn't help noticing the bowl tipping over as I started to stir—she forgot to tell me I had to hold the bowl with one hand while mixing with the other.

"I'm sorry."

"That's OK—I should have held the bowl for you. So, I'll hold the bowl and you try again."

I stirred and folded the ingredients for a minute or so before it got too heavy for me to keep turning. Then Sister Verona took over. When she was about halfway through, she asked if I wanted to try. This time she held the bowl with both hands, and I stood on a stool, looked into the center of the bowl, and tried to continue stirring the forming ball. It was a sticky mess that made it challenging for me to yank the wooden spoon from, but it loosened its grip enough to let it out and splat across my blouse and join the flour already there. Sister Verona coaxed the embarrassment out of my mind when she laughed hardily and said, "Principessa—that's funny. The same thing happened to me the first time I helped my mother make bread."

I felt better when she assured me I wasn't the only one who made that mistake but, whenever she spoke of her mother, I couldn't help feeling cheated. I didn't have a mother.

"Principessa—come on. First, we have to cover the dough and let it rise. That will take about two hours. Then, let's go outside until it's time to finish the bread."

I loved outside—It was the place we both enjoyed most, and where she wove her stories into my life, and where she made me see the beauty in nature—where she brought fables to reality and poked my imagination to create an exciting world for me. Sister Verona called the sizeable gray stone on the edge of a small meadow The Story Rock. She must have told me hundreds of stories on that rock, capturing my attention with the first one—not because the story kept me spellbound, but rather the way she introduced it to me. Then, she took my hand, helped me to the top of the rock, and we both sat.

"Look all around, Principessa, and tell me what you see."

"I see flowers in the meadow."

"Good. What else do you see?"

"Apple trees."

"Close your eyes. I want you to remember the last time you ate an apple. Do you remember that?"

"Yes, Sister. I ate an apple yesterday at lunch."

"Keep your eyes closed, and imagine you just took a big bite. Can you feel the juice squirting past the corners of your mouth?"

"I remember that from yesterday."

"Good. Now I want you to hold the apple to your nose and smell it—can you smell it?"

"Yes, Sister. I can smell it. I can almost taste it."

"Was that fun?"

"Yes."

"Open your eyes and look around again. Tell me what else you see."

"More apple trees."

"Stand up—let's try again. Do you see anything else besides apple trees?"

"I can see a cow."

"That's good. Now, look up at the sky. What color is it?"

She asked the questions to plant the seeds in my memory for the sights, sounds, smells, tastes, and textures of all that surrounded me. She promised that, if I didn't discourage them, the seeds would grow into perfect friends that lived in my mind and that I could take them anywhere and anytime—especially if I were lonely and needed company.

"Let's go, Principessa—it's time to bake the bread."

We went back inside, put some flour on the board, and plopped the bread dough on it. Sister Verona held my hand, guiding the small sharp knife I used to carve a few cuts into the loaf. She sprinkled a little cornmeal on a flat stone and placed the dough on top of that. Then she put the flat rock to fit into three metal hangers in the center of the fireplace. It was fun to watch the fire licking at the bottom of the stone as the fire turned the yellow/tan blob of dough into an ever-expanding, golden-brown shell. Next, sister Verona placed a clay bowl full of water near the embers—she said the steam would help make the bread crusty. It did. Now, the thought of hot bread baking over an open fire filling the air with its essence is all I need to take me back to that moment.

I loved Sister Verona. Whenever possible, we went outside together. We held hands and walked through orchards and gardens where she always paused to tell me about the fruit and vegetables, the trees and the flowers—what was planted and what grew wild—what was good to eat, and what to avoid. She spoke about the many varieties of mushrooms—some delicacies and some death sentences.

I remember scrunching my nose when I saw the inside of the fig for the first time. Sister Verona asked me to notice its color and pattern, feel its texture, and savor its sweetness. Then, with her finger, she traced the inside: "Look, Principessa, it's art hidden in a bit of fruit." I remember it well. I don't know how much time we spent on our Story Rock or in the gardens, nor can I begin to count the stories she told me—the things she taught me—how to speak, read, write, sit up straight, walk tall, tie my shoes, sew, cook, set the table—and to imagine all that's good in the universe. Then, as I got older and stressed or antsy about something, she'd say, "Principessa, don't worry so much—you hear too much noise, go to your quiet place and pray."

"I tried that—it doesn't work—anyway, prayer doesn't change anything for me."

"Maybe it just changes people—and people change things. Or maybe, it's just the silence you need. You can call it relaxation, or meditation, or call it anything you like—I call it prayer."

I didn't realize the depth of her impression on me or how much she influenced my behavior when we were together at the orphanage, but I came to understand it many times as I grew older.

Whenever time allowed, Sister Verona held my hand and walked with me through the acres of fields, and farms, that bordered the Convent. She always stopped us at the gardens, vineyards, and orchards for a while, long enough to teach me something. Sometimes we stayed for just a few minutes to breathe in various fruit trees and wildflowers. But, she never failed to ask, "Close your eyes, Maria—what do you smell?"—see, hear, taste, or feel. Sister Verona was more of a tour guide than a teller of tales, encouraging me to be part of every story she ever told.

"Principessa. You know what dandelion greens smell like—right?"

"Yes. We eat greens in salad sometimes. I love them."

"Well, in Germany, some people eat greens they call Rapunzel. That's what our story will be about today. Are you ready?"

I closed my eyes, and imagined Rapunzel tasting like dandelion greens, and waited for Sister Verona to continue.

"Once upon a time, there was a husband and wife who wanted so much to have a child. For a long time, they waited, and no child came to them. They lived in a small, gray stone house, surrounded by beautiful vegetable and flower gardens—just like the ones near us."

It was easy for me to conjure up the surroundings—the one she described was so much like ours.

"One day, she looked out the window and noticed a bed planted with the most beautiful garden greens she ever saw. It was Rapunzel—the one thing the lady liked most to eat. Each time she looked at it, she craved it more. The husband knew she was getting sick because she was so hungry for the Rapunzel, but they were both afraid to go near the gardens because a wicked witch owned them. Then, one day, the lady told her husband she would die if she didn't eat some Rapunzel very soon."

Sister Verona kept me in my familiar surroundings and wholly engrossed in every turn in every story she ever told. She described in detail the beautiful Princess and how the Prince climbed up her golden braids to rescue her in the story about Rapunzel. I could taste the perfectly ripened, mouth-watering juicy plums when she told me about Prunella. I felt terrible for the hungry fox when he failed to reach the grapes after trying again and again.

Besides her many books, Sister Verona had an extensive collection of magazines, travel brochures, old newspapers, postcards, and souvenirs—most of them portrayed and described the various places she had traveled with her family. She often used one of those articles to illustrate people, places, and things I had never seen before. Sister Verona wrapped my entire world in her heart, tied a beautiful bow on it, and kept that in her mind. I loved her so much.

Chapter Four
Maria
Discoveries

As I grew older, Sister Verona changed her stories from Handsome Princes, Powerful Kings, Beautiful Princesses, and Lovely Queens to the world of travel. Her stories became about trains and steamships, snow-capped mountains and deep blue oceans, cities, towns, artists, and musicians—real people, places, and things she showed me pictures of and placed them in my mind's eye.

"This is an automobile, Maria. See. It is metal, glass rubber, leather, and many other things."

She always took the time to explain what she thought I should know—especially when it was relevant to the story she was telling.

"The wheels on this automobile are made of rubber. Our erasures and rubber tires come from the same material—it's a milky-like liquid found in the barks of trees mostly grown in Brazil."

Sometimes I got impatient waiting to learn more about the automobile while she redirected our attention to her side story—about rubber in this case.

"It takes six hours to drain the liquid from the tree. It's called latex. In the early days, people would dip their feet in the latex and allow them to dry. After several dips and dryings, they could peel a shoe from their feet. Next, they smoked their new rubber shoes to harden them. Can you imagine that?"

She asked me to smell an erasure and my belt.

"Try to remember what rubber and leather look and smell like."

When I assured her that I would remember, she continued her story.

"OK, close your eyes—let's pretend to walk over to the automobile I just showed you. We are now standing in front of the back wheels. Stoop down and feel the rubber tires. Can you smell the rubber? Now stand up—we're going to sit down inside—I'll hold the door open for you. Keep your eyes closed. You'll have to step up high to get in. Can you smell the leather upholstery?"

When she felt my imagination held strong images of transportation systems, and when my senses could feel the roads, taste the air, hear the birds, and touch the people, she announced that I was ready to take a trip with her.

"You're ready, Principessa. Next Sunday afternoon, we're going to take a trip to Rome. We'll meet at our Story Rock—I should say the Train Platform."

I was anxious to make the imaginary trip, so I arrived at our Story Rock that Sunday almost thirty minutes before she did. I closed my eyes and placed myself on the train platform waiting for Sister Verona.

"Hello Principessa—were you waiting long?"

"Not so long. I closed my eyes so I could wait for you on the platform."

"This Train step is higher than the one into the automobile—I'll help you up. Did you see all the people waiting to get on this train?"

"Yes, I did. I wonder where all those people are going?"

"I don't know. I'm sure some will get off before we get to Rome."

"How long will it take to get there?"

"Oh—about two hours. You can look out the window and watch the scenery change once we get out of the station. How do you feel—are you too warm?"

"Yes, I feel hot."

"It's warm today and hot in here because there are so many people on the train. Can you feel the train moving?"

"Are we going fast?"

"Not yet. We're just leaving the train station. What can you see? What do you smell?"

"I see lots of people standing up. Close together. And I smell salami."

"There are lots of people standing. They are holding onto straps attached to a pole that runs the whole length of the train car."

"Why?"

"So, they don't fall when the train bounces side to side. Do you see that man wearing blue shirt and black trousers? I think he has a salami sandwich in the brown paper bag he's holding."

That was the first of many big imaginary trips I took with Sister Verona, and it was a great one.

"Let's sit down across the road—next to that olive tree, Principessa. You must be getting tired."

"My feet are burning."

"Hmm. You should have kept your shoes on. We talked about how hot the cobblestone streets were. And you know very well how hot the midday sun can sometimes be."

"What else is near the olive tree?"

"Can you see the vineyard off in the distance? It's like the one near the Convent."

"No. I can't see it."

"Look way past the olive tree—on the right side in the distance. Can you see all the clumps of grapes hanging from the wires?"

"Yes. Yes. I can see the vineyard now."

"Can you smell the grapes in the air?"

"Yes. I'm going to pinch the juice out of those purple grapes—they look ripe and juicy."

"I hope you're going to pinch them with your teeth and swallow the juice. It would be a waste and a shame to pinch the juice and let it fall to the ground."

"OK. I did it. I put one great big fat grape in my mouth and chewed it."

"How did it taste?"

"Very sweet!"

"Was it warm?"

"Yes. It was warm and juicy."

After we sat for a while and I pretended to eat a few more grapes, we continued our walk until we found ourselves on the side streets of Rome.

"Look at all the people here, Principessa. What do they look like to you?"

"They look dressed up?"

"It's Sunday—maybe they're all dressed up for church."

"Are they all going to church?"

"No. I'm sure lots of them are visitors—like us—here to visit the Vatican. Look over there—can you see that little old lady sitting on the sidewalk?"

"What does she look like?"

"She looks old. Like Mother Superior but older. She's wearing a long black dress, black stockings, and black shoes. She has a black scarf on her head, and it's tied in a knot under her chin. Her face is wrinkled. Her head is resting on her hands—palm to palm as if she's praying. There are four little children—also in dark clothing—two sitting on each side of her."

"Why is she sitting there?"

"She must be destitute—she's begging for God or anyone else to help her feed her hungry children."

"Is anyone helping her?"

"No one that I can see. Some are making fun of that poor lady."

"Will anyone help?"

"I don't know."

"Not even God?"

"I don't know that either."

One day, like so many others, we were wandering in the orchards and through the flower gardens, and, as I passed them, I remarked:

"I love the sweet taste of figs."—"I love to see crystal clear dewdrops on ripe, red tomatoes."—"I love the smell of wildflowers."

"No, Principessa. You appreciate them, enjoy those things, and like them quite a lot, but you don't love them. You can only love yourself or other people."

"What do you mean?"

"I can't explain it properly. I like all the same things you do, but I love you—and that's very different."

"You mean—you like me more than you like how figs taste."

"Of course, I do, and I'm sure you like me more, too. But when I think about you, or other people I am especially fond of, I get a different feeling than when I think about things. There are no things that I can care for as much as I care for you. Nothing. You fill my heart with happiness."

"You told me you were happiest when we were here, together, in the orchards with everything that grows, and looks pretty, and smells nice."

"Yes. I am always delighted when I'm here with you."

"Would you be just as happy if you were alone here?"

"Maybe, you can answer your question—are you happier to be here when you're alone?"

"No. I don't think so."

"Do you know why?"

"I'm not sure."

34

"It's the human connection, Principessa. You and I can do so much more than you and things—or I, and things. We can share all our senses with other human beings. Things don't have senses or feelings to share with us. Do you understand?"

"I know they can't hear, see, touch, or taste, but sometimes, I think things like flowers, and birds, talk to me."

"Sure. That happens to me, too. But, mostly, when I am still and quiet—when I clear my mind from all distraction and listen carefully to the voice that lives inside me—telling me everything will be OK."

"Is that when you love birds—or flowers?"

"No, Principessa. That's when I love myself."

"How do I know if I love myself?"

"That takes a while but, if you wanted, you could practice by taking the steps that will lead you to love yourself."

"What steps?"

"Be kind—thoughtful and considerate. Be mindful of others' feelings."

"When will I know I if love myself, or some other person—besides you?"

"You'll know, Principessa. You'll know."

"When will I know, Sister—how old do I have to be?"

"Hmm. That may be the most challenging question you have ever asked. That's a great one, and I'll do my best to answer it, but it's complicated. I told you I love myself when I relax, stay still, quiet, and listen to the voice inside me that says everything will be alright."

"How long do you have to be still and quiet before the voice talks to you?"

"You have to be patient, Principessa. That's like everything else. For me, the more I practice, the easier it becomes, and the less time it takes to find reasons to love myself."

"In religion class, doesn't the Bible say, "Love your neighbor as yourself?""

"Yes."

"Doesn't that mean I already love myself?"

"What it really means is that you can't love someone else until you love yourself. If you don't have a love for yourself, then it's impossible to give love that you don't have. Think of it like this: You eat when you're hungry and drink when you're thirsty. You flee from danger and never hurt yourself intentionally. It makes you happy when someone takes an interest in you—tells you a nice story, or gives you a compliment. And when you're sad, you always feel better when someone comforts you. So caring for yourself and accepting the goodness of others is loving yourself. Doing the same for others is loving your neighbors."

"What if I don't have food to give a hungry person?"

"You always have something to give, even if it's just a warm smile."

"What good is a smile to a hungry person?"

"Sometimes people hunger for emotional food, and your warm smile may be all they need to satisfy their hunger. Besides, Principessa, you have a million smiles sleeping on your beautiful face—all of them worthless until you give them away."

I don't know why or how Sister Verona's patience with me never wore thin. It didn't matter what or how often I asked questions. She always took the time to answer them. Other teachers let kid questions hang in the air or tell them, "There's time enough for you to learn that when you get older."

"Principessa, meet me at The Story Rock when you finish your chores."

"OK."

Since Sister Verona named it "The Story Rock", I never bothered to ask her why she wanted to meet there. I knew there would be a story or an essential lesson waiting for me there, so I skipped my way to the big rock, pushing tree-sitting birds to the air and sending small furry ground animals scurrying for cover.

"Ciao Sister."

"Ciao Principessa."

"What's the story for today, Sister?"

"I saw you standing alone by the statue today, after class. You were sobbing. What happened?"

"Nothing happened."

"Did anyone do or say something mean to you?"

"No."

"Principessa, you don't cry for no reason. In fact, I think the last time you did was when I changed your diaper."

I couldn't help snickering when she said that.

"I guess I was feeling sorry for myself."

"About what?"

"About being here. About my mother and why she would leave me to fend for myself."

"We talked about this before, Principessa. There's no way to know what she was going through at that time, but I promise you she didn't leave you to fend for yourself. We can't know where she came from, how far she traveled, or how she got here. It must have pained her more than we can imagine, but she knew you would be cared for here at Sisters of Mercy. She loved you enough to make sure you had a chance to survive. That may be more than she could have done for herself. I'm sorry that you're feeling sad. At the same time, I am grateful that you have come into my life. You have made my life worthwhile. I hope I can do the same for you. I love you, Principessa."

"I just don't understand."

"Unfortunately, in life, there are many things we just don't understand. Sometimes, we have to accept what happens, try to find the good in it, and move on."

"What good can come from my being abandoned?"

"You could also ask how much worse it might have been if you weren't. But, unfortunately, we can't know what the future will bring—we can only be patient, wait, and see. Remember. You can look for the good, or you can look for the bad—you will find whatever you look for."

"I'll try. I hope I will only ever find the good."

"That is my hope for you too, but that will not assure you that only good things will happen. It's important to know that nothing lasts forever—not good or bad. Calm will always follow a storm. Light will break after the darkest hour, and the sun will always rise to give us another chance to appreciate all the wonderful things that are right with the world. Patience, Principessa. Your world will unfold in front of you. As it should."

I could never imagine my life without Sister Verona, and I prayed every night that would never happen.

Chapter Five
Signore
Lucci Opportunity

Signore Federico Lucci was a wealthy landowner whose vast landholdings were in the mountain valley area of La Valle. He lived in Castellucci, a nearby village, where his great grandfather bought all the land owned by the Lucci families ever since. Generations of sharecroppers whose families grew up working on Lucci land enriched the soil and the Lucci families. Long days, warm nights, plenty of sunshine, and shade cast by mountains stretching to eight thousand feet surrounding a vast expanse of the valley floor, created an agricultural pot of gold. Grapevines decorated most of the mountainsides while plums and lemons shared space closer to the mountain tops. Farms, farm animals, fields, groves, gardens, and orchards presented a harmony of life and growth—apples, figs, vegetables, and wildflowers sang the tune of breathtaking landscape and painted a living picture of the Horn of Plenty.

Of all the Lucci family members overseeing their land and businesses, Signore Federico Lucci was the most sympathetic toward his workers and their families. With practically no economy in Italy at the time, a sharecropper relied on his share of crops to barter for things their families needed to survive—Signore Lucci more than satisfied that need for anyone willing to work for him. When a church Pastor mentioned his need for a convent and requested his help in funding it, Signore Lucci provided all the material and labor required to build it for him. They constructed the Convent on the eastern edge of the valley in a small LaValle village and named it Sisters of Mercy. The building was much larger than the pastor requested or needed to house the women who would train the nuns.

However, Signore Lucci's foresight served to accommodate more than a home and training ground for aspiring nuns. The building also became a safe harbor for helpless, hopeless, and abandoned children. Despite his demanding work schedule, Signore Lucci always made himself available to help with the needs of the pastor and nuns at the Convent, and he was always welcome there.

One late Sunday afternoon, I heard the sound of his car coming in the distance. When Signore Lucci reached the front gate, Mother Superior beckoned Sister Verona to follow her, to greet him at the door. Most times, he brought good news, and something good almost always happened after his visits. I was curious to learn what good things might happen from that appointment. After a brief exchange of pleasantries, Signore Lucci got to the point.

"Reverend Mother—as you know, I have many friends who live in America. One of them has a sister and brother-in-law who wish to adopt a child. So I immediately thought you might have a child who needs a good home."

"Yes. Sadly, we have more than just one. Do you know these people who wish to take one of our children?"

"Not personally, but I trust my friend, who I have known since he was a child. He is close friends of the couple, and he can vouch for their character."

"Can you tell me anything about the couple?"

"They are in their early forties—married for ten years—childless—unable to conceive on their own, and they are very eager to have a family."

"Can they provide a better life for the child than we can?"

"They are both professionals. Doctor Patricio and Doctor Rose Marinelli. He is an orthopedic surgeon, and she is a physics professor teaching at Philadelphia University. Both their parents emigrated to America in 1880. And, they will make a significant contribution to the orphanage."

"Are they wishing to adopt a baby?"

"No. The couple prefers a female between the ages of eight and twelve. They feel best equipped to handle and provide for such a child."

"This sounds wonderful, Signore Lucci—this will be a great opportunity for a special child I have in mind."

"Excuse me for asking, but may I assume this child is well adjusted and without behavioral problems?"

"Oh! Heavens yes, Signore—she is ten years old, well behaved, and very bright. She was days old when she arrived, and Sister Verona has cared for her exclusively ever since."

"Mother Superior is correct, Signore Lucci. Her name is Maria Della Notte—she deserves to be in a family who can provide for her. She is a pleasant, happy little girl—the brightest student I have seen in my eighteen years teaching here. But Signore Lucci, there are other girls you may wish to consider."

"The child both of you have described seems a perfect match for the couple seeking to adopt her."

"Forgive me, Signore Lucci. Perhaps my concern is unfounded, but how can we be sure the match is also perfect for the child?"

"Surely you agree that her opportunities would be more significant and her future brighter in America."

"I understand that opportunities and the promise of a bright future are important considerations, but will she get the love and care she needs to grow beyond her personal desires?"

"How can you be sure that any child leaving here will get what you want for them?"

I pinched my nose to stifle a sneeze, not wanting to miss a word the three were saying, nor did I wish to be discovered hiding just a few feet away.

"I may be out of order, and no offense is intended, but if I have a voice in the decision, I would ask that you let Maria remain in my care."

Mother Superior interrupted, "Indeed, Sister, you are not attempting to prevent a better life for any child here, are you?"

"Of course not, but this child is extraordinary. She appears to be content and happy with the care and attention I have afforded her from the moment I assumed full responsibility for her."

"I know how attached you are. However, as much as it is our responsibility to take these children in and nurture them physically, mentally, and spiritually, we are equally responsible for allowing them to thrive in an outside environment. In this case, Maria will be in the custody of a loving, professional couple capable of providing a good home, education, and future for her in America. We must let her go."

"I am concerned for this child having to travel alone on such a long trip. How will she manage?"

"Don't worry. I have communicated with all the agencies, and all necessary paperwork is pre-filed."

"I appreciate your concern, Sister Verona. I would never think to let any child manage on its own. I will drive her to the pier in Naples. I will introduce her to the guardian I have selected to watch over her during the passage. Signore and Signora Marinelli will meet her on the pier in Philadelphia when she arrives aboard the SS Taormina."

"I'm sorry, Signore, I didn't mean to offend you or imply—"

I was dumbfounded. I couldn't believe that Mother Superior and Signore Lucci were talking about me as if I were a crate of grapes they were preparing to ship somewhere. And Sister Verona—why didn't she refuse to send me? She had no idea where I would end up.

"Not at all, Sister. Maria will be in the care of the Romano family, whom I know and would trust with my life. Signore Romano and his boys have worked for me on the very fields that surround this Convent. I have helped them on their way to America, where they have lived and worked for nearly two years. They have well-paying jobs—able to save money. My friend has assured me they are pleased there. Unfortunately for me, I may never find anyone else as hard-working, honest, and loyal as those men."

"Why would you send them away if you valued their work?"

"Because that family deserves a better life than I can provide, or they can have here. Now, they have sent for the rest of the family to join them. Sofia— daughter Giada—and two sons, Angelo and Luca, will depart Naples on 26 May and arrive in Philadelphia on the 11th. I have spoken to Signora Romano and asked if she would keep an eye on a child during her trip if I were fortunate to find a girl suitable for adoptive parents. She has agreed. I will meet her on the pier and make the introduction."

"Well then, it appears you have done all you can to assure safe travels and a good home for Maria."

"Mother Superior? Sister Verona? I appreciate all that you do for these children. But, of course, I wish no child would ever need to be here. And, I'm pleased to know that, like me, you can see a better future for children with parents who care for them and who can provide suitable homes and opportunities—especially in America."

I strained to hear every word, but sometimes I only heard phrases, mainly when more than one of them spoke simultaneously. I had a hard time believing Sister Verona wanted me to go since she told me how much she loved me a thousand times. What was I supposed to think—she said my mother left me at the Convent because she loved me so much? Now, someone else who loves me is sending me away. Was I supposed to be happy because they had a plan for me in America? I was much too confused to be pleased.

Sister Verona mothered me since a few days after my birth—not from her body, but she fed me in every possible way. She was there for me at bedtime, and when I woke up in the morning, she bathed me and saw that I was always well-nourished. Besides teaching me during my school classes, Sister Verona told me stories—fairy tales at first, then read literature and poetry, and told me her life story, explaining what I might encounter in my life. She taught me how to cook, and sew, how to be polite, how to dress, how to eat, and set the table. By her actions, Sister Verona showed me kindness and love. She had invested her life in mine—why would she want me to leave? Ever.

When she left her father, Sister Verona said he gave her wings to fly and anchors to their home, where she was always welcome. If Sister Verona thought she was doing the same for me, then she was wrong. It was her choice to leave her father—she didn't offer me an option, or chance, to decide if I wanted to fly. I trusted her. I gave her my love, heart, and soul—she tore all of them to shreds.

A few days after Signore Lucci's visit to the Convent, I met Sister Verona at the Story Rock. That time, she wanted to talk about our lives and how we had changed since I arrived. I hoped I misunderstood the whispers, so I waited to hear what she wanted to talk about.

"I will always remember the moment you came into my life—so tiny and so beautiful. The Reverend Mother told me you were a gift to me—heaven sent. She appointed me to be your guardian and to assume the role of your birth mother. I was terrified. I never planned to be a mother, but I did pledge to obey my superiors. I was scared, but I was also obligated, so I accepted that destiny put us together, and I promised myself to be the best mother possible. I never—not for a second—looked back in regret over what was happening to me. I prayed for the ability to care for and nurture you, but most of all, I prayed for love to bind us."

"When did you stop being scared?"

"The moment I stared into your newborn eyes and saw the innocence in them. My entire body felt your need to be nurtured and loved. So the moment I dedicated my life to that purpose, I gave you my whole heart—you rewarded me with your love in return."

"When did you stop caring about me?"

"Never. And I never will."

"What was I like in the beginning?"

"I didn't have much experience before you, but you cooed, crawled, stood, walked, and talked much quicker than I thought you would. You are everything I hoped for and prayed that you would be."

"I remember the white dress you crocheted for my First Communion. I was so happy and proud to wear it."

"Mm. I can still see you whirling and twirling when you tried it on. Then, when you finished dancing, you pinched the bottom sides of the dress and spread them wide—with your heels touching and your toes wide apart, you bent your knees and bowed ever so slightly. You stayed in that pose for at least a minute—looking at me and smiling."

"I remember that, too. So, what were you talking about with Signore Lucci?"

"I've told you before that Signore Lucci gave his land and built this Convent long before I arrived. He has supported it and our mission ever since. He has worked tirelessly to help children and adults find a way out of poverty—rampant, especially in this southern part of our country. You must respect Signore Lucci for all he does for us."

I was still sitting on the fence of uncertainty. The only question I had was about Sister Verona and Mother Superior's conversation with Signore Lucci, and she didn't answer that one. I held the hope I wasn't bound for anywhere and that my imagination was filling in the blanks for unsaid or unheard whispers. I begged myself for the patience Sister Verona had, but it never came.

Chapter Six
Maria
Telling Me

The following day as I was finishing my breakfast, Sister Verona came to me, kissed the top of my head, and said, "Principessa, after school, when your homework and chores are complete, please meet me in the apple orchard, by the Story Rock—I have something important and exciting to tell you."

"Yes, Sister, I can't wait."

That evening, Sister Verona watched as I emerged from behind a small stand of apple trees. I stumble-ran through fallen apples as fast as I could—waving my arms as if trying to stop a freight train. I stretched a smile across my face as I got closer to the best friend I had in the entire world. For a split second, a strange feeling came over me—despite the hot evening, I sensed a chill in the air.

"Sono qui, sono qui! I'm here, I'm here," I shouted as I approached her.

"Benvenuto (Welcome)," she replied.

"Tell me, Sister, tell me—I waited all day to hear your important, exciting news."

"OK," she said, "I have so much to tell you. But, before we discuss anything, I want you to listen closely and remain silent until I finish. Some things I say will make you very happy, and some may make you a little sad. I need you to listen to everything—carefully—and think about how important it is. Please close your eyes—I want you to imagine living in a good place, where everything is possible—where you can have all the things you want or ever dreamed of. Everything I tell you will be fun, exciting, and perfect for you. Promise to listen quietly, OK?"

"Yes, Sister, I will remain quiet until you say it's OK to speak."

"You and I have talked of many things from the time you were able to speak and understand until this very minute. We have always been open and honest because we know that friendship and love must begin with trust. I love you, Principessa—I love you so much that I sometimes feel I have no love left for anyone or anything else. So, trust me when I say that I am doing this for you, and in the end, you will be happier than you ever thought possible.

"Try to picture the stories I told you about other people in other places. Imagine the beautiful things that happen in the world outside of Sisters of Mercy—the stories about busses, trains, boats, and cruise ships—about the art in Rome and Firenze—about music in Salzburg—about the New World in America, where anything,—anything—is possible. That's not so here in Italy. Here, if you are born to wealthy parents, there's a perfect chance you will have a smooth path to follow that would assure your good health, excellent education, and, with that, some wealth of your own. But, on the other hand, if you are born a peasant, there are no smooth paths—there are only long days of hard work and poverty." She continued.

"Principessa, Signore Lucci came here a few days ago to tell Mother Superior and me that a wonderful, well educated, and wealthy American couple want to be your parents. He has made all the arrangements for your safe travel. Signore Lucci will drive you to the Steamship in Naples that will take you to America. He said Signore and Signora Marinelli would meet you when the ship arrives in Philadelphia. They will take you to their home and, in the fall, you will continue your education in an excellent school which they have already arranged for you to attend. They will show you things and take you places that you could only imagine or dream about."

I bit my quivering lip, trying hard not to show how sad and deeply hurt I felt, but I sat quiet and straight as Sister Verona went on.

"Signore Lucci even made arrangements for you to travel on the boat with a family going to the same place. In America, children must attend school until they reach age sixteen. You will probably start school there in sixth grade, maybe even seventh grade, and finish high school in grade twelve. After that, you will, most likely, continue your education at a college or university, where you can learn the skills you will need to make a career of your choosing. You are a brilliant little lady, Principessa—you can become a nurse, or a doctor, a teacher, an artist, or musician—anything you want."

I could tell by her eyes that Sister Verona was trying to sense my thoughts or feelings throughout her thirty-minute, one-way conversation, but I wouldn't let her. Just as she asked, I sat quietly and still the whole time. I was fuming inside, my head was spinning, and my stomach was churning, but I refused to show any signs of excitement, disappointment, or restlessness. She must have thought things were going great because she remained upbeat and excited. She had no idea how despondent I was or cared about the awful, massive pain I was feeling in my heart when she stood up, cupped her hands against my cheeks, and squinted into my eyes.

I didn't like how I was feeling one bit—her hands were warm on my face, but my fingertips were cold, but my hands were sweaty. I was burning up inside and shivering. My mind went blank and filled at the same time with endless, why questions. Why was she sending me away? Why did I have to go? Why America? Did she think she was doing me a favor? Why can't I have a choice to stay or not? Why did someone dump me here in the first place? I was anxious, upset, confused, and completely lost in my self-pity. If what was happening to me was a good thing, then I couldn't understand or believe it. I couldn't pretend to like any part of it.

My only thought was to kick Sister Verona in the shins with my face still cupped in her hands—hurt her, and make her cry. I wanted to stamp on her feet—slap her hands away from my face—push her to the ground. I wanted her to feel how I felt. But, instead, I closed my eyes, took in a slow, deep breath through my nose and let it pass slowly through my barely parted lips. And waited.

"That was a lot to listen to, Principessa. I love you so much. Now, you stand up and give me the biggest hug ever, and I'll answer all your questions."

"Hug you?" I responded. I sneered at her and said again, "Hug you? Why would I do that—so you can tell me more stories and lies?"

I began to sob. "What have I ever done to you that was so bad you can turn your back on me and send me away?"

She tried to hold me, but my flailing arms and kicking feet kept her away. Tears were streaming down my face—I was crying loudly and spewing words at lightning speed. But, I didn't hold anything back.

"You said we would be together for a long time and that I could be a Nun just like you when I grew up and that we could do so many things together. You lied. Everything you told me was a big fat lie." I drew in a deep breath

46

and continued to pour my soul into my unrelenting rant. "You say you love me just like the lie story you told me about my mother."

I sucked in more air and went on, "You told me how hard life must have been for my mother and how sad she must have been, but she loved me so much, and that's why she put me in this place so I would have a chance." Another deep breath.

"I guess that's why she left me on the stupid grass at the front gate. Maybe she thought I would be lucky enough that the wild dogs around here would eat my body and chew on my bones."

Gulping air and spitting my anger, I went on, "She loved me, you love me; if that's what love is, I don't want it anymore! I don't want to go with Signore Lucci, I don't want to go to America—I hate America! I hate Signore Luci, and I hate you most of all! I'll run away, you can't stop me. I hate you. I hate you."

I collapsed, kicking and pounding the grass with both fists until I had nothing left to say. I lay silently on the ground, soaked with sweat and tears, furious and exhausted. Sister Verona looked stunned, but she laid down next to me, and put her arm over my shoulder, and waited. And waited. Almost an hour passed without a word between us. Then, finally, she stood up and took two steps back to our Story Rock. I stayed, lying on the ground, face down, sobbing tears into the grass through my crossed arms. She spoke first.

"Maria, I know you can hear me, and I know you're angry. You don't have to talk to me, or even like me, but going to America will be good for you. There are a few things I wanted to discuss with you before you left. I thought we could talk to each other about them. I never expected you not to speak to me again. For now, please listen—someday, you will understand."

On and on, she droned.

"Maria, I told you about the places I've been, the things I've seen, and the people I've met. None of that would have been possible if my parents were poor. Neither of us chose our parents or whether we wanted to be wealthy or not. I was fortunate—my parents were wealthy. In that way, you weren't so blessed—you didn't get the same opportunities that I did, but now, you do have a choice. You can choose to run away, or you can choose to change the course of your entire life. That's up to you."

Nothing was up to me—if it were, I wouldn't go anywhere.

"I think you will agree, my Principessa, that we have been happy, together, for a long time."

I put my hands over my ears, but she went on.

"I know you don't believe your mother loved you. Someday, you will understand that her love for you was overwhelming. She knew she couldn't care for you or give you the kind of life she hoped for you. She was thinking of you—not herself—when she placed you in our care. She must have known we could do that better than she could. Her action was unselfish, and it took a great deal of courage for her to take it. I know a tiny bit about how she felt, Maria because now I feel the same way. I love you so much. I want to run away with you—just the two of us, but running away is not the answer. I wish I could take away the pain you are feeling right now. I wish I could take away all your troubles and smooth every path you will ever travel in your lifetime. But, the truth is, I can't."

What was she talking about? She didn't care about me any more than my mother did. Liar!

"Please, open your mind, Maria. Let every person you meet teach you something—you can learn something from everyone. Promise yourself to learn, grow from your knowledge, change with the times, and change yourself when the situation warrants change. When you have a good experience—savor it—cherish it—and hold it for as long as you can. Just know that those good things rarely last forever. When something terrible happens, learn from that, too, and move forward.

"Most importantly, when things get unbearable, remember: Nothing lasts forever—not good times, and not bad times. Whatever comes your way, good or bad, try to learn from that experience. Even in your darkest hour, remember the sun will always follow. May God bless you, Principessa, and keep you always safe—always near people who love you—and who you can love in return. Finally, please don't lose the self-addressed and stamped envelope I placed in your suitcase. If nothing else, just put that in a mailbox—that will tell me you have arrived safely. Goodbye, Maria."

That was it. My best friend—Sister Verona—turned and walked away.

Chapter Seven
Maria
Getting to Naples

The sun had already tucked itself behind the mountain tops—it wasn't dark yet, but it would be soon. Sister Verona took a seat next to me in the convent library. She wanted to talk. I didn't. I trained my eyes on the gray/brown images of mountains in the distance. I longed to be outside to smell the air and feel the freedom that comes in its freshness. Instead, I was trapped inside a room warmer than I like, smelling the wood aging on the walls and the volumes of paper and leather-bound books squeezed together on stacks of shelves.

"Principessa?"

"Don't call me that!"

"Maria. Please. Let's talk—we may never get the chance to talk again."

"That's your fault—not mine."

"Maria. I'm sorry…"

"If you're sorry, then tell Signore Lucci I'm not going to Naples."

"It's too late for that. Signore Lucci arranged everything already. Your foster parents are waiting for you to arrive. They are anxious to give you a home and for you to be a part of their family."

"You, Mother Superior, and Signore Lucci want that. That's not what I want."

"You're right! We do want that because we know what a great opportunity it will be for you. Your life in America will be far better than if you stayed here."

"Did you ever go to America?"

"No, I have never been there."

"Then how do you know it's better for me?"

"Our country has long suffered the results of bad government, crime, corruption, and so on—you're too young to understand. Here, there is little chance for education beyond a few years of primary school—especially now, for poor people like most of our population—that's what I know."

"Is everybody in America rich?"

"I suppose not everyone. But most Americans have the opportunity to have good educations and good-paying jobs and professions."

There was nothing I could do or say that would change anything—I felt like I was talking to the air. I turned my back to Sister Verona and refocused my gaze to the darkness outside. She kept talking.

"Maria. Be sure to take the suitcase and two cloth bags on the floor next to the front door. The bigger bag has two loaves of bread, some apples, and a few pears inside. The other has chunks of cheese, salami, and prosciutto. That should be enough food to hold you until you reach Philadelphia. Don't let those bags out of your sight. If you lose them, or if someone takes them, you may be without enough food unless someone has plenty to share with you—you can't depend on that."

I don't know if she was trying to scare me or what, but talking like that didn't help me. So I pretended I didn't hear.

"I packed all your clothes in the suitcase. The skirts, blouses, and sweaters I packed should be enough to wear for the whole trip if you're careful and keep them clean. You will have to wash your underthings every few days. Otherwise, there's not enough to change into clean ones every day. I'm sure they will have water where you can wash them. I also packed your communion dress. I thought that someday, when you have a little girl, maybe you will let her wear the same one you did."

I loved that dress. I wanted to talk about it and remember what fun we had when I made my First Communion. I tried to laugh about the clumsy dance I did when I showed off and how proud I was wearing it. At the same time, I wanted to burst out in tears and beg her one more time to let me stay with her forever. I did neither and remained silent.

"One other thing. At the bottom of the suitcase, I put a stamped, self-addressed envelope, several pieces of writing paper, and a pencil. If you don't want to write a letter to me, please seal the envelope and mail it. That will tell me you have arrived safely, and I can rest easy. The suitcase is heavy—maybe, too heavy for you to carry for a long distance. I'm sure someone will help you if you ask. I put your favorite books inside—that's what weighs the most."

The knock on the door told me Signore Lucci had arrived.

"Good evening, Sister. I'm sorry to be so late. Two of my workers tried to push a plow out of a mud hole and got trapped under it. They had to be rushed from the lower farm this afternoon to the hospital."

"Will they be alright?"

"I spoke with the doctor before I left the hospital—he assured me they would be fine and feeling much better in the coming days. But, unfortunately, one suffered a concussion and the other a broken leg. So, hello little lady, are you ready for your big trip?"

I wished I dared to tell him and Sister Verona how I felt, but I knew that wouldn't help me. So I just bit my lip, tried not to cry, and walked to the front door to wait with my bags. I was only a few steps away when I heard Mother Superior, Sister Verona, and Signore Lucci exchanging whispers, but I couldn't make out what they were saying. I assumed they didn't want me to hear their conversation. After a few minutes, with Sister Verona walking behind her, Mother Superior came to the front door and wished me a safe journey. Then, Sister Verona stooped to hug me. I didn't reach to hug her back, but I let her hold on to me until she let go.

"Be safe, Principessa. I will keep you in my heart forever, and wherever your life takes you—if you look for me, I will always be at your side—always."

I didn't know what she thought when she said that. She was standing directly in front of me when I begged her to let me stay. I wanted her at my side that moment, and forever—it was her choice to send me away.

"Time to go, young lady. I'll get your things. My! Your suitcase is so heavy—are you taking all of Italy with you?"

"No Signore—it's my books that make it heavy."

"Ah. You'll be happy for the books—you will have plenty of time to read on the boat."

Signore Lucci signaled the driver to put my suitcase and bags in the trunk. Then he opened the back door and seated me next to Signore Lucci. I looked straight ahead as we drove away. The place where I spent every day of my life was growing smaller behind us. There was no life left for me back with Sister Verona—I willed myself to look away and never look back.

We climbed up one side of the mountain and down the other—all the while, Signore Lucci pointed to things he thought might interest me—like why we had to switch back and forth across the mountain instead of driving straight up. So back and forth, we drove across the hill, and when we reached the top, we did the same thing going down on the other side of the mountain. I started pulling on my ears as we approached the top, and he asked, "Do your ears hurt? Did you feel them pop, little lady?"

"Yes. Why did that happen?"

"That's because the air pressure is lower on top of the mountain than it is on the bottom. So, when the pressure in your ear gets higher than the outside air pressure, sometimes, you will hear your ears pop. If you swallow a few times, chew, or yawn—that should help."

I was glad Signore Lucci told me that—when my ears popped halfway up the next mountain, I yawned, chewed, and swallowed the hurt—that helped. Of course, I couldn't see too far off in the distance because it was dark, but seeing the city lights below when we got to the tops of mountains took my mind off my popping ears. They looked like stars on the ground—I never saw such a beautiful sight.

"We're almost there, little lady—it shouldn't take us more than half an hour—are you tired?"

"Yes."

"I'm not surprised. It's been a long day for you—it's almost 10:30."

"Will we go straight to the boat?"

"No. We'll do that in the morning. Tonight, we'll stay with my brother and his family—they live near the Port of Naples—it will be a twenty-minute drive from their house."

I didn't care where we stayed—I was so tired. From the time Sister Verona told me I was leaving—fighting with her, crying nonstop, and now sitting in the car for two hours past my regular bedtime drained my spirit and left my body empty. All I wanted was to go to sleep.

I woke up on the outskirts of Naples early in the morning of April Sixth. I stretched, yawned, looked around—confused about where I was and how I got there. Then I heard Signore Lucci's voice, "Maria, Maria—it's time to get up—come down—everyone is waiting to have breakfast with you."

I didn't say much the night we arrived, but I liked Signore Lucci, his brother, and his family. They were friendly to me, and everyone tried to make me laugh. I especially liked that they didn't ask me a whole lot of questions or force me into a conversation. Still, I was apprehensive. Everyone was a stranger—everything was new to me. I just wanted to run away—just run—until I could be away from everything and everybody. I wanted to be alone.

"Here, Maria—eat—we have some warm milk—some bread—salami—and an egg for you."

How could I ignore these people? They were so kind. I tried hard to be polite, but I would have much preferred to be hungry and alone. I thanked them, drank the milk, ate a little cheese and salami, and told them it was delicious. What I didn't eat, they packed into the bag Sister Verona had prepared for me. They said I would be happy for it along the way. I heard Sister Verona's echo when they said that, "It will be a long trip, Maria—more than two weeks—you will need to eat a little bit each day—so you have enough to last until you get there."

When the time came to leave, I had the same feeling I had when I left the orphanage—I didn't want to go, but I tried to get away as fast as possible. Standing at the door, Signore Lucci hugged his brother—sister-in-law—and three little kids.

"Ciao—Arrivederci," Signore Lucci said to no one in particular.

"Ciao, Mio Fratello—Arrivederci, Zio (Goodbye, my brother—goodbye, uncle)."

I said my goodbyes too. "Ciao, Signore e Signora Lucci. Grazie di Tutto."—"Goodbye, Signore and Signora. Thank you for everything."

The car was outside with the engine running and waiting to take Signore Lucci and me to the Port of Naples. The driver held the back door open for us. He was dressed, head to toe, in black, except for a rumpled white shirt that looked like he slept the night in it. The thing I remember most about him was his nose. His nose was narrow under his eyebrows, then grew bulbous to the middle of his face. It had the color, look, and size of a sickle pear. But he was a lovely man. Friendly. He picked up my additional bag and placed it carefully in the trunk. He asked if we were comfortably seated before he took the driver's seat and drove slowly away—giving us a few extra moments to wave our farewells.

When we arrived at the pier, Signore Lucci instructed the driver to place my bags and not let me out of sight while looking for the group I would be traveling with. Standing on the pier, I watched the afternoon sun pushing its way through the last bit of mist left by the mid-day rain. I traced a rainbow's arc with my finger starting on one side of the sun and stopping where the sky touched the water's edge on the horizon. I watched fish squiggling and squirming below, and droplets of sunlight dance on top of blue/green, crystal clear water. The tide splashed and lapped at the rocks. All these sights and sounds were new to me—different—beautiful. I thought, maybe, there was some truth to Sister Verona's stories. I was daydreaming—relaxing—meditating—the way she told me I should have a hundred times. Then, I heard Signore Lucci calling through the crowd of people.

"Signora Romano, Signora Romano, dove sei?"—"Mrs. Romano, Mrs. Romano, where are you?"

"Sono qui—sono qui (I'm here—I'm here)," she answered.

With me in hand, Signore Lucci walked up to Signora Romano—introduced himself and me. She shook his hand and presented her children to him—Angelo, Giada, and Luca. Everyone exchanged Buongiornos—and Ciaos. We children smiled tentatively at each other while the Signore and Signora chatted about what each expected from the other.

"Signora Romano—I know it may be a lot to ask since you have yourself and three children to look out for on this long trip. However, I don't expect you to do anything more than be sure this little girl does not wander off alone. If Maria can stay close to your family—that's all I can ask."

"Si, Signore, I and my family will keep an eye on her"

"Here, take this."

"A thousand thanks, Signore Lucci. Goodbye."

Signora Romano stuffed the envelope in her pocket, took my hand and Luca's. Then, with Angelo and Giada trailing behind, we melted into the crowd and waited for an official to call her name. Signore Lucci was still visible when the call came, walking off the pier and into his waiting car.

"Sofia Romano! Sofia Romano! La Famiglia Romano—Vieni subito." ("Sofia Romano! Sofia Romano! The Romano Family—Come quickly!") came blaring through the loudspeaker.

Scooting us along, Signora Romano rushed to the man holding the papers. Without a trace of a smile, he barked at her, "Si dice moglie e tre figli; che è questo?"—"This paper says wife and three children—who is this?

"Questa è Maria Dellanotte—Signore Lucci ha detto—" ("This is Maria Dellanotte—Signore Lucci said that—")

"Ah sì, si, Signore Lucci—andare." ("Ahh, yes, yes—Signore Lucci—You wait here.") said the Officer in Charge.

As instructed, we waited in place for about ten minutes before the officer returned and ushered us into the ship. I thought we were in for a treat—hoping he would lead us up on the deck. Angelo and Luca walked side by side, behind their mother—Giada and I followed them. We walked past the stairs leading up to the deck and headed down the steps into the middle of the ship—the area typically used to transport cattle.

When we reached the bottom stage, I saw the officer directing dozens of people ahead of us to the front. I envied them first—I wanted to be upfront, but I settled down a little when I saw many people taking places behind us. At the time, I didn't know that being assigned to berths in the middle of the boat would benefit third-class travelers—maybe, the only benefit.

Chapter Eight
Luca
A Better Life

My name is Luca Romano. I am the last son of five generations of last sons before me whose families were sharecroppers in the small village of La Valle, Italy, Province of Avellino, fifty kilometers from Naples, in the region of Campania. I have three older brothers, Antonio, Marco, Angelo, and a sister, Giada. There were two stillborn boys after Giada—I was born six years after her, on 25 September 1923. Our parents are Giovanni and Sofia Romano.

Being last in a large family has its advantages. For me, I always felt safe surrounded by so many people who loved and cared for me. Besides, I had teachers of various ages with abundant experiences I could learn from without suffering the pains of living through bad experiences firsthand. I loved to work in the fields with my father and brothers. They were the ones working, but they made me feel as though I was contributing something. I was too young to realize I was a heavier burden than any of them needed, but they never complained.

I thought my life and my world were just fine. I didn't have to carry a load of poverty on my shoulders, so I couldn't understand why so many friends and neighbors left our village to find better lives in other countries. I was heartbroken when my father and two oldest brothers left for America. They said we would join them in America when the time was right. Too many nights, I cried and wondered if the time would ever be right.

For as long as I can remember, I was never alone. I lived in my parents' small home with three older brothers, one sister, and my grandmother, Nona—my mother's mother. Ours was one of many homes built close together on the west side of our small village. My family lived in the same house for generations—just as my aunts' uncles, cousins, friends, and neighbors had.

The Lucci family owned all the homes, hundreds of acres of land, livestock, fields, gardens, pastures, vineyards, fruit, and produce. Our families planted, tended, raised, and harvested everything that grew there. We were sharecroppers.

As a child, I didn't know anything about wealth, class, or even poverty. Our home was clean, I had clothes to wear, and we never went without food. As far as I knew, that was the same with our extended family, friends, and neighbors—they were the yardstick I used to compare myself to, so my life was good. I could see that my father and brothers worked in the fields every day but Sunday, but so did every man and boy more than ten years old. The women and girls stayed home to cook, wash clothes, sew, keep the house tidy, and take care of the sick that needed help. Sometimes, I saw my mother and sisters wander off toward the railroad tracks and return with their aprons full of coal. I didn't know it at the time, but they gathered coal that dropped from the trains onto the railroad tracks and burned it in the stove we used to cook and heat the house.

I wasn't anxious to go to school, and I tried everything to make my parents understand that.

"But Ma. How am I supposed to get strong sitting in school?"

"You're already strong enough to go to school."

"I want to be outside and work with Papa, Antonio, Marco, and Angelo."

"Five more years, and you can work in the fields with them, but now you're going to school."

"Why? Nobody else had to go to school."

"Giada did."

"She's a girl!"

"And you're a boy—and you're going to go to school."

"I'll ask papa—I bet he won't make me go."

"That's a good idea. Ask tonight after supper. Better yet. The conversation will be shorter if you ask your father before supper.

I couldn't wait until my father came home. He was always anxious to greet me after work—throw me into the air, hug me, and ask what I did that day. I was confident he would see my point and convince my mother I shouldn't have to go to school. Everything was working according to my plan until I made my announcement.

"Papa. I don't want to go to school—momma says I must."

"She's right. You do."

"But you didn't—and none of my brothers went."

He gave me that look—the one where his eyes spoke, and I knew what they said. If the following few words out of my mouth were anything but 'yes Papa', there would be consequences. I never got to know what the results might be, but I knew when to quit.

"Luca. We'll talk about this after supper."

I kept my mouth quiet when my mother ladled three meatballs on top of a heaping bowl of pasta she served my father and until my sister, Giada, took his empty plate to the washtub. I didn't know what to think or expect. I only knew that my loving, caring, happy-go-lucky father had a serious side, I knew he meant business, and I had better pay attention.

"Luca. What's this about you don't want to go to school?"

"When I get big—I want to work with you—like my brothers."

"And that's exactly the reason you're going to go to school. Working in these fields is not what I want for you."

"Why?"

"Because I want a better life for you. My father, his father, grandfather, and great grandfather all worked in these same fields. So there are five generations of us working long, hard days under the hot sun—there's a sea of Romano sweat in the soil of these farms, orchards, and vineyards—and for what? We have nothing. With education, perhaps, we could have become doctors or lawyers or teachers who work in clean clothes and make more money in a week than we do in a year."

"But don't you have everything you need, papa?"

"Maybe I do. Someday, you'll understand."

I started school with thirty-two other children who entered first grade with me—nineteen girls and thirteen boys. I was five years old and the youngest in my class. I was a little more eager to be there when I learned that other kids I knew from the neighborhood were also in my grade. That didn't matter too much since we could only talk with each other outside during lunch and recess. Once inside, we just spoke when asked and never to another classmate. The teachers talked, and the students listened. That was a sign of respect and the rule mandated by the teaching nuns, enforced by the supporting priests, and reinforced at home. I learned a lot about that at home, and I resolved early on to observe the rules at school, knowing that my parents expected nothing less.

My school was approximately a mile and a half from where I lived. It took my friends and me about an hour to walk both ways, which made a long day away from home. Classes started at eight a.m., and the closing bell rang at five p.m., with an hour for lunch and half-hour recesses mid-morning and mid-afternoon. As time went on, I became more interested in school and learning new things. Because nuns and priests were the teachers, they taught a lot about religion which I already heard about at home and church. But at school, they went deeper into the stories and the characters involved in them. Sometimes, when I was daydreaming, the teachers chased my fantasies away when they talked about hell, and it didn't seem to take much to get there. Lunch and recess remained my favorite times of day, but I also enjoyed Geography. Learning about different places and the people that lived there—what they planted or made, what they looked like, what they ate, and how they dressed—most of it was strange to me but very interesting.

Math was my favorite subject. Progressing from learning numbers to simple addition and subtraction allowed me to move to simple division and multiplication. Nine was my favorite number to multiply. I liked how nine times two equals one -eight—times three equals two-seven, and so on—so that the numbers on the left go up one at a time, and the numbers on the right come down one at a time. Also, the sum of the two numbers always adds up to nine.

They started to teach long division in fourth grade. I remember that because I was anxious to tell my father when he asked at supper what I learned that day in school, but I never got the chance—he had more important news to deliver that night.

"Sofia. It's time for all the family to know."

My mother drew in a deep breath, put her arms across my shoulders and Giada's, let out a soft sigh, and said, "It will be hard, but I'm sure it will be best for all of us. Yes. Tell us."

"Angelo? Giada? Luca?—We're going to America. Me, Antonio, and Marco will go first. We'll be able to work and save the money we need for you to come, too."

"When, papa?" I yelled."

"Soon. Signore Lucci said his friend in America has jobs for us and ten other men. They have arranged for our passage and places where we can live until we can find our own."

I cried the whole night, and for days after, I heard them talk back and forth across our supper table. They said life was better in America—how could they know that—they were never there. And better for who? Not for me!

I wasn't as strong as them, and I knew I couldn't work as long or hard as they did, but I would be old enough to work with them in the fields in a few more years. I wanted to help, but I was just a kid, not quite ten years old—I didn't know, care, or understand anything about Mussolini, Fascism, Depressions, or World Wars. My child's eyes saw that life was pretty good right where we were—why did they have to leave us—when would we see them again—maybe never. I cried until I couldn't cry anymore. The only consolation I had, was that some of my friends were facing the same situation, and we had each other to talk with about our problems. But neither the talk nor all the crying kept them from leaving.

My grades started to slip toward the end of my fourth school year. Weeks passed, then months. It seemed like years since I last saw my Pop and brothers. Finally, on 12 November 1933, a letter arrived—it was postmarked, 7601 Pitt Street, Northdale, PA. My father asked our family friend to write a letter for him and told her what to say. My mother waited until after we were almost ready for bed to say that our family had arrived and settled in an American town called Northdale—near Philadelphia. They were living with friends of our family who had lived there for the past several years.

Pop and the boys had found work—he hoped to tell us sooner but decided to wait until he could send some money home—then he had to wait for Theresa to write the letter. He and the boys were "… busy finding work, and settling in". Papa apologized but hoped we would understand how little free time they had. He missed us terribly and couldn't wait until we were together again. When our mom finished telling us about the letter, she gathered us in for a hug and said, "Thank God they're safe. Pray that everything goes well for them and that we will be together, again, soon."

I cried and prayed, as my mother asked, but I knew in my heart that "soon" would never be soon enough.

Chapter Nine
Luca
The Journey

During the first few months my father and brothers were away from home, I wasn't on my best behavior at school. But at least by the end of that school year, I wasn't crying myself to sleep every night. Twice each month, we got a letter telling us that they were homesick, that they missed all of us, that things were different in America, that they were doing fine, working hard, and earning money. Papa assured us that he, and the boys, were putting money aside so that, one day, we could have our very own house in America. Occasionally, he reminded Mom to save all she could to pay for our voyage when it was time. I was so happy when those letters came—each one bolstered my hope that we would be together again, and they reminded me that every letter we got brought us two weeks closer to that time. In a mid-March 1932 mealtime conversation, my mother announced, "A letter came today, and I couldn't wait until your bedtime to tell you about it. I'll read it to you."

To my Dearest Sofia, Dear Angelo, Dear Giada, and Dear Luca,

I met Signore Francesco Bevilaqua earlier today—the man gets a little bit from my pay each week. He delivered the news to me from his very close friend, our Padrone, Signore Federico Lucci, who spoke very well of our family. The two men have arranged for your trip to America. Signore Bevilaqua talked to the authorities in Philadelphia, and Signore Lucci has done the same in Naples. So you will have to make your way by bus and train to the Pier in Naples, where Signore Lucci will meet you and assure your safe passage. He will give you an envelope, which I will deliver to Signore Bevilaqua when we are together in Northdale.

The ship you will travel on is called the SS Taormina. It will depart Naples on 26 April. Tonio, Marco, and I will meet you at the Pier in Philadelphia on May 11. We can hardly wait for you to see you all. We wish you a safe journey.

Love always,

Gio, Antonio, Marco and pop

My mother's watery eyes glistened in the firelight—she was so happy. The rest of us were overjoyed, too—each of us clapping, whistling, stamping our feet, singing, dancing, and hugging. Angelo grabbed me under my arms and twirled me around until I was dizzy, then staggered and stumbled into my mother's wide-open, waiting, welcoming arms. I was giddy over everything that was happening. In less than a month, I would take my first ride on a bus, a train, and a boat—this was going to happen—before long, I would be on my way to see my father, and brothers, and America. At that moment, nothing else could have made me happier.

A few days before my life-changing journey, my emotions were red-hot and raging. I was sky high thinking about my father and brothers—seeing them, touching them, feeling their strong arms wrapped around my body, making me feel happy and safe. In the next instant, I remembered saying goodbyes to my friends and how sad I was that they were leaving LaValle for places like Brazil, Argentina, Canada, and some, like me, bound for the U.S.A. Sadness weighed heavy on me when I told my friends that I was leaving. Hearing them echo my thoughts just made it worse: "We may never see each other again."

Still, I would have shed my skin for the chance to leave that very second. It was beyond me to understand how I could be giggly happy and next to tears in the same instant. We back-slapped, half-punched arms and push-tripped each other the way boy-children do to say—I love you. When the roughhousing slowed, we sat in a small circle trying to reassure ourselves that, someday, someway, we would meet again. We had to. We were friends, and that would never change.

I didn't know why my mother insisted I continue going to school every day since we were going to America, and I was never going back to my school anyway. I knew there was no sense arguing about that, so I went. She probably didn't realize how hard it was for me to see my friends every day, knowing that I may never see them again. Those last few days seemed like an eternity. My relationships with friends changed. Leaving Italy, my mixed emotions—I was sad to leave some family, friends, and familiar surroundings behind, and happy in our sense of adventure. The ones staying became envious and hostile—taunting us to believe the ocean would swallow all of us before we reached our new world. Some neighbors stopped talking to us altogether. When I spoke with my happy friends, that were leaving, I was pleased with them because I had visions that we were all going to the same place and that nothing would change when we got there. When I talked to the boys, who were sad that we were leaving. I was sad too. I felt like I was the rope in a tug of war. My body was pulling me to stay with my friends, where I lived my whole life, where everything was familiar, and where I was comfortable. But my heart was pulling a little harder toward my father and brothers. I couldn't spend too much time worrying over it—there wasn't anything I could do about it anyway. I just had to wait and see what happened.

After school, in the days before we left, I spent as much time as possible outside walking around waving at everyone I saw—even the ones I didn't know. I'm not sure why I did that—maybe I was waving goodbye to my way of life, but I was pleased to see their waves coming back to me. I walked to where I could see the stream behind my house and saw the same mothers and daughters as always—washing clothes in the stream, wringing them out, and laying them on big rocks to dry in the late afternoon sun. I hoped there would be streams, orchards, farms, and gardens near my new house in America to help me like it there as much as I liked it in La Valle.

I went home as soon as I heard my mother calling for me. There were people inside—cousins, friends, and neighbors—some were excited and happy while others were sad, and some were crying. They were there to wish us well on our journey, to offer us their love and support, to remind us not to forget them, and to give us some food from their meager supply because they could get more, and we might run out along the way.

That evening, my mother and Giada gathered everything we owned, stuffed it into one giant canvas suitcase and two pillowcase-sized cloth bags. Besides our clothes, they packed several loaves of bread, hard cheese, and meats like prosciutto and salami that would travel well. We talked about reconnecting with the rest of our family and what we might expect along the way. I don't know how long my sister, brother, and mother continued the conversation, but I was sound asleep before eight. I felt like I only slept for a few minutes when Angelo shook me awake.

"Get up, sleepyhead. It's time to get dressed and ready to go."

I rubbed the sleep from my eyes, then leaped out of bed and into Angelo's arms. My emotions were sky high one second and down in the dumps the next. I could barely contain my excitement about reuniting with my father and brothers. They were gone for such a long time it was hard to remember what they looked like. My mother had a few fading brown pictures on her nightstand, but they were old pictures taken for special events like confirmation, communion, and weddings. Unfortunately, that's not how they dressed most of the time, so looking at those old pictures didn't help me that much. I wished we had recent photos of what they looked like in their everyday clothes—the way I remembered them.

I was never so happy and excited for anything more than our family would be together again. On top of that, I never rode in a car, bus, train, or boat in my life. I couldn't believe that, now, I would travel on all of those things in a matter of weeks. For the first time in two years, time was moving faster than I could process what was going on—everything kept me flying higher than a kite until I hit bottom, recalling the comments about the ocean swallowing us whole. Pushing my worry aside, I dressed and hurried to the kitchen—the last place we would be together in our home before leaving it. Angelo grabbed the suitcase, which was too heavy for anyone else but him. Maybe helping us carry our things was the reason my father left him behind to travel with us.

We must have been quite a sight walking to the bus station, everyone, except me, struggling under the weight of our baggage. But as we drew closer to the station, I noticed many other people dressed similarly and carrying bags they could barely lift—all headed toward the bus station. When we arrived, my mother bought the tickets and guided us toward the bus. I led the way to the back and sat on the bench seat wide enough to accommodate the four of us sitting side by side. It took fewer than five minutes to board the rest of the passengers. The driver pulled the door shut, backed up, then slowly inched the bus forward and merged with the road traffic. I looked back for a minute to see all I was leaving. From then on, I would only look forward. We were on our way to America.

My mouth was dry as a bone when we reached the Pier in Naples. I had been breathing through my gaping mouth from the moment I stepped into the bus station until I got off the train at the Pier in Naples. My jaw dropped even more when I saw the size of the boat we would soon board and live on for the next sixteen days. Having lived my whole life in a valley surrounded by mountains, seeing the bay and beyond to the sea—that massive body of water—left me speechless. A new world was opening up for me. I was excited and anxious to become a part of it and have it become a part of me.

There were people everywhere, but not everyone appeared to be as excited as I was. Unlike mine, most other faces looked sad, angry, anxious, and scared. When I asked her about it, my mother said she couldn't answer for anyone else's looks or feelings, "but" she said, "our family should be thankful because the day we were praying for has finally arrived." So she gathered all of us in under her hand-made, oversized, black shawl for a big Mama-hug and some reassurance that everything would be fine. Just then, a husky baritone voice rose above the din of the crowd.

"Signore Romano, Signore Romano."

Angelo, Giada, our mother, and I walked toward the calling voice until it came close enough for my mother to recognize it. It was Signore Lucci. He was with a young girl about my age. I wasn't paying much attention while exchanging names and greetings, but I noticed that Signore Lucci handed an envelope to my mother, which she stuffed into her coat pocket. After that, he turned, walked away, and left the girl with us. I wasn't thrilled when I heard the girl would stay with us during the trip—I would have preferred a boy my age who I could have talked with about boy things. But no. A girl.

My mother said I should be nice to her and not make her feel like a stranger. What was that supposed to mean? Bad behavior wasn't tolerated in our house, so I wouldn't be mean to her naturally. I just wasn't ready to redirect my attention from all the amazing things around me and start paying attention to a girl I didn't know or care about. So I decided to let her be the one to choose whether be friendly with me or not.

I turned my attention back to the other boats coming to and leaving the shore. There were different boats, some with people rowing them, and others with tourists taking pictures and pointing in every direction at things they saw on land. I was most interested in the fishing boats and watching fishermen cast their nets and haul them back full of small fish. I began to imagine my life as a fisherman and how exciting it would be to work on the water all day—it looked more like fun than work to me. Before I had a chance to let my mind wander too far into my seafaring adventure fantasies, I heard my mother call: "Luca! Come back here!"

"What? What's the matter?"

"You have to stop daydreaming and pay attention. People are already pushing their way to the front. We have to stay together and be ready to get on that boat when it's time."

I shuffled my feet a few times and stretched my neck, looking backward—taking my last glances at the fishermen and wishing I were in that boat with them.

"Attention! Attention! Please, may I have your attention!"

Whoever was talking on the loudspeaker stayed quiet until everyone on the Pier stopped moving and listened.

"Thank you! Our ship has been staffed, stocked, and all cargo is loaded—everything is in place, and final safety checks have been made. We ask that you please remain in place. Do not push or attempt to move to the front—an officer will call your name. He will ask for tickets and documentation for all passengers. If you're traveling as a family, please have all parties together. If all is in order, the officer will direct you to your berths. Please follow instructions, and maintain order—only in this way can we board quickly and safely."

I didn't know what I expected to find inside the steamship, but I noticed many people approaching the Pier behind us as I looked around. Most of them were well dressed—more like Signore Lucci and much fancier than anyone in our big group. They were directed to the other side of a thick rope separating us from an empty space on the other side. Those passengers must have presented their papers to an officer before they stepped foot onto the Pier because they went straight to the ship. I tried to see where they were going as they entered the boat, but all I could see was that they went upstairs. Seeing everyone head upstairs, I was anxious to get inside, thinking we would have a good look at the ocean when we traveled across it. It took about half an hour for them to board and another ten minutes before I heard our name.

"Sofia Romano! Sofia Romano! La Famiglia Romano—Vieni subito." "Sofia Romano! Sofia Romano! The Romano Family—Come quickly!"

Chapter Ten
Luca, Maria, and a Storm

On the pier in Naples, and for the first few days on the ship, each of the Romano's family took turns trying to engage me in conversation, but all I gave them were half-smiles, nods, and a rare Grazie, in exchange for a slice of apple or a crust of bread they offered. The days were long and tedious. Despite the Romanos' efforts to include me, I felt strange being with them all day, every day. So, I wandered—not too far—to stretch my legs and just to move around a little bit. When I wasn't doing that, I read the books that Sister Verona packed for me. Otherwise, I stayed by myself in the area around my bunk. Finally, on the tenth day, I decided I would open up if Giada started a conversation, and she did.

"How are you doing today, Maria?"

"OK. You?"

"Do you know we only have six days left on this ship?"

"Uh, huh. I draw a line on paper every night before I go to sleep—I keep count of the days that way."

"Do you like the boat?"

"No, not really. It's not at all like the cruise ships I heard about—like people standing on the ship's deck and watching fish swim—or looking for boats—or whatever else might be on the ocean."

"Yeah, I heard those stories in school, too. But, maybe they don't do that on the way to America."

"I don't know—maybe."

"Why don't you come over by us when you finish reading? We're talking about all the stuff we used to do before we left for America."

"OK."

I never minded listening to the Romanos, or the others, when they talked about the loved ones they left behind. But since I had nothing to offer in that regard, I remained silent. Whenever they spoke of the big family gatherings, feasts, and other things they celebrated together, I wondered why they would ever turn their backs on that. Even though I was grouchy most of the time, some of the stuff they talked about made me laugh inside—like when Angelo and Giada talked about pranks and some old guy they knew.

Luca started, "Giada, do you remember when old man, Giacomo, was chasing Marco and yelling at him for drinking wine right out of his barrel?"

"Yes. Boy, was Papa mad."

"Yeah. I remember Papa telling Marco he better not do that again because it was stealing. But then, Papa asked Giacomo why he ran around like a crazy man after Marco and told him off. "You did a lot worse when you were his age—take it easy, old man, before you die of a heart attack."

"Good thing he and Papa were good friends. How about while Giacomo was chasing Marco, and Antonio scooped a pile of donkey poop and dropped it on Giacomo's doorstep—I thought Giacomo was going to shoot Antonio."

"You boys are nuts!"

While I was listening, it made me sad to think I never had those kinds of connections—or memories. Signora Romano must have noticed that I got a little misty-eyed, so she put her arm around my shoulder and asked, "Are you OK, Maria?"

"Yes."

Giada lowered herself, hugged me, and asked, "Do you feel sick?"

"No."

Then she whispered into my hair, "It's OK to cry if you want to—sometimes a good cry can make you feel good."

I did not attempt to escape from her soft hug. Instead, I stood quiet and still, with my head down and hands at my side. Luca tapped Giada's arm, nodded his head to the right twice as if to say, let me try. Then he started talking to me.

"Maria, when I'm alone and have nothing to do, I play a game with buttons. I'm going to sit over there. If you want, I will teach you how to play."

He took a few steps toward a space against the wall, sat down, and watched me turn away from his sister and walk toward him. He skooched over a few inches when I got there, and I sat down next to him.

"I have two coat buttons and two pieces of string—here's yours. I'll show you what to do, and tell you how to do it, OK?

"Yes," I said as I studied his face and listened carefully to his instructions.

"See? The button has two holes—one up and one down."

I smirked while he was telling me about buttonholes. I knew how to sew—he didn't have to explain buttonholes, but I listened.

"Put the string through the top hole—and then through the bottom hole. Now tie the two ends of the string together—Perfect! Finally, wrap the string around one hand."

I did.

"That's it—do the same thing around the other hand, but keep the button in the middle, and spread your hands as far as they go."

"Like this?"

"Yes. Now put your hands a little closer together, and twirl them in front of you, and keep going until the string is tight."

I followed his instructions precisely—twirling my hands in front of me until the twisted string was tight against the button.

"Pull your hands apart—pull your hands apart—quick—quick!" he said, almost yelling. The button spun and bounced. I stretched my hands wide apart, then quickly brought them close together again. The string whirred and untwisted.

"Put your hands together—pull them apart—together—apart—together—apart."

He encouraged me until I had the button spinning, reversing, bouncing, and whirring, just like his. Then, he looked full face at me and said, "I call this game, Bingela-Bingela."

I smiled when he said that. I thought the game, and what he called it, was silly.

One morning, about a week before we arrived in Philadelphia, I saw a spot along the ship's wall, with room enough for me to stand and watch the people. After about ten or fifteen minutes, Luca appeared in a cluster of people standing by the opposite wall. I stood with my arms folded in front of me and smiled tentatively in his direction. I bent my right hand up slightly, at the wrist, wanting to wave at him—but not really. He saw my feeble attempt at trying to be friendly, so he walked up to me and started talking.

"Buongiorno, Maria," he said. "God willing, this long trip will be over soon."

"Yes," I answered, "are you afraid?"

He looked at me quizzically and asked, "Afraid of what? Why should I be afraid? We will soon see my brothers and my Papa, again—we haven't seen them in such a long time. No, Maria, I'm not afraid. Just the opposite, I'm so happy and excited—I can't wait to see them."

Whenever I asked about his family, Luca's eyes lit up. Nothing excited him more than sharing stories about them. He told me they were poor and that his Papa, and brothers, worked on a vegetable farm, crop sharing for a wealthy landowner. He was the youngest in his family, and that, if they weren't going to America, he would begin working on the farm, too. He, and his sister Giada, were the only ones in the family that went to school. He liked to talk about the fun he used to have grown up with his brothers, sister, and many cousins. I asked him how many cousins he had.

"I don't even know—maybe a hundred and fifty? Everyone I know is a Zia or Zio (Aunt or Uncle). Even if they aren't, that's what we call them. We don't have much, but no one else does, either. That's why we're going to America. All I know is—whenever I'm around my big family and friends—that's when I'm happy."

I listened. Everything Luca said was interesting to me. More than that, I enjoyed how expressive and animated he was when he described his life among so many people. I remember thinking that his life was the exact opposite of mine. Everything in my life was planned, organized, and orderly. It sounded like his life was a confusing, jumbled-up mess. I knew that sooner or later, he would start to ask me questions, and I dreaded that.

"What about you, Maria? Tell me about you and your family."

"There's not much to tell. I was an only child—my parents died when I was very young. I don't remember much about them. Someone who knew my parents moved to America. Now, they want me to live with them and."

When my voice trailed off, he looked at me quizzically.

"Maria, my father, and my brothers have been in America for almost two years. We have cousins and friends there, too. My mother gets letters and reads them to us. Mostly, they say how much they miss us, but my father always says how happy my brothers are for the work, earning money, and buying things they need. They saved enough money so that we could all be together there. So don't be afraid."

I liked Luca, and I wanted to believe him when he said I shouldn't be afraid. I wanted to believe Sister Verona, too, when she said the same thing. But neither of them knew how I felt. How could they?

Startled awake, at 3 a.m. on our twelfth day, I squinted my sleepy eyes through the yellow hue of dimly lit bulbs scattered about in the ship's belly and scanned the crowd. The scene looked to me like a very slow-moving picture show. The whole group—adults, and children, standing, sitting, jostling against each other, falling to their knees, falling to the floor, holding on to each other, holding on to something—anything. Their faces frowning, contorted, eyes wide open, and darting side to side looking skyward—hands pressing hard against faces—some looking down at their tightly clenched, white-knuckled fists—others scared, fingers up—praying.

Fear! I could see and hear the bodies screaming. It was all around me. Fear! I could smell it, and I could taste it in my bile. Suddenly, my head jerked toward the pounding sounds of waves knocking hard against the ship's sides and along its underbelly. Thunder roared. Hard driving rain pelted the deck. Lightning flashed all around the boat. Waves approached two hundred feet high. The ship rose—its nose pointing to the sky, its back end pointing down to the depths of the ocean. The boat stem rose to its peak, threw grown men to the floor, and bodies rolled over each other when the stern turned on the wave tops.

I watched in horror at men biting their lips—women screaming—children squirming, crying, wetting themselves—older people, self-soiling, and others puking next to them. For eighteen hours, I ground my teeth, chewed my nails, and sweated under the strain of seeing people pushed against the sidewalls, against their bunks, and each other. The storm was relentless. The ship rose— fell—rose, and fell again. Side to side, the ship banged against the swells. Water climbed over the ship's rails, seeped into the crevices, and found its way among the passengers—cramped and stinking in the ship's belly.

Everywhere, people were groping for bedposts and stanchions, grabbing and holding on to them. I sat transfixed with my arms and legs wrapped around the heavy wooden bunk post, holding on with every ounce of my being. Then, I spotted the Romanos—all huddled together, holding onto things, and holding on to each other. My mother dumped me off at an orphanage, and Sister Verona told me I was lucky, but I wasn't feeling so fortunate. Luca's the lucky one—he had a family to hold onto."

Finally, at 7.20 p.m., a hush came over the ship. The setting sun started to paint the blue-black sky with long, vast swaths of bright, orange-red. Prayers of thanks, sighs of relief, and a ship full of hands clapped at the sounds of calm, still, and quiet. It was the sign that offered a better tomorrow—"Red sky at night—sailor's delight"; everyone looking forward to that promise of good weather in the morning. Luca came over to my bunk.

"That was a little scary," he said.

Still trembling from the commotion, I replied, "I don't know about you or your family, but after a while, I didn't even care anymore. I never thought I'd see so many big people yelling, screaming, crying, and looking like they didn't know what to do."

"All I did was hold on," Luca said.

"Did you cry?"

"No."

"Neither did I. It was still scary, though. How much longer will it take?"

"My mother said we should be there in four days, but she didn't know if the storm would make a difference."

"I wish I never got on this boat."

"My mother said the worst was over, so we should be happy about that."

"Nothing worse—uh-huh, I have heard that story before."

Chapter Eleven
Maria Meets the Marinelli

The first time the Marinelli greeted me, they hugged me and said how grateful and happy they were that I was there with them and how excited they were to finally become a family. I wished I could have expressed the same sentiments, but my doubts about my new surroundings prevented me from even pretending to be overjoyed. My personality was usually happy and friendly, but I guarded my feelings more carefully since my long friendship with Sister Verona ended abruptly. Still, Sister Verona taught me to be polite, so I was.

We left the pier and started walking toward their waiting car—I stepped between them—Signora Marinelli held my hand, and Signore carried my things. She had a strap over her right shoulder that crossed her breast and attached to the big, shiny, black handbag she was carrying. Signora used her free hand to hold the underside of the pocketbook, which was almost as big as my suitcase, perhaps, fearful the straps would break. I couldn't help wondering what she was carrying in that big thing.

"Here's our car, Maria. I'll put all your things in the trunk. So you can have a back seat all to yourself."

I sat in the back seat, gawking at everything while they sat in front talking—probably to me. All I heard were indistinguishable sounds that I didn't invite and didn't interest me. I looked for the flower fields, the orchards, the sights, and sounds familiar to me as I watched the landscape passing by my window—struggling to find any signs of what I left behind. Instead, I saw blacktop roads, concrete sidewalks, and people—lots of people, and automobiles and trolley cars. Here I was in the New World—"paved with gold"—but I didn't see any signs of gold paving on our way to the Marinelli home.

I had no vision of what the homes would look like—I was expecting to see their home in a setting with a cluster of other houses surrounding them. But, straining to see everything in front of me, what I saw when we turned off the main road and into their driveway surprised me. I saw a straight, wide path of light gray cobblestones leading to a circle—the drop-off to the grand entrance hidden from the street. A replica of the Statue of Liberty stood inside the ring, reminding me of pictures I saw in geography books of Ellis Island.

Behind the home was a patio, and behind that were side by side greenhouses; vegetables grew in one, and flowers in the other. The house, and grounds, looked like the mansions and castles that Sister Verona used to tell me about in stories and fairytales. In an odd sense, it looked similar to the orphanage—both were gray stone, imposing, and off by themselves, but that's where the similarities ended. The Marinelli home looked a little smaller but L-shaped.

The main structure was behind the circle at right angles to the rest, on my left side. Six wide steps led to the top landing, where four tall, white pillars propped up a white, wooden, triangular-shaped roof. Below the roof were five sets of tall windows with two windows in each. Massive wide, white double doors provided the entryway into this unbelievable estate. I don't know how much land the Marinelli owned with their home, but it was a lot—and it was beautiful. It wasn't as expansive as the property I knew growing up, but it was plenty big. Their home was grand inside, too.

It's hard to describe the home's inside—there were far too many architectural treatments and nuances to cite them all. Besides, I don't know what they are, anyway. The house had nine bedrooms, and most of them had a fireplace. All the bedrooms, and bathrooms, were styled with chic marble and ceramic imported from Italy—Wainscotting and Crown Molding added an air of elegance to the home. First, I wondered why two people needed so many bedrooms and bathrooms. Then I assumed other family members or friends lived there with them, but no one did. Finally, I learned that two gardeners worked for the Marinelli, caring for the outside of the house, the pool, and the grounds. They didn't live there either.

I slept a lot for the first few days, but the first week in my new home with my adoptive parents was a whirlwind for me. Beyond the long, grueling, and very tiresome trip, I had an enormous amount of information to process. I wondered if I would see Luca again or Sister Verona. Would it matter—would the Marinelli like me—would I like them—would I appreciate America. If I were forced to leave, again, where would I go—what would I do—how would I get anywhere. Whenever I thought I had an answer, five more questions surfaced. Fortunately, when I wasn't sleeping, I was off somewhere, seeing, doing, and discovering things far beyond anything I could imagine.

On my first Monday in America, I had to go to Town Hall with Signore Marinelli to make my adoption official—I had mixed feelings about that. My name, Maria Della Notte, wasn't especially appealing, and it wasn't a longstanding family name—but it was my name, and the only thing I had that was mine. That didn't seem to matter to anyone else but me because I was Maria Marinelli when I came out of Town Hall. Maybe that shouldn't have made any difference, but it was one more thing I had no choice about—my name—the only thing I called my own was gone, and I didn't like that.

As soon as we got outside, Signore Marinelli lowered himself to my eye level, put his arms around me, and gave me a long, tight hug.

"Congratulations, Maria. You don't have to call us Signore, Mr., or Signora, or Mrs. Marinelli. You are officially our daughter now. You may call us mother, father, mom, dad, or something like that. OK?"

That didn't feel right to me. Of course, I knew very well what fathers and mothers were, but since I never had either, I wasn't comfortable calling anyone by those names—and I said so.

"I'm sorry, Signore Marinelli. I don't mean any disrespect, but that will be hard for me. I never called anyone that, so I'd like to keep saying Signore and Signora."

I know I hurt their feelings when I said that, but they said they understood. I thought a good compromise would be to address them without a title. So when they spoke, I answered. When I spoke, I just said 'excuse me' and started talking.

That evening, Signora said, "I'll draw your bath." What? When I arrived at my private bathroom, a tub, filled to overflowing with bubbles, greeted me there. What? That was fun, relaxing, and cleansing all at once. Sitting in that warm, soothing, relaxing tub filled to the brim with bubbles, I felt relief in my worn-out, overtired body, and the burden of my life I was carrying began to wash away.

I can get used to this, I thought and slinked into the tub until only my chin was visible above the bubbles.

It was Tuesday morning when I finally woke up feeling refreshed. The three weeks before that, I went to bed tired, woke up tired, and felt tired most of the day, especially after the big storms we had on the boat. I might have been more homesick if Signore and Signora Marinelli mistreated me, but they made me feel extra special. They seemed to know before I did what would make me happy.

"I have the day off today, Maria. So you and I are going on a shopping trip."

"A shopping trip?"

"Yes. We're going to downtown Philadelphia and buying you some new clothes."

"But I have clothes."

"I know, but this will be fun. We'll get you some play clothes for school, some dress clothes for special occasions, some casual clothes for most of the time, and a few fun clothes."

We took a train to the city, then walked to the nearby department stores—Strawbridge and Clothiers, Gimbles, Wannamaker's, and Lit Brothers. I saw more clothes in each of their Children's Department than I thought existed in the entire world. The children's clothing was not like the scant Italian, hardly fashionable collection of outfits I brought with me.

We shopped for hours—I don't know how many.

"Maria. Look at this pretty blue print dress—see the cute little pink rose on the side? Try it on."

I tried the dress on.

"Oh. It fits perfectly. Do you like it?"

I didn't even have to answer. If I smiled, Signora Marinelli bought it.

"Look at this dress, Maria. And shoes to match!"

I bit my lip, trying not to smile, but she bought the dress and shoes anyway. I didn't even want them. I didn't need so many things to wear—it didn't make any sense to me, but we shopped, tried on, and shopped some more. Finally, when she thought I had enough shoes, dresses, sweaters—you name it—she paid the clerk and took a small bag of things.

"Someone will come to pick up the rest."

"Thank you, Mrs. Marinelli. It's always so nice to see you."

I didn't say anything, but she asked if I were hungry at the end of our shopping. But, of course, I was hungry even before she asked, so I said yes.

"We'll go to Horn and Hardart. There, they have the world's largest vending machines. It's at the train terminal—it will be quick and easy."

Everything she said and did was a discovery for me.

"What are vending machines?"

"You'll see."

When we arrived at Reading Terminal, we stopped in front of an endless row of glass panels displaying a vast array of sandwiches, pies, cakes, fruit, and drinks, sitting on shelves behind locked glass doors.

"What looks good to you, Maria?"

"Maybe an apple, a piece of cheese, and a glass of milk?"

Signora inserted the required coins, opened the door, and, one at a time, handed me an apple, a piece of cheese, and a glass of milk, and, to my delight, a bit of lemon meringue pie. Again, I was wide-eyed and speechless, seeing all that food behind little glass doors—another incredible, marvelous discovery.

On Wednesday morning, a big yellow taxi waited in the driveway to take Signora Marinelli and me to the school where I was pre-enrolled. It was a short ride—maybe twenty minutes, but it was pleasant, and it gave me my first chance to see my new surroundings. It was more an area than a neighborhood—the homes were few, far between, barely visible behind high hedge walls and vast, lush, green lawns.

As we passed by, Signora pointed to several homes in the distance beyond the green and floral landscape and announced, "The Mayor lives in that one" or, "That white brick home, with the two tall evergreens to the right—that one belongs to the President of the Golf and Tennis Club." I reminded myself of Sister Verona's words: "You can learn a lot about a person if you listen carefully when they speak."

Less than a month earlier, I was pounding the ground with my fists, watering the grass with my tears, and hating Sister Verona for forcing me out of her life. There was no place in my mind where I could have imagined what was in store for me, but I was in a constant state of amazement at everything I saw and all that had happened to me since I left. My former world was a cold, stone building living in the bosom of beauty—the beauty of a mountain valley with orchards, pastures, and wildflowers that teased my senses and filled my heart with pleasure. In thirty days, my tiny world evolved into a universe where everything was monumental—cars, homes, schools, roads, everything. Time would tell if this new world was too big for me.

We met the principal and several other teachers who arranged for me to take a battery of tests. Except for a few English words and phrases I needed help with, I completed the tests in the time allocated and without much difficulty. Based on the results, they decided I would start my school year in seventh grade. When we were through, we went into the school library. Rows of shelves stretched end to end, held more books than I thought existed. Besides volumes of textbooks, hundreds of other books included biographies, autobiographies, and novels in every genre. There was also a clothing section of the library—upstairs.

Signora Marinelli bought all the books I needed—books she thought I should have and more books for my reading pleasure. She also purchased the required gray-black-white, plaid skirt, white blouse, black sweater, black saddle shoes, white socks, and all the appropriate accessories she said I would need. I was familiar with that type, and style, of school clothes—it was the same as I wore at the convent. Hmm, I had come full circle in that regard—what a useless waste, I thought. Why didn't we just buy these clothes in the first place, instead of spending all that time and money on clothes I didn't need.

On the Wednesday of my first whole week in school, three seventh-grade girls stopped at the cafeteria table, where I was sitting, with Jaime Williams and Marylin Andrews—both of whom were in most of my classes. The three girls didn't ask to join us or make any attempt to sit—they just stood in front of us, looking at each other, smiling and giggling. Jaime said their names—I only remember hearing Sonya Everhart's.

Finally, Sonya looked at me and said, "I know—you're that orphan girl that Dr. Marinelli adopted." I wanted to throw up. I had a hole in my stomach and a lump in my throat as big as a golf ball. I was humiliated—dumbfounded—I wanted to pull her hair out and scratch her face off.

But instead, I managed to say with conviction, "Yes. Yes, I am."

I wanted to lash out and say things to her and about her, but I stopped when Sister Verona's voice popped into my head, "We should think of our words as feathers in a pillow. Once they're out, you can never get them all back. So, if you can't say something good, don't say anything."

I couldn't find something good to say, so I didn't say anything. Instead, I turned to Jaime and Marylin and took comfort in the look on their faces, shocked at Sonya's rudeness. The kindness in their eyes gave me all the support I needed to weather that uncomfortable exchange. I left no ill-conceived feathers to retrieve.

I spent as much school time with Jaime and Marylin as our schedules allowed. They confided in me, and I was willing to share my feelings with them to the small extent I did, but the nasty remarks Sonya made when we met still stung. Since she was one of the most popular girls in the school, I assumed most of the girls were friends of hers, and I wasn't about to set myself up for more humiliation from her or her friends. On the other hand, I was much more at ease with the young people I met at The Club, so I went there whenever I could after my last class rather than hang around at school.

Few, if any, of the kids I knew from school were Club members—at least, I never saw any of them there. Although I didn't have much more than tennis and swimming in common with The Club girls, that was fine with me. I was delighted that there was never a stitch of gossip among us. Our competitive spirits, not what we disliked about other girls, inspired us. Like me with my school work, Priscilla and Muriel dedicated themselves to being the best swimmers and tennis players possible, and The Club programs allowed us to try.

Both programs offered Intra and inter Club competitive play. Prissy (Priscilla) Bigelow and Murry (Muriel) Von Krumpf played in the same group—Over Eleven. Excuse the boast, but we were good. Players were matched, not by age, but according to our ability, and we were always matched up with girls, at least two or more, years older than we. Collectively, we were responsible for bringing more championship trophies home to The Club than any others in the teams' history. I thrived on the competition.

Chapter Twelve
Maria
Exploring

So much activity blurred my first summer in America, where nothing stood still for long. I tasted foods I never knew of, saw things I couldn't believe, and heard the excitement in the daily sounds of routine life in America—all of it far beyond my imagination. My first American vacation with the Marinelli was a car tour. I saw and did more with them in three weeks than I had done in ten years of my existence.

"Come on, ladies. Old Bessie has a tank full of gas, enough air in the tires, and plenty of oil. We're just waiting for you to hop in."

We packed a few things for overnight and put them in the trunk. It was early morning when we started on our way with some food Mrs. called, snacks, to munch on—I was too busy gawking to think about food.

The landscape changed quickly and dramatically—the hustle and bustle of the city grew quieter, and the numbers of people, cars, busses, trollies, and trains faded away. We left that noise behind and welcomed the new day with the sun shining down on cornfields, pastures, and dairy farms. Big and small animals populated the areas we passed as the city streets turned to small-town roads, then to countryside with rolling hills and cornfield miles. First stop—Lancaster, PA.

"Maria! Look! In front of us."

"Oh my gosh! It's a man and a boy driving a black buggy."

"They're probably going to the market. See? The wagon is filled with fruit and vegetables and homemade things to sell."

"This reminds me so much of home."

"Yes, I'm sure it does, except these people are Amish. They do everything themselves."

"What do you mean?"

"They grow their food—like fruit and vegetables, and they raise animals for the meat, eggs, and milk they provide. They make their clothes and help each other build their homes and barns."

We did practically the same things at the orphanage, so I didn't find that bit of information very exciting.

"What's that big thing that looks like a fan?"

"That's a windmill. The Amish don't use anything modern—they don't even use electricity. So, they use the power of the wind to do for them what electricity does for us."

"Are they American?"

"Yes, but the first ones came from Germany and Switzerland. They share religious beliefs and mostly marry people from their community. They live a simple life."

I was fascinated to hear that the Amish didn't have anything compared to the Marinelli and, now, me—no cars, telephones, no electricity, or plumbing—not even a tub or a toilet. All the men's and boys' clothes looked the same—the lady's and girl's clothes were alike. I didn't need all the clothes the Signora bought, but I was happy that I didn't have to look like everybody else.

"Hey, back there—are you getting hungry?"

"No. Not really."

"Well, Missy, we can't leave here until we have a taste of some Shoo Fly Pie or some Funny Cake."

I didn't answer right away. Neither one of those things sounded very appetizing to me. I couldn't think of anything funny about a cake, and I sure wasn't interested in a pie that had anything to do with flies.

My adoptive parents and I spent a large part of our first few months together at The Club. Oh Boy! That was another astounding discovery. The Club boasted luxury, grand style, people, places, and events, new and foreign. In addition, I was informed, the Club was the place to socialize—swimming and playing tennis and a place to "make some good connections," which was a priority set for me by Signore Marinelli. "It's not what you know, Maria—it's who you know that makes the difference." But, of course, I had no idea what he meant by that, and I didn't bother to ask.

Anything you might imagine was available at The Club—swimming pools, golf course, tennis, squash, racquetball, courts. They even had a polo field, where competitors came from around the globe to play. There were several cafes and two restaurants—one for casual and one for fine dining. There were bars inside, outside, and poolside. We spent a lot of time at The Club—we ate there at least twice every week. My newly acquired parents attended club meetings, social events, special dinner dances, fundraisers, and whenever business moguls or movie stars were on hand. So, they played when they could and, I thought, drank more than they should.

"After all," they professed, "our professions are demanding. We work long, hard days, so we are entitled to some fun, free time."

At school, I worked hard, studied, behaved, completed my homework, and always finished all my assignments—It didn't take long to feel confident that I could keep up with the class. Halfway through the seventh grade, I was already among the top three students in most of my classes. Except for Sonya Everhart and her friends, I enjoyed the challenges and all that the school had to offer. But, most of all, I wanted the campus for its beauty, fresh air, and, when I could find it, the solitude.

It wasn't like I wanted to be alone, but going off to a quiet place on campus reminded me of Sister Verona, my old school, and the kids I knew there. We didn't say mean things or make fun of each other for no reason. Any hint of that kind of behavior was unacceptable. I tried to think of reasons why Sonya and her friends would laugh at me. Why? They didn't even know me. I shrugged it off when it first happened, but it hurt my feelings, and I didn't know what to do about it, so I smiled to cover my hurt.

There was nothing spectacular about my seventh and eighth-grade school years. I got better acquainted with Jaime and Marylyn in seventh grade—we studied and spent as much time as possible together during breaks and after school while waiting for the bus. They lived across town from me, so I didn't see them much outside of school. Occasionally, I got permission to invite them to The Club, or our house after school, to swim. That was fun to splash around, attempt some diving tricks off the low board and see who could hold their breath longest underwater.

Sooner or later, we gravitated to the corner edge of the pool where Jaime and Marylyn sat together, and I sat at right angles facing them. We talked about school, teachers, and subjects we enjoyed or disliked most and exchanged ideas on finding ways to enjoy the things we didn't already—at least how to make them tolerable. Yet, somehow, the subject of boys always managed to seep into our conversation. Someone was handsome, pleasant, or friendly, an honors student, basketball star, played in the band or possessed any of many other characteristics that led them to swoon, giggle, laugh out loud, or bring them to tears. Unfortunately, I failed miserably in all discussions in that category.

I liked Jaime and Marylin almost as much as I disliked Sonya, who made me shudder whenever I saw her in the halls or outside, laughing and giggling with her friends. They never spoke loud enough to hear, but I knew whatever they were saying was about me, and it wasn't good. So I did all I could to avoid her even when she called me "Annie"—like Orphan Annie. When she said that, I stood as tall as I could, and while my heart was tearing apart and my emotions bleeding to death, I smiled wide and walked away. I would never, ever, give her the satisfaction of knowing how deeply she hurt me.

Midway through eighth grade, I began to feel more accepted and better connected to the students beyond those in my classes. I could handle the coursework more quickly than most of my classmates, but I studied extra hard because I wanted to be at the top of my classes. It didn't take long to discover that being an orphan wasn't the only thing on Sonya's reason to taunt list, but I stopped caring. Since Mr. had some strict rules about "No boys!" I avoided them to a fault, but even not dating drew snide remarks from Sonya's crowd:

"Who does she think she is, anyway?"

"She's such a snob."

"Snooty."

Although I wasn't interested in boys beyond our common school interests, I loved it when a boy talked with me when Sonya and her friends were nearby. I felt warm inside when those girls glared at me in those situations. Sonya's group ignited a competitive spirit that didn't exist before I met them, which wasn't all bad. However, a small part of me was disappointed when I heard that Sonya was transferring schools at the end of the year. Her family was moving to the Midwest to take advantage of a great job offered to her father. One side of me wanted to say goodbye to bad rubbish, but the other wanted to compete with her academically and otherwise. I was disappointed to learn that wouldn't happen.

High school was not a whirlwind of fun for me—Signore made sure I understood that I was there to work. Sometimes, he delivered his message subtly, but more often, his tone was louder and more demanding—especially when he pointed to his road to success.

"I had to work hard, get good grades, find my sport, and participate in extracurricular activities. I made sure I was the best—no matter what. There is no royal road to success, Sweet Pea—and remember, boys will only get in your way."

"But in some classes, boys are assigned to be a teammate. I can't avoid that."

"Look! I don't want to argue with you. Working with boys in a class is one thing, but don't get involved with them otherwise."

"If you mean dating—don't worry. Where would I find the time for that?"

I had to work harder to make the soccer team than I did tennis. I had good hand-eye coordination, quick reflexes, and stamina which enabled me to play tennis competitively. I thought those qualities would help me on the soccer field, but they didn't. But what I lacked in strength, I made up for in speed and agility. During soccer tryouts, I had to dig deeper into myself to earn a spot on the JV team. In practice, whether it was jumping jacks or push-ups, I always did one more than requested, and I always did one more lap than required. If I was dead tired and with little energy left in the tank—after the last jumping jack, push-up, or lap I sprung to my feet, stood straight up, and grinned. It wasn't enough for me to beat my competition—I wanted to destroy them.

When it was time to make the JV team selection, the coach said, "Maria—I'm happy to tell you that you're on the team, but it's not because you're a better player than some of the kids that got cut. What you have is grit, determination, and a strong will—I can teach kids how to play soccer, but I can't teach them what you have—that burning desire to win."

Thank you, Sonya.

My high school soccer career was a bittersweet experience—I spent half the JV season playing well enough to get advanced to the varsity team, where I sat on the bench for the second half of the season. The following years, the team did OK, and so did I. We ended two seasons in third place and two seasons at number two. We got very close in the finals, and the games in both seasons went into overtime, but we didn't have quite enough in ourselves to win a championship.

Some might say I had an enviable school experience—mainly for having come from a foreign country, and advancing to seventh grade when I belonged in the sixth, and progressing on an honor's path all the way to my senior year. And, doing well in sports was quite an achievement—they said. But, frankly, I felt better about spending the three weeks of vacation with Mr. and Mrs. every year. Those experiences were eye-opening, and I thought they sincerely cared for me during those times.

Perhaps it was my immaturity that kept me hostile toward my adoptive parents. Except for the fun conversations we had during our vacations, all they ever wanted to talk with me about was my schoolwork and extracurricular activities having to do with school or sports. If I wasn't at the top of the heap, they wanted to know why. Beyond that, all mealtime conversations centered around their work and professions. If not that, then they rambled on about their golf tournaments, charity work, fundraising events, or rattled off a current list of who's who at The Club.

I wasn't especially interested in any of that. I wish they would have pried a little deeper into my life just once. Maybe they could have helped me understand the likes of Sonya or assured me that I was not inferior whether or not Sonya implied otherwise. Deep down, I knew my adoptive parents wanted the very best for me. But I wasn't convinced they knew what that was.

My America sightseeing took me from the rocky shores of Maine to the soft white sands of Southern Florida. We visited zoos, museums, historic buildings, and battlefields. We crossed the Mason Dixon Line, the Mississippi River, and the Continental Divide—I was experiencing everything new to me—from sea to shining sea. We went, saw, and enjoyed ourselves every minute, every time, and everywhere we went. I saw the plains, the deserts, the mountains, and the many treasures of the country's amazing National Parks

One year, we took a long train ride from Philadelphia to Texas. I prayed my head wouldn't explode from absorbing all that was passing by my window—skyscrapers, and slums in the northern cities, cornrows, cotton fields, and pickers in the deep south. I saw mines in the mountains of West Virginia and the river and the mud in Mississippi. Every year, for three glorious weeks, the wonders of the world were unfolding before my eyes. I was in the company of two people who catered to my every whim.

I had it all—but, somehow, it didn't feel that way. I had everything I could possibly ask for but, what I wanted and needed most was their precious time, more than three weeks a year. I'm sure they convinced themselves that they were more than loving and caring for me, and for those three weeks, I was also confident that our ordinary lives waited for us at the door when we returned.

When I opened my suitcase to unpack, my guardians began singing their familiar tune—Signore sang the lead.

"Vacation's over. It's time to get back to work. If you expect to amount to anything, you better plan on being at the top of your class in college. Don't waste your time with anyone who can't make you better than you already are. When the time comes, marry someone better off than you. Meanwhile, no boys!"

It was clear how much my adoptive parents wanted me to succeed. They tried to provide what they believed would fulfill me and assure my happy life. But even as a teen, I struggled with their description of a happy life. By their definition, they had all the ingredients for their own happy life before I came along—they were both well educated, accomplished, and well respected in their professions, in the community, and among their peers. They owned the most beautiful home in the neighborhood, they belonged to the best Country Club in the area, and they enjoyed every pleasure that their accumulated wealth could provide. Creating a family by adding me to their extensive list of assets would have been the crowning glory of their long list of achievements. Having a family should have cemented their happiness. Unfortunately, I'm sure that's what they thought, but it didn't seem that way to me.

I didn't quite understand that if money guaranteed happiness, why the doctor and professor weren't happier. But, of course, besides earning good salaries from their professions, they also got money from the stock market. But the stock market, money, and every subject related to money were always the basis for their high-temperature conversations.

"Another of our investments filed bankruptcy—we might have to slow down on spending."

When those discussions were going on, they were always loud enough for me to hear, and when I noticed, they were clubbing less, drinking more, and still preaching about what I had to do to be happy.

In mid-July, for nearly a century, people gathered in Hammonton, New Jersey, a town between Philadelphia and the Atlantic Ocean, to celebrate the Feast of Our Lady of Mount Carmel. They came from all across the nation, but most lived in southern New Jersey and Philadelphia. The Sons of Italy Social Clubs chartered busses to gather people from towns farther away, so they could enjoy the festivities, too. I arrived on one of the buses from Philadelphia. On the same day, Luca came on a bus from the Northdale contingent.

Chapter Thirteen
Luca
Welcome to Northdale

We just barely made it onto the bus heading to the train station. My family was the last to board, and the driver wanted to split us up because the bus was already filled. Still, a few people squeezed together to make room for my parents; then a few more invited my brother and sister to their seats, and I wiggled my way onto the bench in the back of the bus. I saw Maria still standing on the Pier and assumed she had missed the bus and that we'd meet again at the train station. If not, then in Northdale for sure—that's where I thought the whole boatload of people were headed. She waved, and I waved back until I couldn't see her anymore.

The bus ride from the Pier to the train station took about 45 minutes. I didn't get to see much along the way because it was hard to turn and look. I was sandwiched between two big men, and the pressure of their arms against my small body made it hard to do anything but sit still. I couldn't see much, anyway—the men were too tall for me to see over their heads, so I had to look straight out of the small section of the back window behind me. I saw cars, buses, people, and smoke that looked like what I saw in Naples on our way to the Pier. I was excited to arrive at the train station. There were so many people walking every which way—and trains. I never saw so many railroad tracks and so many trains.

When our train pulled in, it was so long I couldn't even see the end of it. When we were ready to take our seats on the train, the conductor moved one seat to face the other—my father took an aisle seat and let me have the window seat next to him—he and I rode backward. Giada had the window seat next to my mother. Marco and Angelo sat across from my mother, and Tonio sat alone across the aisle from my father. I felt like a big shot—riding backward just like my Papa and oldest brother.

"We're moving," I shouted, happy to get the last leg of our very long trip started.

"No," my father replied, "it's the train next to us moving."

He was right, but it sure felt like it was us.

As the train rolled farther from the station, I noticed the changes in scenery. There were fewer cars and people. Houses were farther apart, trees were more plentiful, and there were pastures with cows walking, grazing, watering, or laying down—maybe, taking a nap. Somewhere, between the Reading Terminal and the Northdale train station, the monotonous, clackety-clack rhythm of wheels on rails weighed heavy on my eyes, and I fell into a sound sleep. I don't know how long I slept—it felt like it was only a minute before my father's arm over my shoulder shook me awake.

"Wake up, Luca. We're here. Finally, we are all together, again only this time in America. Our family, and friends, and some of our old neighbors are here and anxious to meet us."

I rubbed my sleepy eyes and confused head, long enough to see that my father and I were the only ones left to get off the train. I quickly looked at the platform outside to see my mother, sister, brothers, holding, hugging, and kissing people I should have recognized as relatives and friends from our village in Italy. But, at that moment, I couldn't pry their faces loose from the deep creases in the memory part of my mind.

Counting my family, I saw about two dozen people in our group on the Northdale Train Station Platform—all of them cross-talking louder than the noise trains made passing by. Laughing, sobbing, smiling, weeping, hugging, shaking hands, and waving arms were sights and sounds among the people on the platform I was proud to call Zia, Zio, and Cugini. They were there to greet us, help us with our baggage, and show us the way to our new American neighborhood. It was only a short walk along the railroad tracks, across the parking lot, and through a ball field, behind a long row to the home where I would live on Pitt Street.

The Pitt Street neighborhood had a small reception for us when we arrived. Extended family and friends of the families settled in Northdale several years earlier were on hand to welcome us and celebrate our safe passage. They were waiting for us at The Sons of Italy Social Club—a place where the neighborhood gathered to lounge, laugh, lavish, welcome, wed, and weep together. What a party! I was practically dead on my feet, but seeing kids and cousins I hadn't seen since I was barely old enough to remember them kept me awake far past my usual bedtime. I don't know what time I fell asleep on the floor at the party, but Marco carried me home across the street.

Sunday was as hectic as the night before, with people coming and going to welcome us to the neighborhood. Between the food and drink they brought to our house and the leftovers from the party, there was enough food in our home to feed a small army. Before I was allowed to meet and play with the neighborhood kids, I had to suffer through endless introductions to extended family members, friends, and neighbors. Almost every one of them pinched my cheeks. The ones who remembered me most fondly knelt to my eye level and pinched both cheeks. The men were worse.

I squeezed my eyes tight shut, trying to picture why I should know the man who threw me to the air or the one who shook my hand with a shattering knuckle grip, or the guy that patted my head as if he were driving a nail into the floor. Thankfully, I managed to survive all the love I was getting in the form of hugs, pinches, taps, pats, squeezes, and shakes, with enough energy left to meet and play with kids my age—outside.

It didn't take long for me to get in the groove of my new neighborhood. Half the faces were familiar and, somehow or another, we were related—the other half were friends of the family. I couldn't have been any happier living in any place other than Pitt Street in Northdale. So there were many boys to play with, talk with, listen to, learn from, watch, imitate, and avoid. There was always something going on somewhere. Stickball, tag, hide and seek, marbles—games that could be played with anyone, anytime, anywhere. I even learned how to throw pennies "for keeps" against the bottom step of the Sons' Club.

On warm Sunday mornings, after Mass, the male elders were either digging in their gardens or sitting on their front porches talking over the fences with their friends—maybe over a glass of wine or a jigger of Anisette—solving problems. Wives and women were indoors cooking.

West Pitt Street ran for a mile—from Broad Street to Artillery Avenue. The aroma of garlic, onions, peppers, sausage, meatballs sizzling, or some form of braciola sitting under a bubbling pool of tomato gravy (aka sauce), and hot, crusty, Italian bread, from Mike's Bakery, filled the air. Sunday dinner was cooking inside every home in the entire neighborhood.

Late Sunday mornings were fun for my friends and me. It's when the Crapshooters assembled on the ballfield behind the houses. We used to hide in the bushes and wait for one of the elders to call the police. Presumably, the yelling disturbed their peace, so someone always made the call. Within minutes, a car with two policemen came to a screeching halt behind the backstop, raising enough dust to create an instant family for Adam and Eve. Waving nightsticks high in the air and running like the Keystone Kops, the policemen jumped out of the car and started down the first baseline. Nine crapshooters and a dozen onlookers scattered in ten different directions. Some disappeared into backyard gardens, others behind garages, onto the streets, and into their houses.

When the police reached the outfield, my friends and I sprang forth from the dust and ran to the players' crap table in the dirt and picked up dollar bills, loose change, and dice as fast as we could. The fastest among us got most of the paper money, while the slowest scooped the quarters and halves. There was no dividing the spoils; it belonged to whoever picked it up—end of the story.

That Sunday scene never changed. It was a ritual, like so many other things that never changed in the neighborhood. The bakers, barbers, butchers, farmers, grocers—each were integral parts of my life—all grew through the streets penned inside our triangle—two sides railroad tracks and the base on Artillery Road. No one was ever captured or hauled away. Instead, the younger men got older, and the kids took their turns being the younger men. Consistency, and Sunday morning crap games, made me happy.

There must have been a hundred boys and young men living in our neighborhood, and most families were large. Boys in one family tended to be friends with boys of similar ages in other families. For example, my brothers, Tonio, Marco, Angelo, and I, are friends with Frankie, Peppie, Enrico, and Joey Santucci—two families, eight boys—all friends.

Most of my collection of good friends was the last born in their families— B was two years older, but Joey, Pauley, Gino, and the Farina twins, Tony and James, were my age, and I was happy to learn I would be in the same school and grade with them. They were an enormous help in easing me into the unfamiliar territory of an American, Parochial school.

We walked to school, which was a little more than a mile from our neighborhood—one-half block to the railroad crossing, five blocks, wobbly-balance-walking on the tracks to Main Street, and six more blocks to the school. We passed a few clothing stores, a diner, a jewelry store, a gas station, and Memorial Park along the way. The Park filled an entire block with lush green grass, trees, bushes, and flowers planted along the paths that wound through it all. A war canon served as a silent reminder of the wars that took the lives of Northdale's soldiers lost in service to their country—their names engraved in a marble slab on the ground, next to the flag pole behind the canon. In addition, there was a baseball diamond, with stadium seating, at the far, back end of the Park and a deer pen next to that—all combined to make Memorial Park a pleasant place to be.

A century-old giant oak tree growing through the pavement occupies all but a few inches of sidewalk across the Park. Patches of bark are chiseled off the tree, creating flat spaces for etching hearts—some broken and jagged all telling stories of love and loves lost. Hearts pierced with arrows make the announcements—"John loves Mary", "Frankie loves Brenda." Time tells Brenda to scratch Frankie. The newest, permanent, current, brief report becomes, "Brenda loves Edward" and that "Kilroy was here." No one knows who he is, but Kilroy is everywhere at the time.

All Saints is in the Archdiocese of Philadelphia and situated on many acres of land bought to further develop the parish school system. Besides the school, a church, rectory, convent, and graveyard occupy part of the property. Franciscan nuns and a few Roman Catholic priests teach at All-Saints Catholic Parish School, directed by the church pastor, overseen by the Archdiocese, and supported by church parishioners. The school curriculum is as challenging and demanding as the teachers and the parents who send their children there.

My fifth-grade teacher was a Franciscan nun named Sister Mary Helen St. John. We addressed her as "Sister", the same as we did all the other nuns in the school. However, to differentiate her from the others, we called her "Sister Mary." Except for her face, hands, and body build, she looked the same as other nuns. They all wore habits consisting of long-sleeved, pleated, black gowns covering them from shoulders to toes. Black stockings and plain black shoes cover their feet, and a black veil, trailing a black, squared at the top, hood, cover the head. A crisp, white, heavily starched bib, called a wimple, covers the neck and cheeks. The only visible human features are the face and hands.

At first sight, I thought Sister Mary was pretty. She had a smooth, light complexion and clear, light brown eyes that sparkled. Her eyebrows were brown—I suspected her hair was brown, too, but I couldn't see it, or her ears, either. They may have stuck out a mile, but I didn't think so—the rest of her face was so well shaped and nice-looking. Her nose was pretty small, straight, and turned up at the end. Her lips were plump and had tiny creases on each end, making them look like she was always smiling. I liked her.

"Boys and girls? This is Luca Romano. He has come to us from Italy and will join our class for the remaining school year. Hopefully, he will continue with the class to the end of Eighth grade. Please welcome Luca."

I felt a little goofy standing next to Sister Mary, looking into dozens of other eyes staring back at me. I shifted my weight and shuffled my feet, and tried to figure out the seating arrangement. I counted eight rows of desks –five desks in each row. A boy occupied the corner desk, on the right side, a girl sat next to him, and the other three seats were empty. Rows began to populate more after the third row—the last row was filled.

"Children? Starting with the first row, please take turns standing up and telling Luca your name. For now, first names only. That will be enough to try to remember."

"Katherine!" "Charles!"

"Helen!" "Benjamin!" "Michael!"

"Howard!" Francine!" Bridget!" "Bernadette!"

In the end, the only names I remembered were Katherine and Charles. The rest of them came at me so fast I lost them the moment I tried attaching their names to faces. As for my friends—Joey, Pauley, Gino, and the twins were no help by making faces and trying to make me laugh the whole time. When I looked around the room, I noticed that none of my friends were sitting next to each other—they were at least two seats apart. Since they were so scattered, I thought there was a good chance I'd be sitting next to one of them—I hoped so.

"Thank you, class. I'm sure it won't take Luca very long to know all your names. Luca? Please take your place next to Katherine."

Math was my favorite subject, and except for topics like Civics, I wasn't intimidated by any of my fifth-grade classes. I expressed myself, and I understood most words spoken to me, so my English was acceptable. Grammar was challenging, and I soon learned that speaking English was different than speaking American. When my classmates said things like, "That's a piece of cake" or, "You've got one strike against you", I had no idea what they were talking about.

There were thirty-seven students in my class—twenty boys and seventeen girls. Sister Mary taught every class in the same way, in the same room, every day, rarely raising her voice, and her demeanor was pleasant. But, at the same time, she was firm, with little patience for foolery and no tolerance for anyone unwilling to pay attention and learn. Despite her permanent smile, due to her constantly upturned lips, it was clear when someone –seldom a girl—lit her fuse because she addressed the fuse lighter, Frank in this case, was called Mister, plus his surname.

"Mr. Farina! If I have to say that again, you can go home—now—and stay there until next Tuesday."

I learned a lot during that time, and I was grateful for having Sister Mary be the one to start me off.

I liked school, and I was happy to make friends outside my neighborhood, but I was more comfortable when the semester was over. Since everyone in my family had jobs, I was left in the care of my mother's sister, Zia Carmella, whose children were grown, and she stayed home to run the house. Supposedly, she had the time necessary to keep an eye on me, but she had plenty to keep her occupied besides me. So except for having to go in for lunch, I had lots of outside time that summer.

Chapter Fourteen
Luca
Whistles and Clickers

It didn't take long for me to learn that even kids could find ways to earn money in America. A junkyard two blocks from my house bought old newspapers for two cents, and rags, for three cents per pound. One summer afternoon, one of my neighbors, fourteen-year-old Vito, and his thirteen-year-old brother, Mike, showed me how to find the product, exchange it for money, and, most importantly, when to negotiate with Jimmy at the junkyard. That day I didn't earn anything– it was my first visit to the junkyard, and I was just an understudy. I was invited strictly as an observer—to watch and learn.

The boys waved me over as they were leaving their house with a wagon trailing behind them. It was not a shiny, new, red, store-bought wagon with black wheels, but a wagon made entirely with junkyard parts. Weather-worn, scraps of old, gray, barn wood, bent, and rusted axels, and crooked wheels—most without rubber, cobbled together with mismatched, odd-sized screws and large, repurposed, bent, rusty nails—re-bent to secure the axels to the bottom served the purpose. The left front wheel had a little rubber left on it, but no rubber remained on the right front wheel. Each of the two back wheels came from different-sized wagons, and the wheels' diameters were different from each other. The rear end of the "wagon" tilted slightly to the left, while the right front wheel didn't quite touch the ground.

Turning the wagon required lifting it—usually from the back end because someone had to be behind it to ensure the load didn't fall off. There were no sides to hold the cargo on board. The wagon handle was fashioned from a length of clothesline rope, looped through a hole, chiseled into the centerboard, and tied. Technically, it wasn't a wagon, but it was a means to transport our load.

The process began with collecting old rags and newspapers scrounged from the homes of friends, family, and neighbors. Next, we scoured the streets, along the railroad tracks, parking lots, and from the outsides of nearby factories, mills, and warehouses. Loose rags were acceptable at the junkyard, but newspapers had to be bundled and tied. Otherwise, Jimmy refused to accept them. That day, we collected about five pounds of rags and enough paper to make seven bundles—about five pounds in each bundle. Vito decided that if we soaked one pile of paper—divided it equally, and inserted the wet pieces in the middle of each of the six dry bundles, the weight would be heavier, and the goods would yield a more significant profit. We were on a mission.

I was awestruck when we arrived at the junkyard. I saw piles and piles of twisted metal, wheels, tires, rusted fenders, bicycle parts, papers, rags, and a monster crane with a colossal magnet sucking up metal and transferring it to the tops of metal mountains, adding mystery to the junkyard landscape. Shiny objects grabbed sunshine and bounced it back as bright, white light. I had never seen anything like it before. Then I watched the crane operator lower the magnet and let it come to rest atop a black sedan.

Slowly, he raised the car as far as it would go—as high as a house—before he moved it to his far-right and lowered it, front to back, into a crushing machine. The screeches rattled me, like the crunching sounds of metal, fabric, rubber, and oils forced together by powerful jaws twisting, turning, and reshaping the once beautiful, shiny, new automobile into a nothing, flat piece of metal. I stared at the crane operator—amazed at how his little body could manipulate such a big machine and make it do exactly what he wanted. Meanwhile, we waited for Jimmy, who was busy with someone else, but he walked our way soon enough.

"Come here, Luca. Jimmy's coming."

Jimmy was one of the owners and the man who would pay us for our goods. I was anxious to see how much money the paper, rags, and effort would fetch. Jimmy was broad and muscular—built like an armored truck. He had light-brown hair, hazel eyes, and naturally, dark skin made darker from working outside every day. Jimmy's complexion was ruddy. My young, teenaged friends were taller.

Jimmy had a clipboard under his right arm, a pencil on his right ear, and a chewed up, stubby, foul-smelling cigar clenched between his teeth. He looked menacing to me even before I saw his right hand was missing. In its place, he had steel, claw-hook he could open and close by flexing his bicep. I backed up a little when I saw the claw open. I wasn't about to get my nose caught in that thing.

Jimmy finished his business with the customer ahead of us, then turned to go into his shack for the money to pay him. Meanwhile, we moved our load from the wagon to the scales and waited with extra-wide smiles for him to come, verify the weight, and pay us. With our heavy load, we anticipated a payment close to a dollar.

"I'll give ya seventy cents for the papers."

"What? C'mon, Jimmy, the scales say it's worth at least a buck."

"Seventy cents—take it or leave it."

"Jimmy!"

"I'll give you fifteen cents for the rags—take your papers off the scales and go home—bring 'em back when they're dry."

"We'll take the seventy cents."

I learned a lot that day in the junkyard. For one thing, trying to pull the wet paper over Jimmy's eyes was a foolish idea. He was honest, fair, and one of the friendliest business people I ever met. My first summer in America went by fast, and I learned a lot. But when it was time, I was ready and happy to go back to school.

Spending the last six weeks in fifth grade getting acquainted then playing and earning money through the summer gave me a sense of accomplishment and boosted my confidence in meeting new people and trying new things.

Sister Frauke taught sixth grade. She carried a wooden pointer in her left hand—two-feet long, quarter-inch round, with a black tip on the end and a short piece of white chalk in the other. Most times, the stick was used to point to things she couldn't reach with her hand. Sometimes, though, she used the pointer to emphasize her intolerance for talking, passing notes, interruptions of any kind, or writing left-handed. I can't recall if any girl in my class was ever tapped with the wooden stick. I doubt it because they were well behaved, but, occasionally, an ill-advised boy might feel courageous enough to test the veracity of Sister Frauke's warnings—but he only tried it once.

"Mr. McGinnis. Stop talking and pay attention!"

Sister Frauke turns her back to the class and resumes writing on the blackboard. Thomas McGinnis turns to Frank, the boy sitting next to him, and whispers,

"Psst! Frankie. Answer me. She's twenty feet away facing the blackboard, the chalk is squeaking, and she has that hood over her ears—she can't hear!"

Without a word, Sister Frauke walks toward Thomas, who's seated at his desk, looking skyward, hoping she doesn't stop.

"Make a fist, Mr. McGinnis!"

A whack with that thing was never on a flat hand. WHACK! Thomas, along with the rest of the class, sat bolt upright, paid attention, and that ended any sort of class disruption for a very long time.

Whack stories are the ones that linger and become legendary. Lesser remembered stories are about the thoughtful kindnesses that nuns gave out daily, not seeking recognition for their actions. For example, I forgot my lunch a couple of times. I didn't say anything about it or ask for anything, but a nun noticed I wasn't eating with the group. She took me to the convent, where she gave me a sandwich and a glass of milk—just a sandwich and a glass of milk. At various times, other kids forgot their lunch or needed some extra care or attention. Those kids never went hungry or were left wanting.

There was a church on one side of the school and a cemetery on the other side. On the back end, there were a convent, a maintenance shack, and a play yard. Across the street in front of the school, acres of church-owned land was used for a playground. The playgrounds were great. The one in the back was where busses picked the students up and dropped them off. It was used for morning and afternoon recesses and where we would be marched for fire and air-raid drills. The playground was where we lined up or for processions into the church and where the older boys smoked, "unnoticed" behind a stone monument cradling a giant statue of The Blessed Mother.

"You'd better behave! Mother Mary is watching."

I always liked the playground across the street. It was bigger and used during lunchtime when there was more time to play and enough time to allow all the kids to cross the street. All grades were outside during lunch, so there were kids everywhere, playing all sorts of different games. Usually, the boys' games involved some kind of ball being thrown, caught, rolled, kicked, hit, or avoided. Boys ran full speed toward, or away from each other or, to and from, a hiding place. Girls played games with balls too, but more often, they skipped, hopped, jumped, or clumped in a group together, talking and, just like in my neighborhood, they all spoke at the same time.

One kid, 'Zeezie', pretended he was both airplane and pilot. He wore an aviator cap that stretched over his head and covered his ears, with side flaps that snapped together underneath his chin. When "Zeezie" snapped the snaps, lowered his head, stretched his arms wide, and started to run, the roar of his engine was like no other—Yeeaarrrwwwwooounnn. He taxied at full speed, from one end of the play yard to the other, leaving scores of victims knocked to the ground by the leading edges of his wings.

The outside of the school was a cube-shaped, brick building with lots of windows on all sides. It was two stories high—each floor was divided into classrooms, bathrooms, and offices. The basement was divided into two halves, separated by steps coming down from the first floor. Left of the steps was the girl's "cloakroom"—the boy's "cloakroom" was to the right of the steps, and the boiler room was straight ahead.

The boiler room, which contained the big, coal-fired, steam-generating boiler, was not especially inviting. It was clammy hot and had a strange-smelling mixture of musty walls, coal, ashes, and fire. Moreover, the school's maintenance man was the only person who had any business being in that room—any student caught going in or out would receive an automatic three-day suspension. Nevertheless, every year, a small group of energetic and daring male upperclassmen broke the rules because winter, in the All-Saints boiler room, was the time, and place, to carry forward a long-standing rite of passage, tradition.

The boiler provided heat for the entire school via steam that circulated through big, cast iron radiators placed under the windows in each classroom. On the morning of the coldest day of winter, a small collection of eighth-grade boys made their way into the boiler room, opened the iron door exposing the roaring fire within, and peed into it. Soon after, a horrible stench came steaming through the radiators and permeated every classroom and hallway in the school. The informed students sat patiently in their respective classes, waiting for the news that, at the appropriate time, every nun delivered to her students:

"Classes will be dismissed early today to make repairs to the heating system. Those of you who take the bus, please line up at nine-fifteen. Red Bus students line up next to the fence! Green Bus behind the Statue, and Yellow Bus by the maintenance shack! Tomorrow morning, there will be no excuses for missing or unfinished homework assignments! Class dismissed!"

Like everyone else, I was happy with the early dismissal, even though the details behind that decision were unknown to me at the time. If I knew, I would tell you why the buses were named Red, Green, and Yellow when all of them were Orange.

Whistles and clickers used to inform, instruct, direct, and warn were apparently essential to our education at All Saints. After the students filed, out row by row, and class by class, the nuns used their referee whistles to notice an event—like directing lower grade students to their bus-waiting places. In addition to the "whistle", used only outdoors, every nun also had a "clicker" used everywhere else.

The "clicker" was roughly the shape of an empty computer mouse, with a thin, flat steel band stretching almost to the end of the hollow. Pressing and releasing the steel band made clicking sounds. Press—Click. Release—Click. Press and release—click-click. The nuns kept their clickers unknown since there were no pockets in their gown and no strings or chains attached to the clicker. So, no student knew where the clicker was hidden, but we all knew exactly what it meant.

The "clicker" had two functions: To make a clickety-cricket sound and reposition a nun's eyes from her face to some unknown, obscure place behind her back. While writing some endless sentence, or math equation, on the blackboard—with her back to the class, one hand on her rosary beads, and a stick of chalk in the other, a nun can—all nuns can—see everything going on behind her. "Click—I see you, Mr. or Miss—knock it off!"

Church events provided opportunities for both whistle and clicker use. Thweeeeeeeet! That meant, "Stop immediately! Assemble! Form lines according to your grades! Separate yourselves! Girls go someplace—boys go anyplace else!" Click-click meant "Start to walk! Put your hands at your sides! No talking!"

Once inside the church, there were no more whistles—only multiple clicks. Click-click—Kneel! Click-click—Stand up! Click-click—Sit down! Click-click, click-click-click, click-click meant, "I see you whispering. If I come over there, I am going to pull on your ears until your appendix comes out together with the tonsils of the boy you're talking with. Then, I am going to contact your parents, and tell them you misbehaved IN CHURCH! They will be angry and upset with you and probably give you a good, swift kick in the pants. YOU will end up in Hell, or Purgatory, for a thousand years, at the very least. Go stand outside the door and don't come back until I let you in. Do you want me to call Father Benedict?"

"No, Sister, I'm sorry."

"Pssst. Anthony, be quiet—next time, talk to Jimmy if you have to talk."

Chapter Fifteen
Luca
Father Benedict

Father Benedict was a short, portly man, with a round face and a few white hairs on the sides of his, otherwise, balding head. Behind his round, wire-rimmed glasses, his steel, gray eyes looked more prominent than they were. He wore a white-collar, atop a black bib, beneath a black jacket, over a pair of black pants. He kept his pant legs tucked neatly inside black, mid-shin length, rubber, galoshes with metal buckles—he wore them every day, rain or shine.

On Report Card Day, my classroom was a collection of happiness, sadness, exhilaration, frustration, and determination. Father Benedict reviewed every student's report card in every class and handed out their report cards for the semester. Click-click. Everyone stood. There was no reason to use the clicker to announce his arrival—everyone knew he was coming because the smell of his stinky cigar always entered our room fifteen minutes before he did.

Seconds before he enters, we see the shadow of Father Benedict behind the frosted glass window that takes up the top half of our classroom door. He doesn't knock, but he hesitates before he enters. Once inside, he scans the room and nods at Sister Frauke standing in front of the blackboard. She nods back and remains standing at the end of the desk to his left—he takes his seat behind her desk.

"Good morning, girls and boys."

"Good morning, Father."

"Do you know why I'm here today?"

"Yes, Father."

"It's report card day. Are you all ready?"

Most of the class replies with energetic yesses. A few boys remain silent and slink down in their seats in anticipation of receiving a less than stellar report. Sister Frauke begins calling each student's name alphabetically and asks them to sit on the empty chair next to the priest facing the blackboard. The good Father is half smiling, half threatening—his eyes command us to pay attention and behave.

"I am here to see what you've learned and earned since the last time I was here. Andrew? I see you are having a little trouble with math. The last time you earned a B and, now, you've received a B minus. Is this because you don't understand, or because you are simply not paying attention? I see you have a C in Conduct. I think you had better stop fooling around and start learning how to do the math. What do you think? Speak up, Andrew."

"I see you have all "A" s, again, Katherine. Congratulations, young lady. If you keep up your excellent work, then, someday, you will become a doctor, just like your Father. It makes me happy to present this report card to you. I'm sure your parents will be happy, too. Andrew? You must work harder and behave, like Katherine. You can do it if you try."

And so goes report card day with Father Benedict delivering back pats, and ass kicks, with equal ease, in alphabetical order.

As a sixth-grader, I thought Fr. Benedict was just a mean, cigar-smoking, crabby, old man who always wore black rubber galoshes, who enjoyed scolding, and who everyone feared. But, in fact, he was a nice guy who really cared about kids and was determined to educate them in every way possible. Altar boys got to see Father Benedict in his role outside the classroom, where his personality was more light-hearted, but his wisdom, guidance, and direction remained. I was an altar boy.

We Altar boys were almost guaranteed a two-dollar tip for serving Mass at weddings and funerals. That was great—particularly weddings, which were always fun because people had happy faces, and smiled a lot. Men we didn't even know rolled up a dollar bill, winked, smiled, and "made us" take it. However, I didn't like serving funerals as much as weddings because everyone was sad at funerals—especially Italian funerals, which were a little scary with all the crying and wailing.

Part of our altar boy's job was to fill a crystal glass cruet with water and another with wine—place both cruets on an oval, gold plate, and cover it all with a clean, crisp, white napkin. We also filled the chalice with unconsecrated communion wafers. At the time, only the priests celebrating the Mass drank the wine at communion time. Anyone receiving communion during Mass was presented with a communion wafer only. The priests at our church preferred Sauterne wine which they stored under the counter, in a cabinet, next to a tin can filled with communion wafers.

My friend Chick and I were preparing to serve a Funeral Mass. I reached into the cabinet for the bottle of wine and the tin of wafers—I placed both on the countertop in preparation of filling their respective containers.

"Hey, Luca. Did you ever taste wine?"

"Yeah. At home. On Sundays. My Father lets me have a small glass with supper."

"I don't mean that. I mean this wine."

"No. Never."

"How about the communion wafers?"

"Only at Mass. You?"

"Yeah. I tried both."

"What? You can't do that. That's a sin!"

"No, it's not. So how can it be a sin?"

"Didn't we learn that's a sin in school? It's the body and blood of Christ! It's Sacred! We'll go to hell if we do that."

"Come on, Luca! It's not consecrated yet. That's what the priest does at Mass. We're not going to hell. Here. Eat this!"

I was scared out of my wits. I looked all around to be sure no one was watching. Then I looked around again to make sure no one was hiding—and watching. Finally, I thought I heard something drop. I convinced myself it was Father Benedict about to discover us thinking evil thoughts.

Chick grabbed three or four communion wafers, stuffed them in his mouth, and took a swig of wine straight from the bottle before handing the bottle to me. I took a swig, snapped a wafer in half, and let it dissolve in my mouth. The wine was a gold color and a lot sweeter than any I ever tasted at home. The wafer tasted a little like dry bread and reminded me of the paper-thin covering found on the Italian candy—Torrone. I tingled with fear in anticipation of what might happen next. I tried to rationalize the insignificance of one sip of Sauterne and one wafer each. What harm could possibly come from that? Then, suddenly, the good Father appeared. Again, I hic-gulped at the sight of him and again, when he started talking about honesty, honoring parents, theft, and the perils of underage drinking. How could he know?

That night, at the dinner table, Giada said, "Father Benedict stopped by today." My brain felt like I just inhaled a block of ice—my throat, feeling stuffed with a bale of dry hay, unsuccessfully tried to swallow. "He said he was watching you light the tall candles at Mass this morning and that you seemed to be having trouble finding the wick. He thought you may need glasses and that you may not be seeing the blackboard as well as you should."

That episode could have had a much worse ending for me. I thought about that for a long time afterward and came to realize Father Benedict was a much bigger person for teaching me a valuable lesson in that way. Clearly, I, and everything else about that incident, was wrong. He could have used his position to power over us—given us detention, suspended, or even expelled us from school—if he wanted. He could have told my parents—humiliating them and me in the process. Telling them would have put me in a highly uncomfortable position at home—indeed, he knew all of that. He never even accused us of anything, yet he made his point without ever raising his hand or his voice.

I was in the process of growing up in America and learning a lot of essential and exciting lessons in and out of school. My parents, siblings, relatives, friends, teachers, and people like Father Benedict were educating me about life and how to live it. A lot was going on to keep me hopeful for the future—I made it to and through the sixth grade.

Except for the streets I had to walk on my way to school, my parents kept me confined to the boundaries of our neighborhood. To get to school, I stayed on the west side of town, walking the railroad tracks to Main Street, crossing to the east side at Broad, and continuing up Main to the school. At the time, school, and church on Sundays, were the only reasons I had to wander outside the area set for me.

Two years after moving to Pitt Street, our family relocated to Artillery Avenue and Seventh Street. No move took me farther than two blocks from my original home on Pitt Street, so I didn't need to meet or make new friends. Our home was still firmly planted in the neighborhood called "Little Italy," where I knew everyone's name, and they knew mine. The only thing that changed when we moved was the two extra blocks I had to walk to meet my friends.

One of my first goals in my new location was to see if I could get to school faster if I took a different route. I told my friend, B, I planned to walk straight up Seventh Street, turn right onto Northdale Avenue, turn right, and walk the seven blocks to the school. Since there was much less traffic on my planned route and only one traffic light, I thought I could reach school before my friends. We agreed to walk at our average pace and no cheating.

When I crossed Broad Street and entered the east side of town, I noticed differences in the street names. In my neighborhood, the streets were numbered Second through Eighth. Otherwise, they were an Avenue. On the east side of Broad, the roads were numbered Second through Seventh, and they also had Avenues, Lanes, Places, Terraces, Gardens, Circles, Paths, Drives, and Ways. In addition, many of the homes had numbered addresses written in Script, unlike the ordinary one-, two-, or three-digit numbers on the porch walls of houses where I lived. Then I saw a strange sign planted in the ground between the edge of a lawn and a red brick sidewalk. The address was Two-Seventy-Three Periwinkle Lane. The plain, white sign was about eight inches tall by sixteen inches wide with big, bold, attention-grabbing, black letters.

ITALIANS AND DOGS
KEEP OFF THE GRASS!

I didn't know what to think about that. Of course, I knew what each word meant, but I never saw or heard those words put together that way. When I got to school—my friends beat me by five minutes—I mentioned the sign, and they shrugged it off as if it were yesterday's news.

"Yeah! My oldest brother, Al, told me the cops chased him and his friends off that street; said they didn't belong there."

"Why?"

"How do I know why? That's what my brother told me."

When I got home, I asked my Father what the sign meant.

"Hmm. It means a lot of things. First: you're supposed to be walking to school with your friends—not that way, and not alone. Second: You better not do that again, or anything else like that, unless you have my permission."

"It's stupid to say Italians can't walk on the grass."

"No. You're Italian. You know how to read the sign so you'll listen, and you won't walk on the grass. What's stupid is to think the dogs will read it and listen."

"But we're Americans now, too, aren't we?"

"Yes, we are. Every morning, you say so in school when you pledge allegiance to the flag, but we will always be Italian by our birthright."

"Did anyone ever tell you to keep off the grass because you're Italian?"

"Not exactly in that way. Besides, it's not about being Italian, Greek, Polish, or anything else—it's about people. Some are just thoughtless and mean."

As I grew older, I began to appreciate my Father's wit, wisdom, and humor.

"They may have had a fight with some religion, culture, race—in this case, Italian—who knows why—and instead of working the problem out, he chooses to integrate an entire group, and culture, into his unfortunate experience. The best thing you can do is behave yourself—be kind—not cowardly, but thoughtful in your words and actions. That way, you can avoid being lumped in with bad characters."

His response to those kinds of taunts was always the same. "Learn something from this." In his example with the sign, he offered that I should work hard in school and in whatever else I undertook so that, one day, I can be the man who makes the signs. And, he added, "I hope your signs will say, 'Welcome'."

I preferred physical tasks more than mental ones. I liked school and the things I learned there, especially math, but, given a chance, I chose to take things apart and put them back together rather than reading about how to do it. After I graduated eighth grade, I thought I would go to the public school where they offered shop classes and technical training—I was sure that's where I belonged. However, my parents and the Parish School had other plans.

The school I attended for two years and six weeks was expanding and building a new school. Their strategy was to add one high school grade each year in the old building while making a new grade school without interruption. That meant my class stayed in the old, small building for one and one-half years. Then, we got transferred to the brand spanking new school for one and a half years before getting transferred back to the old one. Ours was the third class to graduate from the old, brand new, High School in the old school.

It took some attitude adjustment to become a lower classman in High School instead of an upperclassman in Grade School. But, adjust we did. Meanwhile, I pleaded with my parents to send me to public school and continued to make my case for the following three years. However, my parents were not easily persuaded, and it finally dawned on me that I would never win that debate. So, despite feeling that my interests would be better served in public school, I was just as happy to remain with my friends who continued their educations in the new parish High School. The work was challenging but manageable. Math was still my favorite subject, but chemistry, physics, and biology ranked high in my mind once we got into it. Those classes allowed me to discover things like the energy created when vinegar is mixed with baking soda and bend light rays. Biology was fun for me, too.

Tenth Grade Biology Class was fun and funny, but it could also lead to detention. By coincidence, Sister Bernadine was teaching the class and selected Bernadette to be my teammate. When Sister Bernadine announced that it was the day for dissecting frogs, the boys yipped and the girls yucked. Frogs, scalpels, and aprons were passed around, and soon all the students focused on the teacher pointing at a huge drawing on the blackboard. It was a frog, lying on its' back, arms and legs splayed like a green man at the beach on his day off. But he was a frog with his chest open, and we were looking at an image of his organs. Unfortunately, I missed some of the instructions due to a self-imposed distraction regarding a prank I planned to execute at the perfect moment.

Before class, I saturated several cotton balls with splotches of red beet juice. Then, I spread the cotton flat and made a hole in the middle of it to line up with a hole I cut in the bottom of a tiny, lidded box I kept in my pocket. When the teacher called for attention and prepared scalpels, all eyes were on her. Except for me, every student was totally absorbed in frog body parts and precise locations for their scalpel placement. Perfect. I took the box from my pocket, stuck my middle finger through the box bottom and through the red splotched cotton, then laid my finger flat against it.

"Psst. Bernadette. I just cut my finger off."

"No, you didn't."

"I really did. Look."

I trembled a little and struggled to remove the lid.

"Does it hurt?"

"Yeah! It hurts like crazy!"

I ripped off the lid. Bernadette peeked into the box and turned white—her eyes got glassy, she fainted and slumped in her desk. Her reaction resulted in the totally unforeseen, uninvited, unwanted, unexpected consequences of Sister Bernadine racing to the scene.

"Luca! What happened?"

"I think she got a little upset when we started cutting."

Thanks, Bernadette. You could have told a story, but you didn't. You were a trooper.

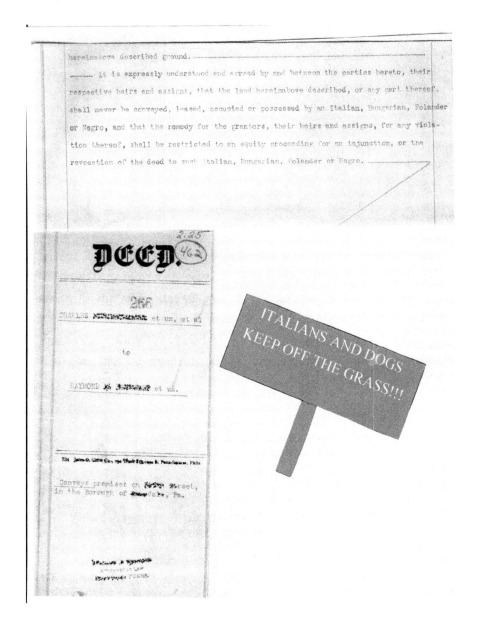

Note: Who cares? On this ship that left Naples, Italy, and arrived in Philadelphia in May 1921, every man, woman, and child on this manifest supposedly had brown eyes and brown hair. Twenty of twenty-three adults were listed as being five feet, five inches tall. Pictured above are the men who helped build the railroads and roadways in their New World. Below are the children doing their part by collecting and bundling papers, rags, and tin cans for the War Effort.

Chapter Sixteen
Luca
Twenty-Two. Forty-Eight. Eighty

There was no such thing as expendable income in my house—everyone worked, and everyone contributed to help maintain their personal and household needs. Everything I needed was always provided, but I had to pay for it if I wanted something more.

"Ma, can you buy me some—"

"No, but when you can afford it, you can buy all you want."

I couldn't wait to get out of school and start earning money. The thought of being poor all my life never occurred to me. I didn't have a bicycle, toys, or many other things, but my neighborhood friends didn't either, so I never really thought about that. Then, one day, a classmate invited me to his house, a short walk from the school. I was struck by the amount of space between his home and the next one, which I couldn't even see from his place. Fifty houses could have easily fit in his yard; he had a barn too.

His mother said, "Now, Edward, please be careful when you ride Cloud." Cloud? What the heck was Cloud, I wondered. Cloud was a horse, and Edward was a good rider. He showed me how to get up on the horse and told me what to do—I fell off Cloud a few times, but I got the hang of it after a while. That whole experience was something I would never think to dream about, but it was sweet and I liked the taste of it.

My working career began at home so work, and earning money, was not strange to me. Besides the simple lawn mowing, trash emptying, errand running, and seasonal snow shoveling chores, there was the garden to tend. That was hard work. From May to October, when there was work for me in the garden or anything associated with growing vegetables, there was no escaping it. Playtime for me was out of the question until after my digging, hoeing, planting, watering, weeding, and picking assignments were completed. There were also vegetables to scrub clean and jars to wash, boil, and fill with garden fruits and vegetables that would grace our table until the following May, when the cycle began again. I certainly didn't do all of it myself—not even a fraction of it, but I was not happy about it. My young self wanted to be anywhere other than in the garden digging or in the cellar washing tomatoes. I'd rather be playing baseball on the street or jumping into the sand and coal bins next door—that was far more exciting and fun.

"There's a time to work and a time to play."

That's what my Pop used to say all the time. He wasn't buying my argument that a good time to start playing a baseball game was in the first inning—not the fourth or fifth inning after chores.

My high school achievements were decent through eleventh grade. Then, when I decided it was ok to skip school on Mondays in my senior year, they fell to the high end of acceptable. After that, I prioritized working and earning money over five full days of school or extracurricular activities, including school sports other than baseball and football. Paying jobs allowed me to contribute to the household funds and always have a little money in my pocket for beat-up old cars, nice clothes, and fun.

From fifth grade through my high school years, I gained a fair amount of work experience while keeping my report cards afloat. I worked in a grocery store, on a huckster truck, a rose farm, movie theater, bowling alley, pool room, haberdashery, laundry, and textile mill. I bagged vegetables, filled rose beds, tied roses, swept aisles, cleaned seats, set pins, racked balls, stocked shelves, and sold clothes. After that, I pressed pants, kept knitters with yarn, folded, packaged, and shipped, sweaters. Life was good, but it was also challenging to balance school, work, and social life.

One sunny Sunday afternoon, a group of us were sitting on the steps of The Sons of Italy Club—chatting, playing cards, and generally horsing around. Then, my friend, Benardo Benedetto, B, elbowed me with an idea.

"Let's go check out the new golf course. It opened about three weeks ago."
"Where is it?"

"On the corner of Main and Gettysburg—where that big farm was."

I knew where it was—I didn't want to go there.

"Why do you want to check out a golf course—golf is a rich man's sport. Besides, we don't know how to play."

"We can start at the driving range—we can try to hit balls, at least."

"I've never even held a golf club."

"No. But you play baseball—you know you can hit a baseball."

"That's different,"

"You're right! It is. But if you can hit a baseball coming at you at seventy miles an hour, you should be able to hit a ball standing still on the ground. Come on, let's go."

He drove, and along the way, he asked me if I planned "to see that girl you met at the Rec."

"Joanne?"

"That's the one."

"No!"

"Why? She's cute, and it looked like you two hit it off at the Rec Center."

"We danced a lot that night, and I thought it was going great, so I asked her for a date. Then she started asking about my friends and what part of town I lived in. When I told her, she refused the date and said she'd never stepped a foot into that part of town and planned to keep it that way."

"Wow! That's a kick in the teeth."

"I tried to tell her that whatever unfavorable nonsense she heard about where I lived, I was none of that. She said her family would disapprove of her dating anyone from north of Main Street and west of Broad."

"Pfff! Forget her, my friend. There is plenty of other fish in the ocean."

As we were pulled up, we could see the Driving Range and the Putting Green—both were to the right of the Pro Shop. The first tee box was behind the putting green. The sign on the pro shop door announced Manfred Schmidt—Course Pro. We walked straight up to the front desk—I was a half-step behind my friend. Acting like he was a player, 'B' asked the Pro behind the desk, "How much for nine holes?"

"You boys can't afford it."

"We'll let you know that when you tell us how much."

"You boys look I-Talian—are you I-Talian?"

"Yeah, what does that matter?"

"I'm the guy that decides who plays here and who doesn't, and you're not playing here—that's what matters; go back with your own people—where you belong."

We both stiffened and glared at Mr. Schmidt—both of us tempted to reach across the desk and slap him across his arrogant mouth. But our father's voices played in our heads.

"Keep your angry emotions to yourself. Never fight a donkey in a donkey barn, and never raise your hands to anyone unless to defend yourself. Don't ever start a fight, but don't ever run from one either."

B and I heard those words a thousand times, always against the backdrop of our having to prove we were worthy of being in America. Then, finally, we turned our backs and walked out the door. That wasn't the first time either of us heard that kind of talk or the first time someone denied us something because we were I-Talian. That hurt, but it was the kind of talk that fueled our determination to work harder, dig deeper, and get more intelligent so that one day, we would be "The guy that decides."

I asked B to drop me off at the corner of Main and Artillery because I wanted to walk and cool off. I didn't mention I was planning to stroll by Joanne's house on the off chance I'd see her outside. I wanted to see her outside the "Rec" and away from her friends, hoping to convince her I was a decent guy and worth dating. I was near the corner of Main and Clementine, where I would turn to walk the following few blocks to Strawberry Lane, where she lived. I saw William Bird walking toward me. Billy was a senior at Northdale High School and a friend of Joanne's older brother. He lived five blocks from them in the same neighborhood. I had seen him around but never talked to him.

"Are you lost?" he asked me.

"I don't think so—why?"

"What are you doing here?"

"Just walking along the sidewalk—minding my business—you should try it."

"Listen, smartass. I asked you a question—I want an answer."

"What was that question, again?"

"What. Are. You. Doing. Here?"

"That's not your business—is it?"

"I'm making it my business—you're in the wrong part of town, boy. Go home!"

"I am home—I moved here about six years ago."

I knew Billy wasn't kidding—he wanted to bully me into running away, so he could brag to his friends what a tough guy he was. I had no intentions of running away. I promised myself to stay calm and wait for him to make an angry, foolish mistake. He pushed me to the ground. I sat still, looking up at him.

"Get out of here!"

He yelled and stepped toward me as if he were about to kick me out of town. When his foot was close enough, I grabbed it, stood up, and pulled his foot up with me. He was furious. I stayed calm. He hunched himself and came at me with his fists closed, arms back, and ready to punch my lights out. I kept my hands open, stiff, and across my heart. He turned his body, slightly left, prepared to send a right hook into my face—I stepped aside and karate-chopped his Adam's Apple. He clutched his throat and straightened up enough for me to deliver a knee to his groin. When he bent from the pain, I bonked the top of his head with my elbow, and he went down. I stood looking down at him for a few seconds before stepping over him to continue my walk,

"Billy! You should try playing at the new golf course—I think you and Mr. Schmidt would get along nicely—say hello to him for me."

I wasn't pleased with that whole experience. I could have—should have—defused the situation by keeping my mouth shut, or simply leaving the scene, as Billy wished. I was upset with myself for carrying my fight with Mr. Schmidt to Billy's neighborhood. But I was satisfied for having stood up against a jerk. At one time or another, most of my neighborhood friends experienced similar episodes with people whose attitudes matched Billy's. Unfortunately, most of those encounters end poorly—nobody really wins.

We didn't do vacations, but I went to an Italian festival in Hammonton, NJ, with a group of family and friends, who chartered a bus to get there every summer. Most times, I hung around in a small picnic area among the group from Northdale. We brought plenty of our own sandwiches, a gallon of homemade wine, and gallons of Kool-Ade. This particular time, I wandered off to scope out the place and, to my delight, I spotted an attractive girl about my age walking toward a candy concession stand. Judging by her tall, trim, erect posture, I suspected she was an athlete. Her hair was the color of dark chocolate and smooth as silk sliding from side to side, across her shoulders as she walked. I inched closer to have a better look.

She stopped at the candy concession and scanned the large block of Torrone—an Italian Almond Nougat—that lay on the counter in front of her. Then, she lifted her chin and turned her face toward the man behind the counter, smiled at him, and asked him to chop a chunk off a big piece of that candy for her. As she looked down at the sweet treat, then up at the man, it seemed like she was moving in slow motion—each slight movement was like one frame in a movie. Finally, when she was halfway into her turn, I recognized that face. I was sure of it, but I couldn't connect it to a time or place.

Her eyes were soft brown with a dot, black as coal, in the center. I wanted to strike up a conversation, but I wasn't as confident doing that since Joanne's refusal to date me at the Rec. I hadn't fully recovered from that insult. I took a deep breath, walked to her side, and with as much self-confidence as I could muster, I asked.

"Hi, my name is Luca—what's yours?"

She looked at me like I was some kind of zoo animal. I was thinking lion, but the way she squinted her eyes and turned up her nose, she may have been thinking more like a monkey.

"What's your name?"

"I don't tell that to strangers."

"I feel like we met somewhere."

"Really? Where?"

Where, where. This girl looked so familiar. I knew her from somewhere. Where?

"I don't know—but I'm sure we met. So tell me, what's your name?"

"I told you, I don't give that to strangers."

"But if we met—we're not strangers."

"Unless you can tell me where we met—you're a stranger."

"Come on—I told you my name."

"Nice to meet you, Luca—I have to go."

"Now that we have met officially, you can tell me your name."

"Nice try, Luca—I have to go."

"Where? Why?"

"Back to my legal guardian."

"What?"

"Long story; he'll get mad if I'm gone too long, and he'll kill me if he sees me talking to you—bye."

"Wait! Wait. Wait!"

I was positive I knew this girl. I raced through the alphabet, trying to find a name I could connect to her face. A E I O U. Uh Uh Uh. Her name had an "Uh" in it—Anna, Olivia, Sophia, Maria. Maria! That's it, Maria.

"I got it! Your name is Maria! I know you!"

As she walked away, she said, "Twenty-two. Forty-eight. Eighty."

I must have said that number a hundred times in the hours and days that followed. I was anxious to see if the girl with chocolate hair and eyes would go out with me, but I didn't want to seem overanxious, so I waited a week before I tried calling her. It was long before most homes had telephones and long before we had one in our house. The closest phone I could access belonged to my Zia Carmella, and her house was two blocks from mine. Besides, I wouldn't use that one, anyway—not only because I didn't want anyone in the house hearing my conversation, but also because her line wasn't private.

There were public telephone booths scattered around the town, and all of them had private lines. There was one in the gas station and two, side by side, at the diner. So I decided to use the phone at Fella's Diner. I picked up the receiver, dropped a dime into the slot, and dialed Zero."

"Number please," asked the operator.

"Twenty-two. Forty-eight. Eighty."

"That will be an additional fifteen cents, please."

I dropped another dime and nickel in the slot and listened to the phone ring at least twenty times before I hung up. I tried two or three times after that and still never reached anyone. I started to wonder if she'd given me the wrong number—or if I heard it wrong. Then, at last, someone I assumed to be her father answered.

"Hello. Marinelli residence."

'May I speak to Maria, please?"

"Who may I ask is calling?"

"My name is Luca Romano."

"And do you know Maria from school?"

"No, sir.

"The Club?"

"No, sir."

"How do you know her, then."

"I met her at the feast—in Hammonton."

Click. All I heard after that was a dial tone. I knew Mr. Marinelli was strict with Maria because she told me as much, but I didn't think he was rude too. Maybe I was overthinking the abrupt ending to our conversation. It was possible that the line just got disconnected—that happened, sometimes. I didn't want to irritate him more by calling back—I decided to wait a few days before I tried again. I hoped Maria would answer.

"Hello. Marinelli residence."

"May I please speak to Maria?"

"This sounds like Luca."

Great! His tone made me feel as if our last conversation ended in a disconnect.

"Yes, sir. It's Luca."

"It looks like you can't take a hint. Maria's not interested in talking with you so, please, don't call here, again."

"But—"

Click. This time, I barely heard the dial tone. Mr. Marinelli slammed the phone down, fast and hard. There was no way I could mistake our exchange— this was more like a threat than a hint. I really wanted to chat with his daughter, but I wasn't sure there was any way to make that happen. I tried several more times, on different days and times—again, hoping she would answer. She never did. I decided to try one last time, but I would ask the operator her address this time.

"Hello, operator. I have the number. Twenty-two. Forty-eight. Eighty— may I have the address for Mr. Patricio Marinelli?"

"One moment, please."

I waited for what seemed an eternity. If only I had a Philadelphia phonebook, I could look up the address myself.

"I'm sorry, sir. Unfortunately, that number has been unlisted. Is there anything more I can do for you?"

"No, thank you."

I finally gave up trying.

I was in the last days of my junior year in high school before I saw or heard from the girl with chocolate hair and eyes again. Call it luck, chance, or just the way life goes, but I was inside the train station in Philadelphia, waving goodbye to some friends returning to their Army base after a short furlough. And there she was—on the platform—walking toward the station. I didn't know if she was coming from somewhere, waiting for someone, or missed a train to somewhere. I couldn't believe my eyes.

My first impulse was to hurry toward her, but I wasn't sure how she would react. She was a little coy when we met in Hammonton, and I knew she was on a short leash with her father. The only thing I knew for sure was that it wouldn't be good for either of us if he showed up and saw us together. So I turned my body away from her, hoping to go unnoticed until she moved past me. In less than a minute, she did.

Chapter Seventeen
Luca and Maria

"Hi, stranger."

She gave me a wry look and replied, "It was your choice to remain a stranger—I gave you my phone number."

"I called—three times—I stopped trying."

"That's a big fat lie."

"It isn't. Your father answered every time—ask him."

"He never told me."

"I wouldn't lie to you, Maria. I spoke with your father."

We talked for a while about what we'd been up to for the past six years. We were most interested to learn how much our lives were the same until after we separated on the pier in Philadelphia and to find out how much different our lives have become since then. She asked again if I were fibbing about calling and talking with her father. When I assured her I wasn't, she got so angry she put her fist on her mouth to stifle a scream.

"Three times—not just once, but three times—three phone calls that I never got or was told about. How mean is that?"

She was so annoyed she started shaking. I took her hand.

"Whoa. Slow down. Take a breath and think about it."

"Slow down? I'm beside myself—I'm so angry. And what is there to think about? He has no right to censor my phone calls."

"It's his phone. He pays the bills—he's your father, and watching out for you is his responsibility."

"Give me a break! Whose side are you on, anyway?"

"It's not about sides. It's about trying to find a way to keep everybody happy."

"It's impossible to keep *him* happy."

"Wait a minute. Do you have a piece of string?"

"I'm about to throw myself onto the tracks, and you're asking me if I have string?"

"I have the buttons, Maria—do you remember the time we were together on the boat? Obviously, we had a whole lot more going on than this, but everything turned out OK."

She thought about that for a minute, took a few deep breaths, and settled down.

"I'll get even with him," she said.

"What does that mean—get even?"

"I should have been told you called."

"He's just trying to protect you."

"From what? Does he think he can keep me locked up like I'm some kind of criminal?"

"Look. Your father is only doing what fathers do."

"That's not true. I know girls whose fathers don't treat them like two-year-olds. I'll show him."

"How are you going to do that? Remember, he's driving the bus you're riding on."

"I don't know what I'll do or say—I'll think of something, and when I do, he'll be boiling mad just like I am now—then he'll know how I feel."

"You're overreacting, Maria. My father always says, 'Stay calm. Think. Don't bite your nose to spite your face.'"

After she calmed down, I directed our conversation back to when we separated at the pier. I told her about my determination to find her after we parted in Hammonton.

"When I thought about it, I remembered waving to you from the bus on my way to Northfield. I was staring out the back window, and I saw you still standing on the pier—waving. So I asked my mother if she remembered that girl who stayed with us when we came from Naples. She said I was right about your first name and that Mr. and Mrs. Marinelli would adopt you. You told me something like that on the boat—that someone wanted to take you—I knew it had to be you."

"Aahh—a detective."

"One time, I came to Philadelphia just to look inside a phonebook—for your address."

"It's unlisted."

"I found that out. So, you know I'm telling the truth. Ever since we met, again, at the feast, you're all I ever think about. I'd like it if we could date, Maria—"

"For your information, Mr. Dick Tracy, I knew who you were when you asked my name."

"How?"

"I don't want to get into that now."

"If you knew who I was—why didn't you say so?"

"I don't know, Luca—that was a silly thing to do."

"So, will you go out with me?"

"I don't know that, either—I mean—how."

"How? I come to your house, knock on the door, you come out, we go someplace."

"Not that easy. First of all, you'd have to find my house. Then, you knock on the door, my father comes out, asks who you are, and when you tell him, he calls the police."

"Why would he do that?"

"Because when it comes to me, he has a one-track mind. He wants me to graduate from the best university, make connections, get a high-paying, prestigious job, so I can be rich, or famous—or both—and live happily forever after."

"Is he rich and famous?"

"If not, he's pretty close."

"Is he always happy?"

"Like everyone else, he has his moments."

"Which moments? Happy or sad?"

"Lately, I think he's more, sad, or maybe, mad is the right word."

"What's he angry about?"

"He's afraid of losing all their money. That would be life-changing for all of us—I mean the three of us—actually, the two of them."

"That's funny—my father doesn't have two nickels to rub together, and he's hardly ever mad."

"It's crazy how often I hear my parents arguing about money. A few weeks ago, they were talking about one of his friends who lost a lot of money in the stock market—he ended up jumping off the Liberty Bell Tower—and died."

"Jeez, Maria—losing a friend like that's enough to make anybody sad...mad—whatever."

"It's almost time for the train, Luca—Mr. will be here any time—how about if I call you; we can set up a time and place to meet?"

"We don't have a phone."

"OK—you call me. I'm usually home on Saturday mornings studying. So they'll both be at The Club. She'll be on the tennis court—he'll be playing golf. Twenty-two—forty-eight—eighty."

"Great! I'll call you next Saturday and let it ring twice before I hang up. You'll know that's me. I'll call right back—if I don't hear your voice, I'll hang up."

"OK—I'll wait for your call."

"Bye, Maria."

"Bye, Luca."

Minutes after Luca walked off the train platform, Mr. Marinelli stepped onto it.

"Hi, Sweet Pea, sorry I'm late, trouble with the track—hungry?"

"Starving."

"Great—let's go."

"Where are we going?"

"There's a small place, food's good—not too far from here."

"How far?"

"Four or five blocks. Wanna walk?"

"Sure."

"Place is called Mc Gillian's—opened up about a hundred years ago."

"Have you been there before?"

"Yes. A few times—with a couple of friends from The Club."

I would be hard-pressed to tell you anything about anything having to do with our dinner that evening. The place was dark and noisy—there was lots of smoke in the air. My father talked about his trip—the convention—I don't know. His words were trapped inside my anger, and the crowd noise—I didn't get much out of what he was saying—I didn't care.

That night, I went to bed pleased that I could hide my anger and manage to behave as if everything was just fine. But, more than that, I was feeling good at having met Luca earlier and excited to think we would meet again. At that point, I was content finding my missing friend. Luca was thoughtful and kind, and I was more than ready for a friend like that.

I was hoping he wouldn't get cold feet after his experience with the last three calls he made, but just as he promised, Luca called on Saturday morning. My heart started pounding as if I had just finished running four marathons. I grabbed the phone before it had a chance to ring the second time.

"Hello. Hello."

"Maria?"

"Yes, Luca. Isn't this the number you called?"

"How was your dinner meeting?"

"To tell the truth, I don't even know what I ate."

"That good, huh?"

"I was so mad that night it's a wonder I made it through."

"I didn't realize I made such an impact."

"Don't be a jerk. You know very well what I meant."

"What I know is—you have to find a way to get along with him."

"I met him like he asked. We walked there—it was a pub—in an alley. The place was crowded, noisy, and my clothes stunk for days from the cigar, cigarette smoke, and beer. I didn't say a word about it."

"Maybe you should have."

"Should have what? Blocked my nose and ears—and thrown my clothes away?"

"Maybe you should have said thank you?"

"For what? Not enjoying my food? Smelling like a barroom?"

"For taking the time to spend with you. Didn't you say you'd like more time with your parents? Maybe he thought he was doing something special with you."

"You always take his side. Why?"

"It's not about sides. It's about getting along. My father's been preaching about that for as long as I can remember. He says, 'Home is the smallest unit of society—you'll never get along in the big society if you can't get along in the smallest.'"

"I'll work on it—I'm not sure where to start."

"I'll put my money on you—I think you'll figure it out."

That part of our conversation with Luca could have gone very wrong if I thought he was preaching. But I didn't feel that way. His tone was earnest and soothing—more like a concerned friend looking to help me put puzzle pieces together than a lousy teacher screaming instructions on how to do it. I knew he was right. I had a chip on my shoulder since I learned that I was bound for unknown places at the convent. But Luca convinced me promised myself to make it harder to knock that chip off.

We talked for hours about our second chance meeting at the Reading Terminal. Our conversation bounced between catching up with our lives and touching on things we both remembered about our trip from Naples. We exchanged stories about our horrible experiences on the ship and the discoveries we made in our new environment.

"I remember waving at you from the Pier."

"I waved back."

"Then you disappeared—then just like that, you disappeared in a cloud of black smoke."

"You did, too."

"That was horrible. I was so sad."

"I thought you would be coming in a later bus."

"I wish."

"You didn't act it when I saw you in Hammonton."

"What did you expect?"

"You knew who I was. I wasn't sure who you were."

"I gave you my phone number, didn't I?"

"We have so much to catch up on—wouldn't it be fun to explore it all? Do you ever have four or five hours—when you have your own free time?

"Yes. Once a month—on Saturdays. This Saturday. The Club has interleague, mixed couples golf, and tennis tournaments—and that's an all-day affair."

"Perfect! Why don't you take a train to Northdale—I'll meet you at the station."

"I don't know, Luca—that's risky."

"You're right. I don't want you to get into trouble at home."

"I get in trouble at home whether or not I go to Northdale. So, see you on Saturday."

I didn't know what to expect when I got to Northdale—would it be a crowded city like Philadelphia, or would it be like what I saw, from the train window—a few houses sprinkled around in large areas of pasture. It didn't matter—all I wanted to do was see Luca again.

As we pulled up to the Northdale Station, I saw a billboard: "Live Work and Play in Northdale. Population: Eight Thousand." From my left window, I could see a set of trolley tracks running toward my train. The trolley track turned right in front of a large hotel at the bend. On the corner at street level, there was a Barber Shop, a Peanut Shop, Soda Fountain, Shoeshine Parlor, and Hoagie Haven under the hotel.

On both sides of my train, the two blocks of sidewalk had small stores on them—hardware, jewelers, feed and grain, clothing, billiard parlor, and a newsstand boasting the best and latest news, cigars, and cigarettes.

As my street-scanning curiosity started to wane, I spotted Luca waving at me. He was wearing blue jeans and a white tee shirt under a one-button opened at the collar, light blue, casual dress shirt. He was tall, tanned, good-looking, and happy. Our last waves were goodbyes—these were hellos, and I couldn't be more pleased.

Luca took my hand and helped me down when I stepped off the train. He didn't embrace me, try to kiss me, bear hug, or crowd me in any way—he behaved like a gentleman. But, of course, I didn't expect anything less.

"Mariaaaaa! Welcome to Northdale. I can't wait to show you around."

"Glad to be here. I'm anxious to meet your friends—will we see them?"

"I don't think so—not this time. But, for now, I want you all to myself."

"Will you show me where you live?"

"Are you kidding? My family, friends, and snoopy neighbors would be all over us like a bum on a baloney sandwich. We'll walk around Main Street—if you want, there's a movie theater on Broad Street—A Star is Born is playing—if you'd like to go."

With Signore's fiftieth sermon on boys ringing in my ears—"You know what boys do to pretty girls in dark movie theaters, don't you?" I opted to forgo the movies. "No. Why don't we just walk around like you suggested?"

"OK. We'll walk—I'll take you by my school, and on our way back, we can stop by Memorial Park and just hang out."

As we walked along Main Street, Luca pointed out things he thought might interest me. First, he showed me the newsstand where paperboys picked up the papers for delivery like when he was a paperboy—a job he started within two weeks of arriving in Northdale. Next, we stopped in at a Shelby's Soda Shop—

where the kids hung out after school for chats and Cherry Cokes. Finally, he pointed to the pool room and narrated: "That place also has a soda fountain, but girls never go inside. It's a dark place where men play billiards, gamble, smoke, and swear. I used to work there racking up balls when I was about twelve. They paid me two cents a rack, but sometimes, the old guys gave me a quarter tip because they thought it was good that I was working."

He pointed across the street to a place he called the Rec. I thought he said, wreck, but it sounded like a fun place when he described it. It was a place for teenagers only—thirteen to nineteen. They had a tennis table, pool table, snack bar, jukebox, dance floor, and a bandstand. It was open on Wednesdays, Fridays, and Saturdays.

They danced to jukebox music on Wednesdays. In addition, high school garage bands played on Friday nights and Saturday nights featuring The Battle of the Bands. Each week, the crowd voted and one band would be eliminated, while the other would fight for the top spot again the following week. At the end of the school year, the top three bands would earn first, second, and third place ribbons. In addition, all the groups won bragging rights. Luca said that some bands were so proud that they used their bragging rights long after leaving school. I thought that was a great, fun place for teens to get to know each other outside of school. I would have preferred to have something like that rather than the Club to occupy my free time.

When we went by his Parish school, Luca showed me the church, the playground, and the cemetery that lay in between. He pointed to the gravestones of family members, friends, and people he knew. Finally, he crossed himself, mumbled a prayer, and then we walked away. I wondered if it was better losing people you loved or never having people love you or love— at all.

Chapter Eighteen
Maria
Navigating Relationships

I noticed a banner hanging outside on the bowling alley across the street from the church—Twenty Lanes, No Waiting. Luca told me he worked there too, and about the perch that Pin Boys sat on, waiting for the bowling ball and having to dodge it, and the pins that came flying back at them. There was nothing automatic. Pin Boys had to depress a foot pedal to set each Duckpin on a spike that rose from the alley and scoop the ball from their pit floor and place it on a sloping rack to return it. The manager let Luca and his cousin, Reds, each work two side-by-side lanes.

"Once," Luca said, "Reds had to take a bathroom break, leaving me with four lanes to set. That was hard work for me and slowed the game down for the bowlers. I learned a lot of new curse words during those fifteen minutes and earned a threat from the boss that taught me the value of staying in my own lanes."

I shuddered at the thought of objects flying at him, the grueling work of handling pins and bowling balls while jumping in out and across four pits and perches. But Luca always laughed telling his stories, and he made me laugh, too. In some ways, he reminded me very much of Sister Verona.

Our arms swung freely as we walked and talked, so from time to time, our shoulders bumped, and I wanted so much to take Luca's hand, but I wouldn't dare. Finally, when we reached the Park, he asked, "Do you mind if I hold your hand?" When he did, I could sense that every part of my body was doing something strange—different—my whole body was out of sync with itself. I had never felt that way before. I knew I was turning red; I hoped he didn't notice.

"Let's take a walk through the park," he said.

Memorial Park occupied one entire city block. There was a baseball field on one corner, and a deer pen next to that—the rest was bushes, and flowers, hugging asphalt paths winding through the lush green grass. He coaxed me up a Revolutionary War Cannon that stood in the middle of the Park—we straddled the barrel. I wrapped my arms around his waist, holding on for fear of falling. But mostly because I wanted to feel his body next to mine.

"Wait here."

I watched him take a few steps, reach into a bush, pull out a cardboard box, and walk back toward me. "Let's have a seat on that bench," he said. We did. I sat next to him and waited as he pulled stuff out of the box—paper napkins first.

"Coke or Pepsi?"

"Coke."

"Hot or sweet?"

"Hot or sweet, what?"

"Hoagie—Submarine—Zep—Hero—whatever you call it."

"How do you know I like it?"

"I took a chance."

"Hot."

That wasn't anything at all like the sandwiches I ate at The Club. But, it was good and, I'm sure, tasted so much better eating it with Luca sitting next to me.

We walked and talked about many things, including what I should do about my troubles at home with my parents.

"I can't seem to get along with him no matter how hard I try."

"There's gotta be something you can agree on, right?"

"I'm going to college whether I like it or not."

"OK, so what's so bad about that?"

"Nothing. But I want to be a nurse or a teacher, but he says I can do better than that, and I'm not setting the right goals and not reaching high enough. He wants me to be like them—that's not what I want."

"What does she say?"

"Once she said it was my life, and I should do what I want with it, but he hit the roof when she said that. Then he went on and on about sending me to a costly school to be ready for the best college or university in the country.

Finally, he reminded her that they both wanted me well prepared for life's challenges."

"Then what?"

"Then nothing—she hasn't said anything since the first time. We start to argue, she leaves the room."

"I don't understand. I rarely hear my parents argue and never about that kind of stuff."

I wasn't ready to go, but it was time for me to leave, so we headed back to the station. On the way, I thanked him for a nice day.

"I'm glad you enjoyed my little town. We'll have to do this again. Sooner than later, I hope."

"We'll see."

"What's that mean? Do you think we're still strangers?"

"No, we're not strangers anymore."

"Does that mean we can go steady?"

"Whoa, take it easy. We just got past being strangers. Besides, don't you think we should get to know each other better before you propose?"

"I'm not proposing—I'm just asking if we can be steadies."

"Maybe it would be different if we lived closer to each other, and dating wasn't so hard."

"But I like seeing you—I have a good time every time we talk on the phone or see each other—don't you?"

"Yes, I do, but I told you—Mr. Marinelli would hit the roof if he thought I was seeing you—or anyone—behind his back."

"It doesn't sound like that's going to change anytime soon."

"That's for sure—I have to finish High School and College—there's not going to be a whole lot of free time for dating. Besides, why would you want to be tied down."

"OK, Maria, but let's do whatever we can to see each other over the summer."

I felt like my world was spinning out of control. Six years had passed since I left my home in Italy and left Sister Verona at the rock with neither of us happy. For a while, I cursed myself for throwing away the self-addressed envelope she had given me. At first, I wanted to write a mean, nasty letter telling her how disappointed, frustrated, and angry I was with her. But I didn't write that letter—I was too mad about that. When I thought about all the good experiences I had with the Marinelli—mainly that they managed to put Luca back into my life, I wanted to write and thank her for all of that, but I didn't write that letter, either. I promised myself that someday, I would.

When there was harmony in the Marinelli household for the first few years, I had every possible thing a child could want. The only thing gnawing at me was Sister Verona. I missed her, and I was upset with myself for being so rude to her when I left. But, on the other hand, I wasn't the one who wanted to leave her. I thought about asking Mr. or Mrs. to help me find Sister Verona. I needed to apologize and tell her how right she was—life was better for me in America. I wanted to ask for forgiveness because she made it possible and was too immature to realize that. But I didn't pursue my thought to find her—someday, I would.

I wished the whole year could have been as enjoyable and happy as our vacations. Every year, for three entire weeks, we personified the happy family. Still, before we finished unpacking our bags, the bickering, shouting, drinking, and preaching picked up where we left it before our three glorious weeks began. Troubling is the right word to describe my world after I turned Sixteen. I was still doing very well with my studies—I played lacrosse and volleyball for the school team, and I was winning trophies at school for tennis and breaking records for swimming at The Club.

But despite my achievements, my home life was starting to crumble. My adoptive parents were spending less time at home and quarreling more when they were home. I hoped that whatever was causing them so much torment would soon get resolved. They probably, hoped the same.

I was about to start my last year in high school in five and a half weeks— I was sixteen years old, and if everything went according to my plan, I would be graduating on 16 May 1940. Meanwhile, I had the rest of the summer to plot ways to see Luca and either strengthen our relationship or end it.

Getting together with Luca proved to be much easier than I thought. Following our three-week summer hiatus, the Marinelli dove deeper into their work lives—they said they must, "because we have so much to catch up to." When they weren't working, they were socializing with their "friends who hadn't lost everything—yet." That was OK with me. That meant I had more unsupervised free time to see Luca.

That summer, Luca and I were together whenever possible. He worked nights in a hosiery mill from three to eleven and Saturdays, seven a.m. until noon. I ensured I was ahead on my summer reading and did all my other chores during Luca's work hours. On the days he couldn't meet me at the Philadelphia train station, I went to Northdale. That was great, and very possibly, the only thing that kept me from going off the deep end.

Luca was happy to show me around and give me an overview of Northdale, especially whenever we wandered around his neighborhood, where his temperament overflowed with enthusiasm and pride. He showed me the coal yard, next to his house, where he played with his friends—marbles, hide and seek, and cowboys. He scared me half to death, showing me the narrow concrete ledges high above the sand and coal bins they jumped into. His fun activities were a far cry from what I was used to at The Club.

We walked past the junkyard, and I couldn't stop laughing whenever Luca told me his junkyard stories. They also made my heart hurt, thinking about how much money and privilege my family had and how little there was in his family.

The next stop on Luca's neighborhood tour was the Italian Bakery, across the street and a hundred yards away from his house. Long before we got there, I could smell that unmistakable, mouthwatering aroma of crusty, Italian bread in the process of baking. He brought me inside to meet his friend, Mike. As soon as I walked into the two by two vestibule, I heard a sound like zzzztt zzzztt…zzzztt…zzzztt…zzzztt…zzzztt.

Chapter Nineteen
Maria
Ding-Ding and the Chocolate Bud Man

"What's that?" I asked.

"Look up—it's a fly zapper."

"Why is it up there?"

"Guess it's because that's where the flies are."

I could see the stainless-steel mixing machines transforming flour into giant globs of dough and screaming hot ovens turning dough balls into crusty sandwich rolls from where I stood. Mike, the baker owner, suddenly appeared through the dusty cloud of white powder. He was short, a little round in the middle, and dressed in white from head to toe—white shoes, socks, Tee-shirt, pants, and baker's hat, all covered in white flour. He stood in stark contrast next to the two broad, black, cast iron doors, sealing in the oven heat. Luca introduced us,

"Mike, this is my friend, Maria—Maria, this is my friend, Mike—best baker in town." With that, he turned me, and himself, toward the door.

"Wait!"

Mike opened the oven door, reached for a spatula with a handle about eight feet long, slid the spatula under a tray full of rolls, and pulled the tray toward himself. A sweet, bread-baking fragrance entered the room immediately before the appearance of golden brown, crispy soft Italian sandwich rolls. The heavenly scent came to rest under my nose and intensified when Mike handed two hot rolls to Luca, then turned to me and said, "I hope you like this one, Maria."

I'm sure Mike gave little or no thought to his small gesture, but I was pleasantly surprised at how thoughtful and kind he was toward me—a perfect stranger. The third time I mentioned that to Luca, he said, "Jeez, Maria, it was just a roll; it cost a nickel—and even less for him." But I will never forget how warm and welcome I felt meeting Luca's friend—a five-foot-four inch old baker, covered in flour dust—a man I had never met before giving me a gift. Those kinds of things always turned my thought to Sister Verona—"Not everyone can paint the Mona Lisa, Principessa, but anyone can be kind."

We left the bakery and headed toward Russo's Italian grocery store, one block away.

"Hi, Mr. Russo—I'll have a stick of Pepperoni. We just came from Mike's—we need something to put in these warm rolls."

"Hey, Luca—are you going to introduce me to your friend?"

"This is Maria, Mr. Russo."

"Hello, Maria—nice to meet you. I've never seen you here before—do you live around here?"

"No. I live closer to Philadelphia."

"Oh. I know. Luca can't find anyone in Northdale who'd have him; better watch out, Maria."

Mr. Russo laughed, Luca blushed, and I enjoyed the banter—Luca was red-faced until we were on our way out with our Pepperoni, and Mr. Russo said, "Luca—don't forget to come back for your free Popsicle."

"OK, Mr. Russo, we'll be back—thank you!"

"What was that about?" I asked.

"Yeah, that's Mr. Russo. I don't know if they do it in Philly, but around here, we can get Hershey's Cream sickles—orange sherbet on the outside and vanilla ice cream inside."

"Yes, we can get them—I love those things."

"Well, around here, if the popsicle stick has Free written on it—you get a free popsicle. So I had a free one coming. Mr. Russo is supposed to turn those sticks in to get his money back from the company. My brothers told me they think he only ever had one *Free* bar. He uses the same one to give free ice cream to the good kids he likes, but primarily, to the kids who can't afford to buy them."

"So, you can afford the pepperoni, but not the ice cream?"

"Come on, Maria, don't be a wise guy—that's Mr. Russo trying to be nice."

We left Mr. Russo with my promise to come back when Luca picked up his free popsicle. We turned right at the store and left onto Maple, circling our way back to Seventh Street—Luca said there was a treat in store for me there.

"What could possibly top Mike's hot out of the oven rolls, and Mr. Russo's Pepperoni and bonus Creamsicle?"

"You'll get to meet Wally Ding-Ding and The Chocolate Bud Man."

"What's that?"

"Not what—Who! These two guys are as much a part of my neighborhood as anyone else. In the next thirty minutes, they'll be on Seventh Street—The Chocolate Bud Man first, then, within thirty minutes, Wally will ride by."

"What's so special about that?"

"Maybe nothing. Maybe everything. Or maybe, it's just the ritual—the consistency—that keeps me grounded in this place—they've been doing the same thing, at the same time, every day, from the time I moved here. And who knows how long before that?"

Just as we arrived at the corner of Maple and Seventh, Luca pointed to the left, about a block away, at a man riding a bicycle. At first glance, he appeared to be stopped. This is because he was moving so slowly. Kids were darting into the street in front of, and behind him—boys reaching over their heads to catch, while other boys, and girls, bent to pick Hershey Kisses from the street, scattered about by The Chocolate Bud Man.

I got a better look at the man and his bicycle when they approached us. He was a tall man—slim—in his late sixties. His thinning hair was white and longer than the other men in town wore theirs. His eyebrows were bushy white, and he had a primarily white beard with black patches. His lips were permanently closed and positioned halfway to a smile. His nose was not prominent, but his deep blue eyes were clear and sparkling. The man wore a barely visible, white t-shirt under a blue/black/white long-sleeved, plaid shirt, with every black button buttoned.

Watching The Chocolate Bud Man on his bicycle was akin to watching a ballet dancer—he was that smooth and graceful. He inched his way along, perfectly balanced, in a straight line, not looking left, right, or even down, long enough to see the chocolate buds he grabbed by the fistful from the wire basket he had secured to the handlebars. Like himself, his bicycle was efficient and straightforward. The frame was lightweight—almost like a racer's bike—it had skinny tires, no fenders, and a cloth seat. But, except for the wire basket, his bicycle was unadorned.

Luca waved and said hello, but he got no response. The Chocolate Bud Man looked straight ahead and continued to coax his bicycle upright and straight, pedaling ever so slightly up the hill, over the tracks, and down, to the next group of kids yelling, "Here comes the Chocolate Bud Man!"

I watched the backs of him and his bicycle—fascinated to see him getting smaller and, eventually, fade into the bottom of the hill on the other side of the tracks.

"Does he ever speak?"

"He's never spoken to me."

"Where does he live?"

"He has a loft above an old factory behind the junkyard."

"Does he work?"

"I think so—I'm pretty sure he does. Very well educated. Two degrees in engineering—Electrical and Architectural. And, he's an artist. I heard he's a genius."

"And you say he's been riding this street for years handing out candy to kids."

"Yep! Never missed a day since I've been here."

"Isn't that kind of strange?"

"Who's to say? He's never been in trouble—never hurts anyone, and he's made lots of kids happy with his chocolate buds—including me."

"That just seems kind of strange. Why does that man do that?"

"I guess he does, what he does because doing it, makes him happy. How many people can say the same? Look quick! Down the hill! Here comes Wally Ding-Ding—he won't be riding as slow as The Chocolate Bud Man."

I looked to my right and saw a grown man pedaling a bicycle on the opposite side of the railroad tracks. He seemed to rise from the exact spot where the Chocolate Bud Man disappeared. I could hear his bell in the distance—Ding-Ding. He crossed the tracks—Ding-Ding. Wally's bike was dull blue, faded white, and heavy. It had wide, balloon tires, and the spokes held two red reflectors on both, fender-covered wheels. There were two more reflectors on the bottom of the back fender—the white one was immediately above the red one, which reached the bottom edge of the fender. He kept a stack of newspapers, possibly two feet tall, on a flat, metal rack that almost touched the back fender until he reached the spot where the newsstand dropped his next load along his route. Ding-Ding.

Wally's bike handlebars were wide-set, with a wire basket attached to the front and between the curves. A light with a switch was fastened above the basket, just left of center. Both ends of the handlebars had dark blue handle grips with red, white, and blue streamers. Ding-Ding. Wally's bell was just above the right-side handle grip and tilted slightly upward, so his hands didn't leave the grip when his thumb depressed the bell. Ding-Ding.

Wally looked directly at us as he approached. He was an average-sized man in his late fifties. The few hair strands visible under his cap were brown, with a few white ones mixed in. There was nothing special about his face that stood out or that I remembered. I noticed large freckles or dark spots on his left hand as he passed.

"Who's going to win the war, Wally?" Luca asked.

Wally grinned. He faced right, quickly to the left, right, and back left toward us.

"I don't know. I hope Pennsylvania wins." Ding-Ding.

Wally stayed on the right side of the street as he pedaled past us. We watched him reach into his basket, grab a pre-folded newspaper, and sling it onto the lawns of his customers.

"Have you ever had a conversation with Wally?"

"No. Not really. Wally would never start a conversation. He only ever answers questions—as far as I know—and he grins a lot."

"At least he answered—not like Hershey's guy."

"Uh-huh. I never thought about it, but those guys are different from everyone else and different from each other, too."

"So?"

"So, nothing. Just saying."

"Do you like those guys?"

"Yes. I do."

"Why?"

"I guess because they're real. There's nothing phony about The Chocolate Bud Man or Wally, and they never try to impress anyone by trying to be something they're not. Neither of them cares about what anyone else thinks about them. Day after day, year after year—for decades, they've been doing the same thing—giving kids candy—delivering newspapers. Yet I've seen and heard kids taunting them. Why? They don't bother anyone."

"Don't they retaliate?"

"No. The Chocolate Bud Man never says a word. And Wally? He just looks at them and grins. If they insult him when he's on his bike—he grins, rings his bell, and rides off."

I look back on that summer as one of my best for having experienced another side of life that was very different from my own. Most people I met in Luca's neighborhood did not appear destitute, but clearly, they were not wealthy. Yet, they were so much more alive than the more formal, stiff people I was surrounded by at home, school, and The Club. I wasn't sure why I felt more comfortable in Luca's environment than I did on my own, but I did. Perhaps I was fascinated by the contrast in our lives or, maybe, I was simply infatuated by his charm. By summer's end, Luca had earned my trust many times over—with that, my feelings for him grew more profound.

When I started school, I found myself getting back into my old routine—studying hard, getting good grades, earning letters, and trophies, in my sports activities. I tried harder to appreciate all that Marinelli's opportunities continued to present and stop resenting their apologies for having missed dinner—again—leaving me alone—again because they had to work late.

I was president of my senior class and enjoyed all the status, benefits, and privileges that go with that. I was on my way to a college of my choice—the guidance counselor told me I was sure to earn a scholarship—maybe, even several excellent scholarships. The Marinelli was overjoyed with my performance and behavior, so life was good.

As my busy school year schedule progressed, I found it more difficult to steal away to Northdale, but despite the short time we had together—or, perhaps, because of it—my feelings for Luca continued to grow. Finally, in October, I asked him if he would save April Fourth for me. "I'd like it if you would take me to my Senior Prom."

"I don't know, Maria. April's a long way off."

"It will be here before we know it. Are you refusing my invitation?"

"Look, I like you a lot—maybe more than I should; we always have fun when we're together, but we do come from different places."

"No, we don't, we both come from LaValle—Italy. Remember?"

"That's not what I mean—and you know it."

"No, I don't know. I'm not asking you to marry me—I'm asking you for a date."

"Look. You live on the Main Line—I live in Northdale. You live in a mansion—I live in the middle of a row of houses in a crappy neighborhood; you'll be off to college—that's not even on my radar screen."

"I can't believe you're saying these things. When you asked me for a date, I accepted."

"Not at first."

"I'm not going to beg you, Luca. But, I'd like it if you would take me to my Senior Prom."

"I'd like you to come to my house on Christmas Eve. Dinner is always a huge deal—all the family will be together—we will have seven fishes—three kinds of pasta—pies, cakes, and pastry you've never tasted—it will be so good. All the family will be together. It will be noisy and fun. Giada will stand up, ask everyone to be quiet, and tell stories about the Nativity, the Three Wise Men, and having no room in the Inn. So tell me now that you'll come—and I promise, I will take you to your prom."

"Thanks for nothing, Luca. I've been sneaking behind everyone's back every time I come to Northdale. Christmas Eve, and New Year's Eve, are big deals for us too—at The Club. It would be impossible for me to skip that."

"So, you answered your question—we live in different worlds—you'll find someone that lives in your world to take you to the prom."

"No. I won't."

"Then your father will find a suitable partner to dance with you."

"Is this a breakup?"

"I think it's reality. I like you a lot. Maria, you're spunky, you know what you want and where you're going, and no one will stop you. I like that about you. Nothing's changed."

"I want you to take me to the prom."

"I'll think about it. I'll let you know in plenty of time—I'll let you know before Christmas."

Chapter Twenty
Maria
No Boys

On 29 November 1939, a letter arrived for me—it was postmarked in Northdale, PA. I was grateful for having been the one to take it from the mailbox because it had Luca's return address on the back, and that would have raised questions I wasn't ready to answer. It was two months since I had seen or heard from Luca. I hoped that his yes answer was in the letter, accepting my request to take me to my prom. Excitedly, I tore open the envelope, held his letter in my trembling hands, and brought it close to my beat-skipping heart. Then I read it:

Dear Maria,

I'm sorry if I hurt you or made you feel bad when we talked about your prom. But of course, I want to take you to your prom. Why wouldn't I? You're beautiful, bright, and so much fun. It's been great since we reconnected. After you gave me your phone number at the feast, I couldn't stop thinking about you. I couldn't believe it when you didn't tell me your name—then, you gave me your phone number. I dreamed about you every night ever since. I couldn't get you out of my mind.

I have to admit, I did a doubletake when I saw how beautiful you looked in the papers last Sunday. From the picture taken at The Club Dance, it must have been quite an affair. I wondered about that good-looking guy—who he was, with his arm locked in yours. Maybe I felt jealous, but I know I have neither right nor reason to feel that way, so I'm happy for you. Really!

The Club, the golf course, and the grounds looked mighty fine in the pictures, too. I can only imagine what it must be like inside. And that golf course—boy, that's a far cry from the golf course I tried to play on. When I thought about it, I realized it's money that makes all the difference—I wasn't allowed to play golf on a Public Golf Course, but if I had enough money, I could play whenever I want, at a private one. I don't know yet how, but one day I will gain your father's respect. Meanwhile, I will live hoping that we will find each other again sometime in the future.

Anyway, yes, I'd love to take you to your prom, but I don't think that's a good idea for you. I hope this doesn't ruin our friendship, Maria. It doesn't have to. Hopefully, one day, something will change to allow us to be more than just good friends. Meanwhile, we should each follow our dreams. Your friend, Sister Verona's words: "Life is meant to learn from it, and to do something meaningful with it."

We're still young. Neither of us knows what tomorrow will bring, but our past has shown us life isn't always easy, but we're in it, and we have to keep trying. So please don't be upset with me, Maria. I'm sure you will find the perfect partner for your prom. Have fun.

Until we meet again,

I will be the best friend you will ever have.

Luca.

P.S.: I can't imagine what life must be like for you—feeling like you don't have real, loving parents. But they have been very good to you—you said so yourself. They have dreams too, and you are part of them—you're just not the whole part.

Soon, you'll be off to college and on your own anyway. You'll get married and, if I'm lucky, you'll marry me. When you look back on your life with the Marinelli, you'll realize they gave you all of everything they could—just like Sister Verona. You'll regret your anger and fight with them. Think about it. Right from the beginning, you've referred to them as Mr. or Mrs.—you couldn't bring yourself to call them Mother, Ma, Father, or Dad. But of course, that wasn't so much for them to ask. Even after providing every other thing possible—best schools, fabulous home, clothes, maids, butlers, country club, the travel, and all the places you've seen and things you've done—you still call them Mr. and Mrs., or nothing at all. Who wouldn't trade their lives with you? They would call your parents anything they wanted to be called and kiss their feet while they're at it.

Your parents do a lot for you. But if there's any hope of us, together, it would be easier if we could all be friends, and that has to start with you.

I care about you more than you know. So please do that for me.

For as long as you wish—I am,

Truly your best friend
Luca

I don't know how many nights I cried myself to sleep after reading Luca's letter. Months, at least—I know that, but I had to push on. That's what Marinelli expected from me, and that's what Luca wanted too. More than anything, I wanted to be with Luca, and I knew he was right. But, to see him, I had to get over myself and start getting along with my parents. So, for the next three and a half years, I directed my energy and efforts to study, get the best grades possible, achieve a place at the top of all my classes, and be more respectful by calling the Marinelli my parents—my Ma and Dad.

On 31 May 1940, I graduated from high school with high honors, and the following month I turned seventeen. The scholarships predicted by my guidance counselor made my parents very proud and happy with my achievements and resulted in my choice to enroll at the City University of PA.

"We're proud of you, Sweet Pea—you're on your way."

"I've been thinking a lot about that lately, Dad."

"And?"

"And I know you want me to study medicine, or law but…"

"You're right—because you have the capabilities—you can lay the groundwork in your undergrad programs, then focus on your goals in your Masters. Then, you can specialize after you get your doctorate. From there, you can do anything you want."

"I already know what I want—I want to spend my life helping people, and I can do that with degrees in nursing and education."

"Are you kidding? You're not going to make any real money in either of those choices."

"Money isn't the only thing."

"Maybe not—but it's pretty far ahead of poverty."

"Money isn't that important to me."

"You can say that because you never had to worry about earning it."

"Ever since I was little, I wanted to be like Sister Verona. She was the best teacher I ever had."

"And she's probably still there, going nowhere, stuck in a dead-end job."

"Why does everything have to end up in a fight with us?"

"It's not a fight. It's a fact!"

"You always say you want me to be happy, but you keep me away from things that bring me joy."

"Like what? Trying to make you understand that I can help more people by being a doctor than you can if you're a nurse?"

"You might be the best orthopedic surgeon in the country or, maybe, the world. And I will always strive to be the best at nursing anyone back to health, regardless of their illness—not just a select group that has bone problems."

"That's a low blow, but I'll tell you what—I'll earn more in five years than you will in your lifetime."

"We're back to money. You and Ma fight a lot about that, don't you?"

"Show a little respect, will you?"

"I wasn't trying to be disrespectful."

"Well, you are."

"You don't respect me either."

"What the heck are you talking about? All I've done for you?"

"Why won't you stop doing for me and let me follow my dreams instead of trying to make me walk in your footsteps?"

"Have it your way, but I promise, you'll be sorry. You're lucky I got rid of that kid who's been after you."

"Luca?"

"That's right. I told Luca to get lost. He was no good for you."

"Who's good for me, Dad? 'No boys' doesn't give me much choice, does it?"

"First of all, you have plenty of time for boys, after college, not high school and certainly not him."

"Who then?"

"There are plenty of well-educated young men who come from good homes and prosperous families."

"Like from The Club?"

"Well—yes. And, the good ones that will show up when you're a junior or senior in college."

"Maybe like the good ones that showed up from The Club, pawing at me."

"Someone was pawing at you from The Club? Why didn't you tell me?"

"What was I supposed to say, Dad? I was standing in the pool when your good friend's son swam underwater behind me and started feeling his way up my legs? Or your other friend, whose son I had to go with, at the Spring Dance?—his hands would have never stopped if I hadn't elbowed him in the face."

"That's so hard to believe."

"And the reason I never said anything about it."

"Then imagine what that Luca kid would have done to you. That's the reason I insist on your keeping a safe distance from any boys."

"I don't have to imagine what Luca would do. He's never been anything but a gentleman."

Like so many of our conversations, this one was exhausting. Deep down, I knew my stepfather only wanted the best for me, and by every account, the life they gave me was very comfortable. I was grateful for everything they did for me, and I should have been better at demonstrating my appreciation, but he had a knack for knocking off the chip on my shoulder I put there when Sister Verona sent me away. The roads Sister Verona told me I would reach were upon me. It was my time to start crossing them.

I completed my college course work and final exams in three years, allowing me to graduate with the Class of Nineteen Forty-Three—one full year ahead of time. That was another source of pride for my parents, but I had to forgo any semblance of social life to accomplish that. As a result, my college life lacked adventure—I didn't join any sorority or find much reason to socialize. The few friends I made were girls I met at the library or in study halls. I went on a few dates, but I learned quickly that those boys were far more interested in groping at me or making out than I was.

As a result, my dates never ended well for my partner or me. Before long, I became known as "One-Date Maria", which was fine with me. I compared my short-date experiences to my times with Luca, who always made me feel safe and comfortable. He set the bar pretty high as far as dating partners went.

After I graduated from college with degrees in Nursing and Education, my dad reluctantly introduced me to a partner in several nursing homes. He would have preferred to set me up with friends who had "connections in a more suitable, prestigious environment" but he bowed to my stubbornness and helped launch my career in his friend's nursing home.

I liked every part of my job, my colleagues, and my management. The general feelings and attitudes of the caregivers, resident seniors, and their families were mainly upbeat and happy ones. The facilities were clean inside and out—it was well-staffed, and the cooperation we received from each other and from area hospitals was exceptional. Meeting and caring for my senior patients was comforting. I played a game to guess which ones, in the parade of wheelchairs, buggies, carts, walkers, crutches, and canes were housing bones repaired by my Dad. There were many more than I thought. More than a few of them commented on his stellar work, his empathy toward them for their struggles, and his bedside manner—several of them whispered to me that he even forgave unpaid bills when they fell on hard times.

Of all the people I met at SSNP, Maddie Madigan was my favorite. She never married, and her visitors were few and far between, yet she was the liveliest of the bunch.

Everything about Maddie was petite except her personality and big heart. She was a great listener and knew how to keep things to herself—I trusted her. She was the first to welcome me into the Personal Care Unit and encourage me whenever she thought I needed a lift. Maddie had fewer wrinkles than most other ladies her age—and younger—she was ninety-two. I attributed her tight skin to her petite frame, which she said hadn't changed since she was twelve. Her clear eyes, sharp mind, and keen interest in my well-being led her to be my confidante. She reminded me of a ninety-two-year-old Sister Verona, so I shared my most troubling thoughts with her—like my graduating college, being gainfully employed, and still having my Dad preach about finding the right partner.

"You said your father doesn't want to hear about your boyfriends?"

"That's what he says, and I believe him."

"You know—parents and their children don't always agree on everything."

"It seems like we never agree on anything."

"I'm sure he wants good things for you—he's probably doing his best to help you get them."

"It would be different if he'd listen to what I want instead of telling me what I want."

"I've got lots of experience in this old head of mine, and I can tell you this: We don't always know, or understand, why things happen—when they'll happen, where, and to whom. We can't change any of that, so we have to look beyond for answers. It's like getting upset when you missed a train, but as you're walking home with your head down, you find a twenty-dollar bill. So, instead of begrudging the things we've lost, we might be better off finding joy in the things we find."

Sister Verona told me she would always be nearby. Every time I had intimate conversations with Maddie, I thought of her as Sister Verona's echo.

Soon after I started working at SSNP, I questioned my wisdom for doing that. My passion for working with younger people never left me, but I had a Eureka moment toward the end of my first year. I realized that the older folks were a treasure trove of knowledge. They were teaching me things I would never discover in books or in a classroom. They had lived through decades of good times and bad times experiencing joy, and agony, in their lifetime memories of weddings and wakes, wars and peace, family fun and feuds, hearts given and taken—they were happy to talk of such things, and I was eager to learn about them. But, most of all, they taught me how to die.

In the end, the patients all seemed at peace—perhaps, with their families, or friends, their lives, their maker, or, maybe, themselves. There are countless times I stood by their sides—sometimes with family members or friends— sometimes, just the two of us. But, almost always, I could see that a smile was their final act. Dying with dignity—I hoped I could do the same.

I weighed my future working with seniors all my life and sacrificing the things I left remaining to learn against following my dream to work with children. I was happy and grateful for the opportunity to work and learn from my senior patients, but helping, teaching, inspiring, and leading children into their futures tipped the scales in that direction. I just didn't know how I could make that happen.

"Relax, Maria, your life will unfold as it should."

Thank you, Sister Verona, but when?

I hadn't seen or heard from Luca since I received his letter refusing to take me to my senior prom. He'd be happy to know I took his advice about calling my parents—my parents. He was right about that. It wasn't long after I began calling them Ma and Dad that my relationship with them improved. I often thought about that letter he wrote and how I might have felt if I saw him in the newspaper with his arm linked with another girl. Would I ask questions about it—or would I just write him off in a letter?

It wasn't like anything was going on with my escort—I didn't know the guy—he was the son of a Club member my Dad knew. I didn't even want to go to that silly event. I tried to explain to Luca that it was more of an obligation to satisfy my parents, but I couldn't reach him,—or his family—I suspected they still didn't have a telephone. Besides, he could have tried calling me, but he never did.

"Your life will unfold, Principessa, and it will give you all the tools you will need to find your way. So relax, Maria, everything will be fine."

Chapter Twenty-One
Maria
A Letter. A Phone Call.

Then it came—another letter. There was no return address, just Luca Romano. This time, I was happy to be home alone and retrieve the message from the mailbox before either of my parents. If Dad had picked it out of the mailbox, I knew there was a chance I would have never gotten it. I tore it open and read:

Dear Maria,

It's been a very long time. I hope this letter reaches you, and if it does, I hope it finds you healthy, happy, and enjoying yourself—and your life. I don't know how much of this letter you will see. If I'm right, you should be in your third year of college now. I wonder what path you have chosen to pursue—I thought, maybe, a doctor or professor of something—like your parents.

Maybe I shouldn't say this—who knows—you probably have five boyfriends, or perhaps you're engaged, or married by now. If any of that is true, please forgive me for saying this: You are still the only girl in my dreams. If you are in a relationship, you may not want to read any further. Now would be the place to tear this letter up and move on. Otherwise, there's a lot I wanted to tell you, so have a seat—this could be a long one.

When you left for college, I started to think seriously about my own life and career path. For a long while, I thought about quitting school, getting a permanent job, and starting to make money, but I knew I had to do better academically to have a chance with you. So I sat down, kept quiet, and paid attention, and before long, my classes started to get more interesting. I didn't make it to the top of my class, but I got close. I have an excellent job opportunity waiting for me when I'm ready. I'd like to tell you all about it, next time we get together—if we do.

I joined the Army soon after I finished at McCoy Institute of Technology. I took my basic training at XXX, then I was sent to XXXX, where I'll probably be until I get out. Right now, we're doing XXXXXX at XXXX XXXXXXX. I like the job I'm doing, but most of the time, I'm scared. One day we had a massive XXXXXXX go by XXXXX our XXXXX. As soon as I can, I'll send you a card and let you know what's up on my end.

I'm sorry for all the rambling. Like I said, I don't know if you're single, engaged, or married, or what, but if you read this far, I'll say the last few things on my mind.

I wish you could know how much I wanted to take you to your prom. I know that your father only wants what's best for you—I would want the same for my child—you would like that too. He has so much to offer you—I have nothing—and he knows that.

I can only offer a heart that burns for you and a crater in my stomach that grows bigger whenever I think of you. I miss you so much. If we can find a way to live our lives together one day, I promise I will do everything humanly possible to make you happy.

Do you remember the night you, me, and B took a fast, round trip ride to Atlantic City and the goofy picture we took in the booth? I've looked at that picture every single day since I dropped the last letter to you in the mailbox. I'm looking at it right now—it reminds me of the times we spent and the things we did together. Of course, there was never anything extraordinary, but the thousand, tiny, little, somethings, we did together—when I think of them, I dream of you—and us, together for all time.

Whatever happens, I want you to know that, wherever we are—together or apart, I will always be your friend.

In your hands, you are holding every bit of feeling, every piece of my soul, every ounce of love I feel for you, and every speck of hope, of having you close, and knowing you will be, always, by my side.

Until we meet again,

Your best friend.
Luca

I cry-laughed, bit my lips, screamed for joy, and wept at the same time, for all the longing I had for Luca and for all the emotions raging in my body. I had a plan for my life. God willing, I would be part of a family with Luca, and I would dedicate my life—just like Sister Verona did for me, to caring for children whose lives I could help shape—that much I knew. What remained unanswered was how I would, or possibly could accomplish that.

My parents and I were on the way home from dinner at The Club, on the evening I got Luca's letter when I told them about it. They seemed interested and immediately asked more questions than I thought they would or that I cared to answer. "How do you know him? Where did you meet? Where is his home? What does his father do for a living?" I should have known that Ma would remain quiet, and Dad would be furious. I didn't care. I knew I might never see Luca again, but it was time for me to take charge of my own life. I was determined to have him in my life.

If time healed wounds, I hoped it would repair my relationship with my parents. When time passed, and they realized that I would see Luca, with or without their blessings, their tone softened if the subject of Luca came up. But I was the one that always carried Luca into our conversations. If one of them mentioned the feast in Hammonton, I told them I met Luca there. If they talked about an Eagles football team, I told them Luca was Captain of his high school team. The more I told them about Luca, the less they bristled at the mention of his name, but they never fully understood or accepted our feelings for each other.

"Maria, if you get serious with this guy, you better make sure you know what you're doing. Your life in America, so far, has been easy. The great depression and two wars have been financially cruel for many others, but fortunately, not us. Do you think for a minute that you can live a happy life with this Luca? I promise you, you won't unless he can provide financial security."

I knew they were right about others having hard times. Sixteen years of depression, and wars, took their toll on people's financial, physical, and emotional stability. Countless families suffered through food rationing and scarcity of other essential goods and services—some starved, others went homeless. But, for immigrant families, who had nothing before the depression and wars, their lives improved. They weren't the ones jumping off buildings. Newly implemented government assistance, and work programs, provided enough food to feed their families and work opportunities to advance their agenda for homeownership—neither of which were available to them in Fascist Italy or other countries under attack during the wars.

'Nothing lasts forever—not good times and not bad times.'

I was at the very edge of my belief in that promise Sister Verona made when I got Luca's letter on 8 July 1945.

Dear Maria,

It's me again. I'm sorry you haven't heard from me before this, but we couldn't get mail-in, or out, of our Base.

My tour of duty ended on 24 July. If all goes well, I will be on a train coming from Jacksonville, Florida, to arrive in Philadelphia at two p.m. on July Twenty-sixth. I called my family from Heathrow airport, in England, before I left there. I told them I would take the train to Northdale from Philadelphia, but they insisted on meeting me in Philadelphia. So I told them I should be arriving at Reading Terminal around six p.m. I thought—I hoped— if it works for you, we could meet and spend a little time together—alone.

We'll be out of touch until then, but I will look for you on the platform or inside the terminal. If I don't see you within an hour, I'll know you won't be there. In that case, I will still have enough time to catch a train to Northdale and be there before my family has to leave for Philadelphia. Until then, I will hold the hope of seeing your beautiful face, tasting the fragrance of pure silk in your hair, and feeling your heartbeat next to mine. I can't wait.

Your forever best friend,
Luca

I was a long way from home with a week's worth of travel ahead of me and plenty of alone time to think. At first, I felt a sense of loss for the servicemen and women wounded and dead in service to our nation, and then for leaving a country and a people I grew fond of, but I took comfort in having helped to successfully complete our mission. The minute our plane lifted off headed for the USA, my nagging bad feelings turned toward excitement about going home began. I thought first about my parents and family—how and what they were doing—then about my friends—who made it home, who was married, who changed, what changed, and Northdale—what was that like after almost three years?

When I thought of Maria, everything else moved to the background. Where was she? What was she doing? Was she working? Was she married? Have children? Widowed? Single? Was she still seeing that guy with his arm around her in the picture? Was she still upset with me for not taking her to her prom? She probably forgot me by now. Why wouldn't she? Why would she forget? How could she forget me after all the time we spent reconnecting? I didn't think of it at the time, but she must have had a good grip on my heart when we met on the boat. I never realized what an impact Maria made on me on that trip. Spending more than two weeks with her, sharing secrets, and surviving torturous seas and scary storms created a bond not easily broken—for me, at least. I hoped she felt the same.

Even if Maria felt as I did, we still had her father standing between us. I tried calling her, but instead, he answered and told me to get lost. When I called again and attempted to talk with him, that didn't end well either. I replayed that conversation in my head over and over again. What could I have said to make him understand that Maria and I were friends and we both wanted him to accept our friendship? If only I could have a chance to redo that conversation. I couldn't get it out of my mind.

"Marinelli residence."

"Hello, Mr. Marinelli. I'm happy to find you home."

"Who's calling, please?"

"Oh. Sorry. This is Luca Romano."

"She's not home, son. I thought I asked you not to call here anymore."

"I called, hoping to speak with you."

"Why?"

"I feel as though our last conversation could have ended better than it did."

"Look, boy, I don't have time to waste. You can tell me why you called if you promise not to call here again."

"OK. If you promise to have a conversation, I promise I won't call there again."

"Go ahead. Start talking."

"I understand and respect that you're trying to protect your daughter. But, I wish you could understand I would never hurt her."

"That's what you think. You already hurt Maria by calling her and having her sneak behind my back to see you."

"I didn't kidnap her—we talked and saw each other because that's what we both wanted."

"You just don't get it, do you?"

"What am I missing? We come from the same place. We have a lot in common."

"You come from the same place—that's all you have in common."

"That's not the only thing. We talked enough to know there's a lot more than that we share."

"I'm a hair's breadth away from hanging up this phone."

"Then you don't mind if I keep calling there."

"Being a wise guy isn't doing anything for you, boy."

"I'm sorry, Mr. Marinelli. I didn't intend to be a wise guy or offend you. I'm only trying to understand why you're keeping boys, especially me, away from Maria."

"Fair enough. I'll tell you why. Maria is a very bright young lady, and she's a good athlete. She has a great future ahead of her if she stays focused on what's important and doesn't get mixed up in misguided youthful romances."

"To my knowledge, I haven't interfered with any of that."

"If you think for a second that I don't know how much of her time you wasted—think again."

"Did she tell you her time with me was wasted?"

"I'm telling you. Maria wasted her time with you?"

"How can you say that?"

"Because I'm her father. I know what's best for her—even if she doesn't."

"I don't deny we saw each other more than you think we should have. And I know Maria didn't like having to sneak behind your back to see me, but you didn't give her any other choice."

"You know what I gave her? In the best neighborhood, a nice home in an affluent town, fine clothes, great schools, membership in a country club, swimming and tennis lessons, summer vacations—that's what I gave her. Should I go on?"

"I was waiting to hear that you gave her a choice in any of that."

"Listen, kid. She will have the choice to meet and marry someone capable of providing a good life for her. So what do you have to offer? I'll tell you. Nothing!"

"You kept your promise, Mr. Marinelli—I'll give you that much. We can end this conversation, but not before you let me finish what I have to say. Otherwise, I keep calling. Deal?"

"Go ahead."

"We both know Maria is strong-willed. The tougher you make it for her to see me, the harder she'll try. I have no interest in holding her back in any way. We're friends. Neither of us is looking to get married any time soon—to anyone. I have a great deal of respect for both of you, and I have demonstrated that by my behavior often—ask her. I know about your 'No boys' rule, but I don't know what kinds of boys you have in mind when you say that. Whatever that is—it's not me."

"Are you through?"

"Almost. I've been courteous and respectful to you this whole time. I've addressed you properly and apologized because, you thought, I was a wise guy. That was never my intention. Yet, you called me son, boy, wise-guy, and kid. You can say, Luca, Mr. Romano, Young Man, or you can call me Three—I'll answer to any of those. But don't say boy, kid, or wise-guy because I'm none of those. Especially, don't call me son. I have a father, and it's not you—he's kind and never rude. Three is the last number on my brother, Angelo's dog tags—they were on a chain around his neck when they shipped his body home from Germany—fighting in a war to defend our country, freedom, and jackasses like you. So, if you prefer, you can call me Three. Have a nice day, Mr. Marinelli."

That conversation with Maria's Dad kept me company during the last leg of my trip on the train to Philadelphia, where my thoughts oscillated between high hopes Maria would be waiting for me and despair that she wouldn't. If nothing else, my internal struggle stimulated me and kept my hope alive over the clackity clack monotony of train wheels on rails. As much as I begrudged his oversight, I thought Mr. Marinelli was right in trying to protect her.

But I would have thought he'd take time to know me before he made any judgments on my character. Maybe I was the one rushing to judgment for projecting Mr. Marinelli's future attitudes toward me based on three-year-old events. He may have softened since then. I know I've changed, and a lot has happened since our last phone conversation.

Chapter Twenty-Two
Luca and Maria
Back in Touch

I left my teen years in Northdale and became old enough to vote and drink legally when I lived in a tent in France for a while. After that, there was no time to think about the past or the future. But that was behind me, and now, every time the train wheels turn and with every tree that goes by my window, I am closer to home and the girl I met when we were ten years old. How could I feel so strong for someone I didn't see for almost three years? I don't know, but she was always on my mind. I wanted to be near her, to hold her, and never let her go.

Sometimes I cursed my military assignments because my job kept me on the move, and trying to maintain a connection to home was virtually impossible. I sent mail from time to time, and I'm sure my folks would have been notified had an emergency occurred on my end. I just couldn't get mail, and that left me with some wild imaginings. I tried to imagine what Maria and her dad might have responded to the letters I wrote them. I could only hope they received my good intentions—if they even received the letters I sent.

Most of my thoughts in the weeks before I got discharged were dedicated to Maria, but now, I had to focus on the things I had to do to smooth the path I hoped to travel with her. Everything that awaited me back home led to her. I needed to secure the job waiting for me there and earn her father's confidence before turning my hope of a future with her into reality. I had written three letters to Mr. Wilson, who promised me a job upon my safe return, but I got no answer.

Now it was time for me to follow up on that promise. Reconnecting with him and assuring my employment was high on my priority list of needs to satisfy. There was no way I could have a meaningful man-to-man talk with Mr.

Marinelli about my future with his daughter without that. Still, rejoining Maria, my family, and friends remained at the forefront of my mind.

I was seated in the middle of three train cars full of men dressed in military uniforms representing all military branches. From my window seat, I could see the train platform rising from the distance and imagined Maria waiting there as she had so often on my trips to meet her at the Reading Terminal. Servicemen passed me in the aisle as I stood standing, squinting into the crowd searching for her. My heart sank. She was always there before—waiting, waving, smiling, and happy to see me, but not this time. There were no signs of Maria anywhere on the platform. Hearing the excitement, seeing the joy and happiness squeezing out from under all the hugs and kisses moving about in every direction but mine made me sad. I was one among a gigantic crowd of celebration, yet I felt alone and lonely. The scene took me back to my first trip to Philadelphia and the Pier. My stomach churned at the thought that Maria may have felt the same way on the train platform a dozen years earlier, and she was only ten years old.

Standing on my tiptoes and looking over the crowd, I inched my way to the Terminal, hoping to find Maria inside. "Maria! Maria!" I called. "Maria! Maria Marinelli!" No answer. What kind of fool was I expecting her to be waiting for me after years without a prior commitment or any communication? This was not the homecoming I expected—at the least, it was disappointing, and the pain of it reached my core. I promised Maria I would be her friend regardless of the path she chose for herself. When I said that, I didn't realize how difficult that would be with her out of my life. I was hurting.

In less than an hour, my family would arrive at the Terminal, and it wouldn't be fair to them if I carried my woes into their arms. I bent to pick up my duffle bag, hoisted it to my shoulder, turned to wiggle my way through the crowd and back to the platform to wait for my family.

Maria

I read his letter so many times the ink faded on the paper under the stains of my dropped tears and sweaty palms.

We'll be out of touch until then, but I will look for you on the platform or inside the Terminal. If I don't see you within an hour, I'll know you won't be there. In that case, I will still have enough time to catch a train to Northdale and be there before my family has to leave for Philadelphia. Until then, I will hold the hope of seeing your beautiful face, tasting the fragrance of pure silk in your hair, and feeling your heartbeat next to mine. I can't wait.

Your forever best friend,
Luca

I couldn't wait either. I counted down the weeks and days until there were only three days left before my every night's dream came to life. I had more clothes than I needed, but I bought a dress, hat, handbag, and shoes, for this special occasion on that very day, for the most special man in my life. I wanted to look perfect when Luca stepped off the train and when he saw me—a grown woman.

The day—Thursday, 26 July 1945—finally arrived. I counted the hours, and minutes, to the moment we would see each other again. I called for a cab and allowed plenty of time to be there, waiting for him to step off the train. I wanted to wave at the window, where Luca would be sitting, and be the first person he saw when his feet touched the platform. I wanted to jump up, and wrap my arms around his neck, and fold my legs around his waist—I would squeeze the breath out of him—hold him, and never let him go.

The cab was ten minutes late getting to my house, and the twenty-minute ride to the train station took thirty. I gave the cabbie five dollars more than the meter displayed, and I didn't waste a second waiting for change. I raced through the Terminal to the platform to find soldiers, sailors, and military uniforms, everywhere—and people all around them—but no Luca.

"Luca!" I yelled, "Luca! Luca!"

Couples and families paraded past me on their way outside to the cars, taxis, and buses waiting to take them home. Even as the crowd thinned, Luca was nowhere in my sight. I started to feel the emptiness that often comes with disappointment, so I jumped up, hoping to get a glimpse of him somewhere in the dissipating crowd. I was excited and nervous—nothing about me looked presentable. I was sweated, wrinkled, upset, and frustrated.

"Maria!"

I heard his voice from somewhere in the crowd, but I still couldn't see him. So I stood tall as I could, stretching my calves to the limit.

"Maria—turn around."

When I did, I saw his flashing white smile, his deep blue eyes, and close-cropped but still wavy, jet black hair. I saw two dimples on his striking face that had never left my mind. The boy I knew looked wiser now, more experienced, more mature—a very handsome man standing straight and tall in his Army uniform. Altogether, it was too much for me to take. The notion I had of leaping into his arms and hugging the breath out of him, disappeared fast when, instead, I fainted and collapsed into his open arms.

When I came to my senses, I considered staying as I was—forever limp—with his strong arms wrapped tightly around me, and feeling the heat of his sky blue, laser light eyes, searching the deepest parts of my soul.

"Maria, are you OK? Take a sip of this water."

I couldn't remember the last time I was more OK.

"Yes," I said, "yes, yes, I'm OK—sorry."

I vaguely remember the indistinguishable sounds coming from the swarm of people huddled around us—it was like the din of a jam-packed restaurant. The nearby crowd looked more like a blurry lump than a collection of individuals. Luca's recollection of that scene was the same as mine—we must have looked and acted like two giddy teenagers, locked in a closed-eyes embrace and utterly unaware of the world around us.

As the time approached that Luca's family would arrive, I thought it best for me to leave and that he waited for his family to come. I was grateful for his thoughtfulness in meeting me first and was encouraged that we were, at long last, able to spend those few hours together. We agreed that his family would be very anxious to see him, too, and that all of them needed some, together time, alone. After another long embrace, we parted and promised to meet the next day.

Later that same day, I went to The Club with plans to meet my parents for dinner. It was arranged for earlier than our usual eight p.m., but when I arrived, Maurice, the manager, gave me a note instructing me to meet them at home for dinner at six. I called to him as he turned to walk away.

"Maury! Did they just hand you a note and say they weren't coming?"

"No! No. Your father called early this morning. A few days ago, he noticed I was a little downhearted. I told him I missed my daughter and her family. Unfortunately, my son-in-law's company transferred him, and the whole family recently moved to Georgia."

"Wow! That must be hard."

"A lot harder than I imagined, and I told your dad."

"What'd he say about that."

"Not a whole lot—except that we all take too much for granted and that he had to find a way to spend more time with you."

"He said that?"

"Well. Yeah. Why?"

"I don't know. Sometimes I get the feeling I'm somewhere near the bottom of the home totem pole."

"That's hard to imagine. Look. You and I have known each other for about six years—I met your dad almost twenty years ago—long before either of us knew The Club existed. We've talked each other through more situations than I can recount. But, for the past six years, *you* are the only subject we discuss that thrills him and makes him proud and happy. He smiles at the thought of you, and when he senses danger, or that he would ever lose you, for any reason—he weeps."

"Gosh. Thank you for telling me all that, Maury. I hope you can visit them, and that your daughter's whole family will see you often, too.

I left The Club and headed home, talking to myself the whole way. My short conversation with Maury struck an unfamiliar chord in the tune I had been singing about my adoptive parents. I believed that my parents cared more about their careers, money, and social status than they did about me. But, according to Maury, Mr. Marinelli shared the human side of himself I never saw.

"There is good in everything, and everyone, Principessa. But unfortunately, you can find evil too, if you look for it. So, remember, whatever you seek most, you will find."

What possessed me to disregard so much of what I learned from Sister Verona. A considerable number of people said nice things about my parents, and when they did, I just nodded and smiled. However, their words chafed against my selfish thoughts of ignoring me, so flames were always present just beneath my nods and smiles. Both parents were caregivers applying their skills to heal, strengthen, assist, and support everyone that came their way.

So why couldn't I see the kindness in their everyday actions? Why didn't I understand their hurt or empathy and compassion when their friend died—when my mother spent a month with his wife cooking, cleaning, and comforting her. That's the month my dad barely spoke to me, and when I noticed him, late at night, sitting in his library in the dark alone—weeping.

From the moment I left the orphanage, I was all about myself.

"Your life will unfold before you, Principessa. Nothing stays the same forever. Observe as the world changes and be open to change yourself when the need for change manifests itself."

I didn't grow up all the way, but I grew some when Maury handed me a note and set my eyes looking in the right direction.

That evening, at six sharp, my parents greeted me from the front door.

"Hello, Maria. Hi Sweet Pea. Surprise! Something different for a change."

"Hi, Ma. Hi Dad; what's the occasion?"

"You know," said Dad, "Ma and I have been talking a lot lately and decided it might be time for a long-overdue family chat."

"Wow! I can't believe you're saying that. There are a few things I wanted to talk about with you too."

"Uh oh," Dad said, "I know—you got married."

"Not quite, Dad, but that may be closer than we both think."

"Why don't we chat over dinner?" Ma asked.

Dad replied, "Well, I was thinking about something quick—like pizza or a cheesesteak sub from Mario's—after that, we can take in a movie."

"Boy, we weren't on the same brainwave on that one," Ma said. "How did you plan to have a dinner conversation sitting in a movie theater?"

"I didn't think it would take long to say what we wanted to, but you're right. Maria has some things she wants to chat about so, why don't we make short work of dinner and get to the chat. OK?"

"Sure," Ma said, "Maria, would you like pizza, a cheesesteak, or something different?"

"I'll have the cheesesteak."

"Sounds good."

"Done! I'll go pick up three of them—I'll be back in twenty."

We did make short dinner work—we finished eating, cleaned up, gathered in the living room, and with our pajamas on, sitting in our favorite chairs before seven-thirty.

Dad said, "You go first, Maria."

"I was hoping you would go first, but OK, I will—I've had a lot of time to think while I was away at college and even more working at SSNP."

"Go right ahead, Sweet Pea."

"I'm sure my attitude toward you, sometimes, makes you think I don't appreciate all the things you've done for me. Nothing can be farther from the truth, but I can't change anything I've said. I am aware of all the opportunities you provided. I can never repay you or thank you enough for my education and the job you arranged for me at SSNP. I love my job, the people I work with, and the people I serve. If I were more mature, I would have known about your excellent work and dedication to your patients. Your reputation follows you, too, Ma. I asked myself why I couldn't see all the goodness that lived in the same home as I did. I'm so sorry for any grief I've given you, and I thank you—from the bottom of my heart, for all you've done for me—thank you!

"And, I have a confession to make. I think you already know part of what I am about to confess, but before I start, please, I want to talk about Luca."

"Maria. Stop! Before you go on, I'd like to say a few words about that."

"Dad. If we're going to argue, that's not going to work—not this time."

"If we can agree on the subject, there won't be any need to argue."

"We never agreed on the subject of boys. In fact, we never really discussed the subject. And what about all the things you said about Luca. Maybe we should stop right now."

"You said you had a lot of time to think while you were away at college. I did, too. Actually, Luca and I have been in touch during that time."

"You what?"

"He called a couple of times, and he sent me a letter."

"Why didn't you tell me?"

"I didn't want to upset you."

"Why are you telling me now?"

"It wasn't the right time before—now, it is."

"What are you talking about?"

"The letter he wrote. He told me about a job he had waiting for him and that he enlisted in the Army. He should be getting discharged soon."

"That's right! He's already discharged. He came through the Reading Terminal on his way home today. I saw him, and tomorrow, I'm going to Northdale—nothing, and no one, is going to stop me."

"Just so you know, I spoke with Jonathan Tolleson, at The Club, about Luca."

"I know Mr. Tolleson—what's he got to do with Luca?"

"He went to college with the guy who hired Luca."

"Are you saying Luca got a job through your connections?"

"Not at all. I'm saying I may have been wrong about Luca. As a result, I wasn't treating you like the little lady you were blossoming into. According to Jonathon, Mr. Wilson—Luca's boss—is very impressed with Luca and said he has a very bright future ahead of him."

"I could have told you that."

"But you wouldn't have been objective."

"So, you had to spy on him?"

"I prefer to think I was standing guard over my Sweet Pea."

"I've been watching myself ever since I got here—do you think I'm not able to guard my own feelings?"

"Someday, when you're the parent of a young, bright, pretty girl like yourself, you might understand how I feel about protecting you."

"When will you stop worrying about having to protect me?"

"I'm afraid that time will never come."

"Phew! I don't know whether to be angry or scream with joy. That's a whole lot to digest, but I'm feeling happy right now. If everything goes as planned, I'll see Luca, and the rest of his family, tomorrow, and I can't wait.

"Like you, we can't change the past, but I can promise you, the future will be different. So, yes, meet your friend, Luca, tomorrow. I would only ask that you continue to keep your eyes and ears open for bumpy roads and the caution signs along the pathways to your heart. We love you, Maria. We want to dance at your wedding—whoever the groom is—and wherever your wedding takes place."

"No one said anything about a wedding. Luca's a friend I haven't seen in a long time. Things were going great then, suddenly, he disappeared. I missed him. There's a lot to catch up on and talk about. Maybe friends are all we'll ever be, but I'm going to find out.

Chapter Twenty-Three
Luca
Welcome Home

The next day was Friday, and by noon I was standing in Luca's home, wrapped in Mrs. Romano's arms. She took my breath away, excitedly telling me how happy she was to see me again. The whole family took turns saying how lucky Luca was to have me for a friend and that, "You are all he ever talked about, ever since he saw you at that candy concession in Hammonton."

Mama Romano was cooking, and Polenta was on the menu—made and served "just like it was in the old country." The cheerful, festive mood made me feel like I was standing on the doorstep of paradise. Fresh Scali bread still warm from Mike's bakery, freshly made sausage from Russo's, vegetables from their garden, dandelion greens and chicory from nearby fields, picked that morning for the salad. The heavenly earthy fragrance of everything on the table waited patiently to introduce themselves and test my somewhat sophisticated palate.

Luca stirred the cornmeal the same way he did as a child—non-stop and for a very long time. Mrs. Romano served the entire evening meal on a large, wooden board Mr. Romano placed on the table beforehand. Dinner was so different from anything I ever had at home and unlike anything I'd ever seen or thought about seeing at The Club. It was fascinating to watch Luca's mother plopping a mountain of Polenta in the center of the board, making a crater in the top, and spooning several scoops of red *gravy* into what looked like Mount Vesuvius erupting.

She scooped heaping portions of Polenta out of the pot with everyone seated and pushed it across the board toward each of her hungry, patiently waiting family. Then she surrounded the polenta hill with the remaining meat after placing two meatballs and two sausages in front of the men and one each for the women—"there's plenty more, so Mangia, Mangia!" Mrs. Romano served her husband first, then me, followed by each of the boys descending age order, then Giada, and last, she helped herself. The Polenta was not a meal I had ever seen on The Club's menu or any menu in any of the restaurants I'd ever been to with my parents. Still, to me, on that day, with that group, Mrs. Romano's Polenta was the best meal I ever tasted. It was a fun day, but it didn't last near long enough. Goodbyes, see you later, Buonanotti, and Ciaos came much too soon.

"I had a fantastic time with you today, Maria. I knew you would make a great impression on my family—they all loved you."

"They were so nice—and so much fun, too. And that Polenta—oh my God, that was amazing, and I'm sure it was because you stirred it perfectly."

"Well, I think everyone had a hand in it—glad you liked it."

"I don't know what I would have thought if you had told me we would be eating our entire meal without plates and from a wooden board—that was different, but it was great."

"There's a lot of things different between us, Maria. I knew that long ago—when I saw your picture in the Sunday papers—when you were at that Club Dance."

"Why do you have to bring that up? I was a teenager, still in school. Didn't we decide we had lots in common long before that?"

"Look—you must know how much I care about you; every dream I have, you're in it. But I know how things work. Your parents want more than me for you."

"What about what I want—does that count?"

"Sure, it counts—just like it counts to know the difference between your being happy having everything you want, or not being happy without all that."

"You think I've always had everything I wanted. Guess what. You found your way to a good job and, eventually, you'll buy the things you want—lots of people do, you know. But there's no way I can ever buy a family like yours or buy the love they've given you all your life."

"I know, I know—I just don't want us traveling down a road to nowhere."

"When I gave you my phone number, when we talked for hours, when I met you here, or met you at the Reading Terminal, or met your friends, waited for three years and met your family—was that the road to nowhere? If it was, then I'm headed for a new road—right now!"

"Can we start this conversation over?"

"We can—if you stop acting like a beaten dog. You may not think it, but I've had to fight my way to see you. If you're not willing to fight a little to see me, then what's the point of more conversation."

"I told you how I feel about you—my whole family told you how I feel about you. I want to be with you always—I don't want you to have to sneak behind your parent's back so we can see each other. I pray we can see more of each other—I dream of that. I'd like to meet your parents soon, too."

"That can happen—you'll see."

The entire weekend was a steady stream of visitors to the Romanos—all wishing Luca a big Welcome Home. Some came to him with banners and flags, expressing their joy at having him back, where he belonged. Some visitors came with homemade cookies and cakes; some came with homemade wine and Limoncello. All his friends came with stories of the good old days when they were kids—before the war—when they were young and without a care in the world.

When Sunday evening came, we left the crowd to spend the last two hours of our day together, alone, in Memorial Park. We sat on a damp bench—still sticky from the day's scorching high heat and clothes-wetting humidity. I could see the big orange sun fading deep into the evening sky and sense the cooling relief that would soon come. But, with Luca's arm around my shoulder, my body temperature started to rise toward near-boiling, but I didn't mind that heat at all.

Luca stood, tilted his head, scrunched his nose, closed his left eye, then opened it slowly, and asked, "May I kiss you?"

Still looking into his deep blue, hypnotizing eyes, I stepped into his waiting arms. "Try it," I said. His kiss was slow and soft—gentle. Again, I shivered against his firm, tight, military-shaped body. Again, I could feel goosebumps growing on my arms and down my spine, and again, I fell limp in his arms. There was no question—I was falling hard and fast.

Too soon, it was time to make our way back to the train station, but having made the trip twice over the weekend and having to rise early for work in the morning, it was time. So before I even climbed aboard the train, I started counting the days until I could see him again.

"Goodnight, Maria."

"Goodnight. When will I see you again?"

"Not for a few days, anyway—maybe a week."

"Why?"

"I have to check in with Mr. Wilson. I don't know when he'll want me to start my job. Truth is, I can't be sure if he still has it waiting for me."

"Why wouldn't he?"

"It's been a long time since we last spoke. I wrote, but I never heard back. That's not surprising since I moved around a lot and never got any mail from home. I plan to call him first thing in the morning—he may want me to go to New York."

"Well, let me know either way, will you?"

"Sure. As soon as I know anything, you'll know. Sweet dreams."

"You too. See you soon."

That night, my dreams were as wonderful as any and sweet as honey—made sweeter since I didn't have to sneak behind my parents to see Luca anymore. Both of them had sent me off with good wishes to have a good time and a safe trip. Maybe I should have told Luca about that, but I didn't.

I woke, feeling on top of the world, on Monday morning. Most everyone at work noticed how relaxed I was and the glow I carried on my face from Northdale.

"There's something different about you today, Maria—you seem happier than your normal happy self."

"Thank you," was all I could muster in reply. Either I had to be experiencing some new kind of mysterious illness, or Luca was responsible for my unusual but pleasant feelings. I preferred to think it was the latter and that love was creating this new feeling in me. One side of me welcomed the unknown territory I was about to enter, but on the other side, I was terrified. I couldn't bear to be left with the same disappointments and scars I carried for loving someone too much and having them disappear. So I decided to keep my guard up, be extra careful, and be sure to keep my toes pointing in the right direction. Easier said.

Sickness and death are routine when caring for elderly patients, and I allowed the sadness of losing them to replace the joys I felt for helping them. Yet, I desperately wanted my life to include more promise—not only for myself but also for my charges. It struck me that the mood of everyone on my floor was lifted by the exceptionally high spirits I carried leftover from the weekend. I recalled Sister Verona's telling me that the smallest gesture of kindness could make a significant, positive change in a person suffering grief or desolation. I never gave much thought to making positive changes in others with a personal attitude adjustment, but at the moment, that idea seemed simple enough.

I resolved to lose my cynicism and be more open and trusting, knowing that wouldn't be easy for me, but I decided it would be best to ease into this new role I was planning for myself. Overall, my relationships were on the rise. I'm sure that my newfound trust in my relationship with Luca was responsible for that.

"Relax, Maria. Look for the good—it's all around us—we just have to look for it. Relax, Maria, let your life unfold."

I may have left Sister Verona in Italy, but she never left me just as she promised.

Luca

Mr. Isaac Wilson was VP of Field Operations. I met him in Northdale when his team was in the early stages of setting up a Regional Field Service facility in the greater Philadelphia area. He chose the Delaware Valley for its proximity to New York, New Jersey, and Washington DC, and Northdale for the site because it was a railroad town with easy access to those places. At the same time, he could take advantage of the railroad spurs used to offload coal coming from the northeast coal region for shipping machines and parts. I got to know him reasonably well during the month I worked for him at their headquarters in New York. I was as confident as I could be with his job offer and promised to hold it, but I couldn't be positive, so I made a meeting with him a top priority. So I made the phone call.

"Yes, Mr. Romano. Please hold for Mr. Wilson. He'll be with you shortly."

"Luca! Hello! How are you! Where are you? How long have you been home?"

Hello Mr. Wilson. Thank you for taking my call."

"Are you kidding? I'm so anxious to see you."

"Me too. I can't wait to get started."

"Whoa. Whoa. Slow down."

My heart sank to the floor and came to rest on top of those words I dreaded I would hear. Mr. Wilson's message to me was mixed. If he was so anxious to see me, why did he say 'Slow down'?

"I'm sorry?"

"I mean, you must have a hundred things to do—take a few weeks to get your feet back on the civilian ground. I told you a job would be waiting for you when you got back. It is, and it will be."

"I don't know what to say, Mr. Wilson."

"Tell you what. You know what our plant looks like, and you know what the product is all about from the time you spent here before you left. I have to go to Harrisburg for a few hours tomorrow. If I take an early flight, can you meet me at the airport for breakfast?"

"Yes, Sir. What's your ETA and Airline?"

"I'll be on Eastern Airline Flight 282, arriving at Gate 4 at 8:20 a.m."

"I'll be there."

I was happy to see Mr. Wilson again and that nothing in his warm and welcoming personality had changed in the least. He was a tall man in his early sixties with traces of white in his otherwise medium brown hair. He was neatly attired, well-spoken, and talked with a calm, pleasant radio voice. He greeted me warmly and easily erased all the time and distance between us during the past few years. It was like meeting a good friend after a long absence. Our exchange felt to me like a comma in a long sentence as we continued conversations we had years ago with hardly a pause before picking back up where we were. I am forever grateful for meeting this extraordinary man and having him be my mentor—the best and only one after my father.

We swapped stories of our lives since we were together last. A few things we recounted were funny. Some were not. Mr. Wilson asked—so I shared the sadness I felt losing a fellow soldier or seeing one severely injured after a skirmish. He told me his son died in a freak accident six months before he met me in Northdale. Mr. Wilson said I reminded him of his son, Michael, who made hand gestures like me when we spoke. "His skin was the color of bronze—just like his mother's. Michael liked taking things apart and putting them back together—another thing you two have in common."

I had earned competency certificates from the Spring Garden Institute of Technology in pneumatics, hydraulics, electricity, and electronics. We talked at some length about the essential parts of what my job would be and what he expected. My years of work with the Army Corps of Engineers and the "on the job training" I had at the company before I enlisted gave me all the confidence I needed to handle technical field service work for Mr. Wilson.

"OK then. I'll set things up so you can start working from the Northdale facility next month. After that, you can use the time to get your civilian life in order."

"If it's all the same to you, Sir, I'd like to start ASAP and take the month next May. Actually, I'll only need a couple of weeks."

"We can arrange that. We've been covering that region from headquarters for the past six months. So, if necessary, we can cover for three or four weeks next May, I'm sure.

"You didn't ask, but I'm planning to get married. So that's why I'd like to delay the time off you offered before I started."

"Wow! Congratulations! When?"

"That depends."

"Really? On what?"

"For one thing, her father has to accept the notion that I'm going to marry his daughter. If he does, I have to make sure my gal, Maria, will have me."

"Hmm. Interesting. Doesn't a guy ask a gal to marry him before he asks her dad for his permission? Suppose he says yes, and she says no?"

"Then I have to keep proving myself to both of them that I'm worthy of her love."

"What do you think your chances are of success on both fronts?"

"One hundred percent. The problem is, I don't know if it will happen on my timetable."

"I have to hand it to you, Luca. You've got chutzpah—enough self-confidence, I believe, to win them both over to your side. I saw that in you the first time we met. Seems like nothing's changed. That's good. Uh oh, I have to go. "I'll have someone meet you at the Northdale facility on Tuesday. OK? We'll figure it all out from there."

"Thank you, Mr. Wilson."

"Thank *you,* Luca. I'm happy you're back."

Chapter Twenty-Four
Luca
Managing

On Tuesday morning at 7:30, I met Charlie Henderson in the same brick building on Walnut Street where I first met Mr. Wilson three years earlier. At that time, establishing a regional technical service center was still in the early planning stages. Like me, Charlie was another of Mr. Wilson's techie proteges hired to train at headquarters to establish a service center—his territory would be within a three-hour radius of Hartford, Connecticut. If sales and growth continued as projected, Business Machine Corp would have service centers up and down the east coast and west to Chicago. Until now, all service was handled from the NY Headquarters. That was the plan, and Charlie and I were excited to be the starting parts of it.

Charlie and I spent the days and into the evenings of Tuesday and Wednesday reviewing blueprints, operational manuals, and troubleshooting guides for earlier versions of the company's machines. Then on Thursday and Friday, we visited existing customers in North Jersey and New York City, all of which had been serviced from headquarters. Those, I learned, would be my customers and territories in the future when the Northdale facility was ready to go. Finally, we spent the weekend and the following week erecting a demo machine, arranging parts, and making workstations for light assembly work. Again, I was in my element, doing what I liked and enjoying every second of it.

On Saturday, we finished our work with a customer in Newark, New Jersey—shortly after 2 p.m. Charlie took himself to the airport, and I took a train to Philadelphia, arriving at the Reading Terminal close to 4:00. I had a feeling Maria might be upset with me for not calling before this but, I had to make the call. She answered on the first ring, and I was happy about that.

"Marinelli residence."

"May I speak to Maria, please?"

"May I ask who's calling, please?"

I knew it was her when she picked up the phone. I don't know what possessed me to ask if I could speak to Maria. I should have told her how pleased I was that she picked up the phone. I cursed myself for trying to be funny when I sensed she was already upset with me.

"This is Luca. Luca Romano."

"I'm sorry. The name sounds familiar, but I haven't heard from him in such a long time. How can I be sure you're Luca Romano?"

"What would you like to hear me say after 'I'm sorry'?"

"Sorry for what?"

"For not calling before now."

"Why would you be sorry? Why should I expect you to call a day or two or three or four after having a fabulous time the whole weekend? Of course, that happened before, but you did come back after three years, right?"

"Maria. Please don't do this. I'm sorry."

"Uh-huh. You said that already. I think I understand the M O. We meet, have fun together, then you disappear—you could be gone for days or years. This time it was nearly two weeks."

"Will you let me explain?"

"What's to explain? Unless you've been unconscious for the past two weeks, whatever you have to say, I won't understand."

"You're right, Maria. I was wrong. I should have told you what was ahead of me in the weeks after we were together last. I didn't. I was wrong, and I'm sorry. Would you like it if I told you now?

"No."

"Do we have to let our feelings die in the wires between our telephones?"

"Whose feelings should we leave to die in the wires, Luca?"

She was altogether right. I was so wrapped up in everything I wanted to get accomplished to win her that I was losing her over one thoughtless act. I should have included her in my plan—make her feel a part of it, and a part of me. If I were upfront with her, there would be nothing to explain. But, at least she didn't hang up on me. She was giving me a chance to make it right.

"I'm so sorry, Maria. If you can forgive me that, I promise I will never do that again."

"Look. I was worried. I thought something terrible had happened to you."

"Nothing terrible happened, Maria."

"Thank God for that, but I had no way of knowing. I had to go to bed every night for two weeks wondering where you were and what terrible thing may have happened to you."

"No excuses, Maria. I can only offer you regrets and my most sincere apology. I'm so sorry."

"OK. When will I see you again?"

"I'm at the Reading Terminal now. I can wait if you can make your way here."

"I can't. Promised my folks I'd meet them for dinner at The Club. I was halfway out the door when you called."

"How about sometime tomorrow?"

"There's an Open House at my work tomorrow afternoon and evening. I promised my old friend Maddie I'd be there."

"Are you brushing me off, Maria?"

"I'm not. How about Wednesday after work?"

"Dinner?"

"It doesn't have to be. I'd just as soon use the time to chat—fill in the gaps in our relationship. I admit I like you a lot, Luca—a whole lot. I just have to know that my feelings aren't wasted on you."

"They're not, Maria. I feel the same about you. I wish I would have—"

"Don't say it, Luca. What does it matter? We both can do better. Wednesday then?"

"Yes. I'll meet you at the Terminal. We'll grab something from the cases at Horn & Hardart and stroll the Downtown."

"Sounds fun. Can you make it there by six?"

"I'll be there."

A few minutes past six p.m. that Wednesday, when the sign announcing Horn & Hardart Automat came into my view, I made a dash for the little glass doors displaying desserts. If Maria were on time and in the building, I knew I'd find her there, but she was nowhere in sight. I scanned the columns and rows of puddings, sweetbread, cookies, and cakes before my eyes came to rest on a generous wedge of mouth-watering lemon meringue pie. That was Maria's second favorite dessert after Italian Crème Cake. I heard her voice behind me.

"That's my favorite pie; is it yours too?"

"No! My favorite is Sweetie Pie, and that's you."

She chuckled, I smiled. We reached in for each other's hug, gave each other a peck on both cheeks, took each other's opposite hand, and strolled the length of the endless columns of glass doors behind which lay our taste-tempting food selections for our dinner that evening. On her tray, she put a small garden salad, a ham, and cheese sandwich on white bread, a cup of coffee, milk, one sugar, and a piece of lemon meringue pie. I chose rye bread for my ham and cheese sandwich, black coffee, and apple pie with a dollop of vanilla ice cream on top.

We walked our trays to a back-end corner table, placed them down across from each other, and I stood until she sat. As soon as I sat, I took both her hands in mine, looked into her eyes, and whispered, "There's nothing I can do to change the past. I know I was wrong in not telling you where I was and what I was doing, and I'm sorry. I didn't mean to hurt you in any way. Can you forgive me?"

"You're kidding, right?"

"What do you mean?"

"What I mean is you hurt me, and I told you so. You already acknowledged that and apologized and said it wouldn't happen again. Is there anything going on under that curly black-haired head of yours? Of course, I forgive you. We wouldn't be here otherwise."

Gazing at each other, we took small bites from our sandwiches, moved our salads from side to side, and sipped our coffee. Finally, after ninety minutes of conversation and the occasional sounds of silverware clashing on plates, the wide end of Maria's Lemon Meringue pie remained untouched, and my wedge of apple pie was barely visible under a pool of melted vanilla ice cream.

Maria broke the spell when she offered, "Looks like a bunch of people over there waiting for tables."

"We should go," I said. "Are you up for a stroll?"

"Let's go," she answered.

Holding hands, we stepped out into the warm summer night and strolled the streets of Philadelphia's Center City, and talked about everything on our minds in no particular order. First, I told her about Mr. Wilson, my job at Business Machine Corp., how the company was growing, and the tremendous opportunities that lay before me there. Then, she told me about her work with senior patients and how it was sad and satisfying at the same time. "Ultimately," she said, "I want to find a way to work with children."

On any other night, we would have seen and heard the sights and sounds of the city—gas lights flickering, people bustling, taxi horns honking, jukebox tunes pushing through open tavern doors, and jazz music seeping through the bricks of old night clubs. Across Market Street, up Broad, past Filbert, and along Arch, passing museums, city hall, department stores, Rittenhouse Square—noticing everything and seeing nothing. Instead, we talked about the fun times of being together and the pains of years apart—aching for our touching hands. We peeked at our pasts and stared at hopes for our futures. We examined our needs and wants and established the importance of keeping them separate.

"You know, Luca—I've never shared myself with anyone so much as I have shared with you tonight."

"Same here. I've never felt comfortable enough with anyone else—man or woman—to talk about all the things we did."

"I can't believe how much we are alike."

"That's not good, is it?"

"Why not?"

"Because opposites are supposed to attract. Have you ever heard that Identical attracts"?"

"No. But I don't think about that stuff."

"What *do* you think?"

"Right now, I'm thinking about you missing the last train back to Northdale."

"Holy cow! It's almost eleven—the train leaves in less than fifteen minutes. Come on, we have to get you a taxi."

"Never mind that. I can take care of myself—you just catch that train unless you plan to sleep in the Terminal or walk home."

I pulled her in for a quick kiss on her cheek and dashed off toward the train platform.

"Call me tomorrow," she said.

"Saturday morning! I'll call you Saturday morning."

"I'll be waiting."

One minute later, and I would have missed the train. As it were, we waved temporary goodbyes at the Reading Terminal that night. At the same time, we greeted the arrival of a beautiful new beginning to our growing love relationship.

I woke on Thursday morning with renewed confidence that Maria would share her life with me.

At first, I thought about asking Maria to elope, but I wanted her to have a wedding to remember, and I wanted to stand proud in front of my family and friends and proclaim my love for her. If it was puppy love we felt before, I went away—it wasn't puppy love anymore. We had more time than we needed to think about ourselves, each other, and what our futures would be together. We shared a commitment to each other to have a loving, caring family and dedicate ourselves to that purpose. I was ready to take the next step, and I was convinced Maria was prepared for me to make a move. I summoned up the courage to inform her Dad of my plans and hoped he would approve. I took a deep breath, swallowed hard, dropped a dime in the coin slot, and told the operator the number I was calling.

"Marinelli residence. May I ask who's calling?"

"It's Luca, Mr. Marinelli."

The silence was deafening. Nothing in the background I could hear to assure me Mr. Marinelli was still holding the phone. I waited. Nothing. Not a sound. I questioned the wisdom of my call. He must have thought I was the same, young, snot-nose, wise-guy, punk kid he talked to before. I waited the minute that felt like an hour. Finally, I heard the drawing of a long, deep, nose-inhaling breath. Would he allow me to speak, or was he preparing to launch an eardrum-bursting yell?

"Are you calling for Maria?"

"No, Sir. I'm calling for you."

"I got your letters. Is there something more you want to tell me?"

"Yes, Sir, there is. I'm not a wise guy, and I'm sorry for how our last phone conversation ended. I plan to see Maria every chance I get until she says she won't. And I'll be asking her to marry me until she says she will."

Another long silent pause. What more did he want me to tell him? I didn't want to play this silly game. If he wanted to engage in a conversation, why didn't he just do it? Finally, the telephone operator broke the silence.

"Please deposit an additional fifty cents if you wish to continue."

I was not especially happy about paying for nothing, but I dropped two more quarters into the slot and waited—determined to remain silent until he spoke again.

"I had it all wrong, Luca—about you and about the strength of the bond between you, two; I had no idea. It tore me apart to hear Maria sobbing, alone, in her bedroom all the while you were gone. I could sense the pain she wore on her sad face and feel the emptiness in her heart when she told me how much she missed her Prom and missed you every day since. It's pure agony to know how much pain I caused to the person I love and strive so hard to make happy. I'm sorry for that."

"It's a new day, Mr. Marinelli, and another chance for all of us to get it right."

"Welcome home, Luca."

"Thank you, Sir. I'll be seeing Maria a lot in August."

"Don't honk the horn—she won't answer unless you ring the bell."

"I'll never honk the horn for her. Should I wear armor in case you answer the door?"

"No, Luca. You shouldn't. I'm happy you didn't give up on her because of me."

"And I'm happy *she* didn't give up on *me*."

We talked for more than an hour, each sharing our deep-felt feelings for Maria, both coming to a better understanding of the complexity of a man's love for his daughter and a daughter's love for a man. I accepted his protective attitude toward her, and he acknowledged that Maria and I had grown separately into man and womanhood toward our goals and to each other. Our tone was tense at the start of our conversation, but it mellowed with some teasing on both sides, then turned to laughter when he shared similarities of his boyhood days as an immigrant's child.

A few times, we both paused to choke back emotions when Maria's Dad shared memories of his impoverished youth. Poverty, he said, haunted him and drove his will to learn, succeed and protect. From that, I knew that, as much as we were different, we were the same. Near the end of our conversation, he asked if I had proposed to her.

"No, Sir. Not yet. I have too much respect for both of you to ask her before you, and I talked about it."

"I appreciate that. Thank you. When you think the time is right, go for it."

"If it's OK with you—would you mind keeping our conversation between us? Especially about proposing."

"I will. That's a promise. Maria's here. Would you like to speak with her?"

"Yes, please."

"Hold on."

That conversation couldn't have gone any better. I got a surprisingly warm, easy-going, pleasant manner from Mr. Marinelli, and the frozen dry ice he kept between us evaporated.

"Hi, Luca. Dad said he had a nice conversation with you."

"Yep! It couldn't have been much nicer."

"What were you talking about for so long?"

"A bunch of things. Your father told me not to honk the horn for you—like I'd do that."

"That's pretty funny."

"I have a full day tomorrow. Can you meet me at Bennett's on the boulevard between six and six-thirty?"

"Sure. Friday at Bennett's? What's the occasion?"

"No occasion. It's a nice place. I thought it would be fun. If you'd like someplace else, tell me where and I'll be there."

Chapter Twenty-Five
Maria
A Dinging Popover

It was six-fifteen when I arrived at the Greeter's Station at Bennett's.

"Hi. My name is Maria—is anyone waiting for me?"

"Yes. Mr. Romano is seated at table six. Right this way, please."

I followed the hostess to a smaller, more private room away from the crowd in the main dining area. Luca walked toward me as soon as he saw me enter the room, leaned in, kissed my cheek, and pulled the chair away from the table.

"Have a seat."

His eyes sparkled, his grin was ear to ear, and Luca made no attempt to disguise the joy he had on display at that moment. I grinned back at him, straightened my skirt behind me, sat down, looked around the room to see if I knew anyone, and saw our waiter approaching our table.

"Hello, my name is Arthur; I'll be serving you this evening. Mr. Romano has ordered a bottle of Dom Perignon champagne for the table." He showed the label to both of us, thrust it into an ice-filled, silver bucket, draped a white napkin over its neck, and placed the bucket on a stand between Luca's and my chairs.

"Thank you!" Luca and I said in unison.

"Wow! You must be pleased about your new job."

"Right now, I'm happy about everything, and there's no one in the world I'd want more than you to help me celebrate."

"Salute! Cent Anni!"

"Cent Anni!"

We clinked glasses and toasted to our unfolding good fortune and to our future. We gazed at each other, mesmerized by the moment, our surroundings, and the fabulous taste of great wine. Our waiter broke the spell when he apologized for not having delivered our popovers before this. "But the chef has a fresh, warm batch, coming out of the oven in the next few minutes."

Before I could count down the minutes, Arthur was back. He carefully placed a wicker basket covered with a white linen cloth napkin on the table next to me. He pulled a napkin corner to expose four hot, flaky, crispy, and very puffy popovers. "You may want to let them cool a bit." Next, he withdrew the champagne bottle from the ice-filled chrome bucket he had plunged it into earlier. Finally, he poured a glass for each of us. "Enjoy," he said and walked away.

Luca looked at me, smiled, and broke open a popover. Holding his gaze, I smiled back and opened my still warm popover. I heard a ding and felt my jaw drop when I saw a diamond ring bounce off the china bread plate and onto the table. Could it be that Luca had an engagement ring baked into a popover? Who does that? He never looked away from my eyes as he calmly and quietly asked, "Please marry me, Maria."

I wanted to shout yes from the rooftop, but I had so many questions rattling around in my mind starting with whether I should pick up the jewel that dropped from my warm popover. He kept his eyes on my face, reached for my hands, and pulled them on top of the ring. Then he placed his cupped hands over mine and said, "You have questions. Ask them."

"I…I…don't know where to start. I dreamed of this day—I just never dreamed it would be *this* day—it's so sudden."

"Can you picture us spending our lives together?"

"Yes, of course, I already have."

"Can we agree that marriage would be the best way to do that?"

"Yes."

"I love you more than I can say—and more than enough to commit my life to you. Do you love me?"

"I think you know I do."

"Will you marry me?"

"Yes—yes—yes—I will," I replied, in a very high-volume whisper, oblivious to the diners surrounding us. Luca slipped the ring on my finger, stood me upright, and planted a soft kiss—first on my forehead, then one each eye, and, finally, on my trembling, patiently waiting lips. I hardly heard the crowd clapping, whistling, and shouting their Good Luck and Congratulations at us. I wasn't the least bit embarrassed. On the contrary, I was anxious to recover my breath, sit down, and get back to more questions.

"Are we thinking about a long engagement?"

"I wasn't," Luca answered.

"A year?"

"No."

"Two?"

"Next May."

"You can't be serious! We're both so busy, there's so much planning and too much to do, we couldn't possibly do it all; what do you think my dad would say if I tell him I'm getting married in nine months?"

"You don't think I'd ask you to marry me before I asked his permission, do you?"

"He'll want us married by a Justice of the Peace, at The Club—and have the reception there too."

"We talked about that. Your Dad said you'd want a church wedding—probably in a Catholic church, but he hadn't been to church—any church—in years."

"He's right about that. I hadn't been to church either—until I went, occasionally, with your family."

"That's the reason I talked with Father Benedict—he said he'd be happy to officiate the marriage at our church, and the 18th of May could work for him. By the way—your parents are OK with that."

"What about the reception at The Club?"

"We talked about that too. I said my family might be a little uncomfortable in The Club environment—and The Club would, probably, be just as happy without such a loud, rowdy crowd, very much in the mood to celebrate."

"So, what did he say?"

"He said he understood."

"Will they invite anyone from there?

"He said there were lots of people from The Club they were friendly with, but few were close enough to invite to your wedding or the reception."

"How about their families—are any of them invited?"

"That was a little touchy when we talked about that. Your Mom doesn't have any family, and your Dad said, sadly, they lost touch with his side when

181

they were in college. Neither of them went back to their hometowns after their parents died."

"Humph! You'd think I would have known all that—they never talked about any of that stuff with me."

"Did you ever ask?"

"Come to think of it—probably not. So, guests and no reception?"

"Maria—of course, there will be a reception—at The Sons of Italy Hall. So half the people in the community will spend the week before the wedding, making and baking and taking all the food to the Hall—most everyone I know will be coming and going and celebrating with us that night—weddings like that happen a lot in my neighborhood. "

"What did my parents say?"

"They said just the thought of that brought back fond memories of their childhood—they can't wait to celebrate like that again. Mr. Wilson and several couples from The Club are already on the invitation list. Your parents agreed that an old-fashioned, Italian wedding reception could be a fun treat for them too."

"Whew! Luca, I'm exhausted—how did you find time to arrange all this?"

"I make time for the things most important to me, and you are the most important. If you decide against any part of what I've told you, I'll understand; we'll just regroup and try something else. You already agreed to marry me—now, we're just working out the details."

"I'm so overwhelmed, I can't describe how I'm feeling right now. I'm so happy—I want to shout my excitement, but I'm nervous and scared, too. People take months—years even—between an engagement and a wedding."

"Long engagements don't guarantee a successful marriage. Look—yes, we're busy, and there are things we want, need, and expect to accomplish. We can choose to put it all on hold and put our lives, together, on hold, for some unknown, undetermined amount of time. You decide."

"Have you thought about a honeymoon in your plan?"

"Yes, I have—I've been thinking about that for a long time. I want our life to be one, long honeymoon. I know that with you by my side, I'll feel as if I'm always on a honeymoon—I promise to do all I can to make you feel the same way."

"Hmm, so after the wedding, we come back home and get back right to work?"

"No, Crème cake, we go to New York City for a long weekend, then fly to a mystery destination for two weeks."

"You can't be serious, Luca. I've waited too long for this very moment—how it came about is a mystery that I'm already fighting to accept. You can't let my curiosity about our destination dampen my excitement about our honeymoon."

"I'll tell you as soon as I'm sure I can make it happen."

"How do you know I want to go where you're planning to take me?"

"I'd bet my life on it. Trust me."

"I *do* trust you. But you shouldn't bet your life that I'll go anywhere without knowing where I'm going."

"OK. But our two-week honeymoon I'm working on may not even take place—I need some time to find out if my plan can even work. If not, you can choose where we go, how long we stay—up to two weeks—and how we get there. I promise I'll be happy as long as we're together."

"Deal! It sounds like all I have to do is show up at the church."

"No, Hon, all you have to do is believe this is what you want and say, I do."

"*You* are what I want and what I've wanted since you handed me two buttons and a piece of string in a crowded boat on an angry sea in the middle of nowhere."

"Now we're talking. And I wanted you to live rent-free in every corner of my heart from the moment you threw your phone number over your shoulder. But, just so you know, I'm waiting for one more hotel to confirm room reservations for our honeymoon."

"In New York?"

"No, Biscotto. Not New York."

"Please, Luca? Tell me so I can dream about it until then."

"Italy."

He had mentioned the possibility, but I was still a little disappointed when Luca confirmed he would be working at headquarters in New York for the first three weeks every month starting Monday. His schedule was to arrive Monday mornings at noon and finish his week on Friday sometime before 2 p.m. That would allow him time to travel both ways and still have most of the weekend for himself. Then, on the last week of each month, Luca would work at the Northdale facility setting up and receiving parts, equipment, and inventory they deemed necessary for an area service center to have on hand. Despite his nightly calls and reassurances, I missed him terribly and longed for the weeks we could see each other every day for nine days straight.

We both tried to stay upbeat and positive during our nightly phone conversations, so we spent the time talking about our days, sharing stories about the best and worst parts of them. Luca enjoyed every aspect of his job—the challenges, the opportunities, colleagues, the machines he was helping to build, and the potential clients he would be servicing. He was as excited to tell as I was to listen to his vision of his future there. I still liked my job and loved the people I worked with and the patients—many of them who became friends—friends who made me sad to watch them ailing and failing.

On Luca's second weekend home, he came to Philadelphia, and we strolled the streets holding hands, talking about how much we missed each other and probing to find what might make our lives better and how to achieve that. Luca was pleased with the way things were going.

"You used to tell me how much you liked your job—what happened?"

"I don't know. I can never get used to the idea that my patients are at or near the end of their lives. I'm only at the beginning of mine—still full of hopes and dreams. The best I can offer them is a smile, a listening ear, a hand to hold, and, maybe, some pills to make them stop hurting for a little while. That's so hard, sometimes."

"You said you wanted to teach. What would it take for you to do that?"

"Well, I'd have to quit my job, take some Course work necessary to teach the hiring school's curriculum, get certified, accept a salary reduction, and start teaching."

"Otherwise, you're qualified?"

"Yes. My degrees are more than sufficient."

"Would it matter what grades or subjects you taught?"

"Not really, but if I had a choice, I think, I'd like to teach children in the lower grades—say, third to eighth grades. As far as Subjects? Any or all. I've dreamt about making a positive impact on children the way that Sister Verona made on me."

"What do you think about my asking Father Benedict if he has any ideas?"

"I guess it wouldn't hurt, but why him?"

"Because they always need help teaching. Teachers start there then leave for higher-paying public school teaching opportunities. Besides, I'm pretty

184

sure All Saints School doesn't have a legitimate nurse there. As far as I know, they never did. The nuns serve that purpose and do the best they can. I'd bet they'd be thrilled to have you."

"Sure. You can see what Father Benedict says. It will take a little time, you know—months anyway. I'll have to give my notice and get certified."

"That's OK. That will allow you to keep making the big bucks for a while."

"Haha. You're a funny guy. You should mention my high-paying job to my Dad sometime—see what he has to say about that."

Luca was right to talk with Father Benedict. He told Luca about a nun who was on loan from the Archdiocese for the past few years. She currently taught fifth-grade but was nearing retirement, so my starting a few months one way or the other was a non-issue.

A week later, I met with Father Benedict, the school principal, and the retiring nun, Sister Ursula. The meeting was actually a mutual interview. We got to explore each other's personalities, attitudes, and goals. They showed me around—I had to smile, remembering the things Luca told me about his going to school there and Father Benedict's presence on report card days. We reviewed the syllabus, and they informed me of their lack of tolerance for poor behavior and total support for any disciplinary I deem necessary in my classes. Under my breath, I said I hoped there would be no need for corrective action in my class. But, if there were, then I wasn't doing my job as well as I intended.

With so much going on, time was moving so much faster than I imagined it would. But, as Luca suggested, I left the wedding *to-do* list entirely up to him. All I had to do was select my wearing apparel, flowers, bridesmaids, etc. and be at the church on time. He'd make sure there would be groomsmen, a church ceremony, a singer, altar boys, a photographer, and a car to take us from the church to the reception. He promised plenty of seats, food, drink, guests, a short honeymoon in New York City, and a special envelope for the altar boys. "Relax, Maria."

Weeks, months, Thanksgiving, and Christmas all passed. Then, finally, I had my Board Certification to teach at All Saints Parochial School in hand—my plan was to start teaching there the following September. I was happy for the week that slowed between Christmas and New Year—I saw more of my parents and Luca's during that week. In addition, my wedding, which was always at the forefront of my mind, was only five months away. So, for now, I decided to breathe easy, relax, wait for Luca's train to arrive, and enjoy New

Year's evening with him. But, unfortunately, things don't always work exactly as planned.

Luca stepped off the train holding flowers in one hand and a small box of chocolates in the other. I melted into his extended arms for a longer than usual squeeze.

"Hello gorgeous," he said.

"Hi, Hon."

"Whew! You look like you just stepped out of the pages of Vogue."

"You don't look so bad yourself."

"Thank you, I think. Was that a compliment?"

"Yes, it was a compliment."

We left the station and wandered aimlessly through main streets that took us past department stores, taverns, bars, nightclubs, the gas-lit side streets past statues, gardens, and the cobblestone alleys that were back ends of old brownstone residences. During the many leisurely walks I took with Luca, I knew I was in love with him when we first walked without a word between us for long periods. Being together with his hand in mine, breathing only steam into the cold night, was all I needed to feel warm and safe.

"Are you OK, cream cake?"

"Why do you ask?"

"You're extra quiet. There's something's bothering you. I won't pry, but if you let me, I'll help you carry the load—whatever it is."

I had a flashback to the time on the boat when his mother and sister tried to console me on a bad day. He wanted to try, and he taught me how to use buttons to forget my troubles. That was Luca. He never changed. I buried my face in his chest and started to cry.

"Maddie died this morning."

Luca held me close. He offered silence, a hug, and stroked my hair.

"There are times when only love can satisfy a hunger."—Sister Verona.

I had a bittersweet feeling when I told my manager at SSNP that I was leaving the first week of February. I was sitting on the decision fence—staying or following my dream to teach—it fell over when Maddie died. I wasn't anxious to keep making friends with people I knew would leave me sooner than I wanted. However, the job at All Saints was waiting for me, and losing Maddie helped me decide to take it sooner rather than later. Sister Ursula was happy to begin her retirement earlier than she thought. The principal, Sister

Mary Helen, and Father Benedict were also pleased with my announcement to join them as soon as they would have me.

Knowing I planned a three-week vacation following my wedding in mid-May, we all agreed to a start on the Fourth of February. We judged that would allow ample time for me to adjust to my new surroundings and familiarize myself with the school's organization, working parts, history, current plans, and future goals. In addition, my working most of the second semester with Sister Ursula would provide a smooth transition for her and me while preparing me well for the opening session the following Fall.

To help my surroundings feel familiar and I feel welcome and attached, Luca sought and received permission from Father Benedict to allow him and his construction friends to landscape a small area of the field behind the school and twenty yards past the statue of the Virgin Mary. Luca never mentioned that he and his friends provided the materials and used whatever free time they had to work on that project. When it wasn't snowing, it was bitter cold the last half of January, just as it was on that Sunday—the day before my first day of work at All Saints—the day Luca revealed his surprise gift. He walked me around the side of the school that prevented me from seeing the project until we were practically on top of it.

"Maria, I'd like to show you something in the field at the other end of the building."

"It's freezing, and the field is coated with crunchy frozen snow."

"I know, but stay behind me and close to the building where there's hardly any snow."

He was too excited for me to resist, so I lowered my head to brace my face against the wind, held onto his hand, hugged the wall, and walked to the end of the building, where I saw nothing worthy of note.

"Now, stay with me. We'll walk to the end of this wall."

"It would have been quicker to go the other way—wouldn't it?"

"No. There's more snow on the other side. Come on."

I stayed close behind him and next to the wall to the corner. Still, nothing was inspiring to see.

"You don't know it yet, but the second-floor windows that wrap around that corner will be yours to look through starting tomorrow. That's the fifth-grade room."

Luca stopped me before we reached the corner to point out an area cleared of snow and ice.

"See that spot? In the Spring, we will plant grass and sprinkle in some wildflowers. There's also room for two apple and two peach trees. It will take a few years for them to mature, but I think you'll enjoy them even as they grow."

Luca pulled me close, placed his arm over my shoulder, and pointed to a large boulder sitting at the edge of the cleared snow and tamped ground.

"Let's take a closer look at that stone."

The front of the stone was polished flat and engraved. I did all I could to choke back my happy tears and swallow the lump that kept me from saying a word.

"Be patient. Relax. Understand.

Appreciate all that surrounds us.

Live. Learn. Love

And be Kind. Always."

In Honor of Sister Maria Verona OSF

Chapter Twenty-Six
Maria
Never Better

18 May 1946—I will remember it always.

The sun was bright that day, and trees were filled with rainbow colors, and more were on display in all the beautiful May flowers in bloom, reflecting innocence, trust, and friendship. I was on the whitest white single cloud-morphed chariot riding against a periwinkle blue sky.

167 guests were invited to our simple wedding. The first two rows of pews on both sides are usually reserved for the immediate families, but our guests filled in evenly on both sides of the aisle. It would have looked silly otherwise. My complete guest list totaled seventeen—the rest was Luca's family and friends.

Luca chose his brother, Antonio, for Best Man; I picked his sister, Giada, for my Maid of Honor. She wore a robin egg blue A-line dress, matching shoes, and gloves—it was an excellent color for Giada, who looked stunning carrying a small bouquet of mixed-colored roses—pink, white, and blue that matched her outfit. Luca's mother wore navy—mine wore pink. Our fathers, Antonio, Marco, and Luca, were dressed in classic black tuxedos, black cummerbunds, black shoes, black bow tie, black onyx studs, and cufflinks on white-on-white shirts.

I wore a white lace, below knee, cocktail dress with sleeves just past my elbows. I carried the small bouquet of blue roses which accented my sheer, shoulder-length, white veil, attached to a rhinestone crown tiara, white shoes, and wrist-length white gloves. I tucked a tiny white lace handkerchief under my bra strap and pulled a small piece up to the outside top of my dress—just enough for the lace to be visible.

The scene felt surreal when looking at the flowers on the altar, the backs of heads in the crowd, and the priest standing tall in a gold robe draped over a white gown. Father Benedict was holding an open bible, looking at me, and waiting patiently. Giada stood on one side facing Antonio and Marco, and Luca stood facing us, on the other side of the aisle—everyone waiting. Gong. Gong. I heard the church bells—then the organ began playing the Bridal Chorus. Everyone stood up and turned their eyes toward the back. I was standing with my father; altogether, it appeared a fantasy.

"How do you feel, Sweet Pea?"

"Never better, Dad."

"Something old, something new, something borrowed, and something blue." I double-checked the list. I had borrowed a pair of diamond stud earrings from my Ma, carried blue roses, and my entire wedding outfit was new. Lastly, the lace handkerchief that Sister Verona had crocheted for my Communion was old, and it also held the most sentiment. I closed my eyes and placed it under my nose to breathe in the fragrance of lace tinged with salt for having traveled the ocean with me. I could feel Sister Verona's presence and hear her soothing voice calming me, assuring me, "You'll know, Principessa. You'll know."

"I'm all set, Dad."

"You can still change your mind, Sweet Pea."

"Follow your heart, Principessa, follow your dreams; there will be crossroads and choices to make; choose wisely—cross carefully."

"Daa-aad!"

My Dad squeezed my hands firmly and kissed them warmly.

"I'm ready too. Good luck, Sweet Pea. It's time. I love you. Go get 'em."

"Thanks, Dad. Thank you for everything—I love you, too."

I stretched to my tallest height, walked gracefully down the aisle, and smiled broadly at the faint images I saw smiling back at me. Then, gliding through my dream-like state, I saw Luca—bright, bold, strong, loving, and kind. He was my everything—I loved him so much. I finally saw a future—a good one, and I was happy.

"Do you take—better, or worse, richer, or poorer, sickness, and health until death."

"I do."

We were once separated by a few orchards, farms, wood, and a meadow, but each journey began in the same valley. Thousands of miles of ocean connected us and tied us together with two buttons and two pieces of string. Looking back helped show me what to take for our long trip—good deeds, kind words, helping hands, understanding, compassion, and most of all, love.

"I now pronounce you man and wife."

Luca slowly and carefully lifted my veil, he looked into my eyes, held my hands, and planted a feather-soft kiss on my anxiously waiting lips. I had read stories and seen movies capturing scenes like that—images of fireworks, rainbows, waves washing up on soft, white sand, sun setting on calm waters, cupids, shooting hearts, and angels. I felt it all.

Unlike my entrance to the church, where I saw the backs of many heads, there were smiling faces, sparkling eyes, heart clutching arms, and kissing waving hands directed toward us on our exit. Rice and confetti rained on us as we stepped out the door and followed us down the steps and to our waiting car. No limousine or fancy car waited for us. Instead, there were several years old Hudson with dull gray paint, nearly bald white-walled tires, and the back door held open by its owner that stood idle for us. If nothing else, the car was roomy inside. "It's Harry's. He's a good friend of our family," Luca whispered to me. "And he's honored to be our chauffeur today." With that, we were on the way to our reception.

Before my own wedding, I had attended five others with my parents whose friend's children married in the past six years, all formal. The wedding parties were grand and chauffeured in limousines to some country club—if not *The Club*, or to a five-star hotel ballroom. While the photographer took formal wedding pictures of the bridal party, guests mingled in the open spaces between the portable bars set up to provide any drink imaginable. Strategically placed hors-d'oeuvres were there for anyone who missed the waiters serving them. Eight to twelve-piece bands played classical music, jazz, swing, and some pop; the guests danced—waltzed, swayed, slow-danced, and jitterbugged across the floor, always mindful of providing plenty of space for the bride and groom should they happen to be gliding by.

Following the introduction of the bridal party, guests settled down for a many-course meal and jovial conversation. The subdued din of the crowd sounded like that heard in an expensive hotel restaurant. Such was my experience at weddings—that is, until I went to my own, where I had no idea what to expect.

Luca and I arrived in front of the Sons of Italy steps at three-fifteen that Saturday. Luca skooched out first from the back seat of the old, faded gray Hudson Terra-plane, then he reached in to help me out. We were immediately showered with confetti and peppered with rice thrown by the crowd of well-wishers and cheered on by passers-by.

We smiled, waved, ducked, and bounded up the stairs to the entry of the grand ballroom. Actually, it was the Assembly Hall inside the Sons of Italy Club, where most of the guests had already started partying in anticipation of the actual party. There was nothing formal and nothing fancy. A fifty-five-gallon beer barrel sat in one corner of the room for any adult if they chose to draw their own, and next to that, a quarter keg of root beer was placed for the kids.

On the end opposite the entrance, two long, white tablecloths covered a series of tables, placed end to end assembled to look like one long table. Mountains of homemade cookies, cakes, trays of pink and white candied almonds, Italian candy confetti, and assorted sweets fought for every square inch of space on the heavily sweets-laden tables. Two cardboard shipping boxes—each approximately three cubic feet stood at the ends. Each box filled to the brim contained sandwiches—each one carefully made and wrapped by family and friends. Every bun held some portion of capicola, prosciutto, ham, provolone, white American cheese, roasted red peppers, and tomato—except the ones that had "everything". All sandwiches were in fresh-baked, crusty, Italian rolls from Mike's.

Behind and above the sweets tables, the stage could easily hold a fifteen-piece orchestra with space leftover for a ten-person choir. It was more than adequate to accommodate the small, perpetual motion band and random singers that wandered on stage to offer their off-key renditions of songs by Frank Sinatra, Perry Como, Jimmy Durante, Dina Shore, Sarah Vaughn, or the Andrews Sisters.

The band comprised family and friends—Dominic played the drums, Caesar played sax, Stretch on the trumpet, Richie and Jerry on the accordions, and four tambourines passed around in the crowd kept the party lively, swinging, swaying, and bouncing. Most guests liked jitterbug, but the seniors proudly and happily strutted their traditional music and spirited dance—the

Tarantella—for the following generation. The lovers, tuned to the swoon dancing, barely moving, cheek to cheek, eyes closed—and likely, dreaming. A dozen of the youngest children were having the time of their lives—some holding hands in a circle that expanded, collapsed, oscillated, disconnected, reconnected, and repeated its way across the floor until a few girls assembled to whirl, twirl, and send big waves to their Moms. The boys, oblivious to the swirling girls' glances, slapped their sides and galloped across the floor every which way, as their untucked white shirts and blue ties forty degrees off-center flew in the breeze. Little cowboys at a wedding.

As I was scanning the large happy dancing chatting group, I noticed a familiar face walking toward the table where my parent's friends were seated.

"Luca! Look over there. That's Carl Brown at that table with my parents' friends, I almost didn't recognize him—he comes to sing at The Club sometimes, he must have come as their guest."

"Do you know him?"

"Not really, but I know his voice, and it's great. I don't understand why he's not famous—more popular at least—like on the radio or something."

"Maybe he doesn't want to be famous. He might be happy being a club singer. Should I ask him?"

"I don't think so."

"OK. How about if I just request a song for us?"

"Don't you think that would be rude?"

Just as Luca was about to answer, Carl looked in our direction, and Luca waved him over. When he reached our table, Carl put an arm around Luca's shoulder, and they shook hands like loving brothers reuniting after being away from each other for many years.

"Congratulations, Luca. That was a beautiful ceremony at the church. How did you manage to keep this lovely lady a secret?"

"Maria? I'd like you to meet Carlo De Bruno. He grew up in this neighborhood, singing his way from birthday parties to wedding ceremonies into nightclubs, and right out of the area. Someday, if he wants, you'll see him in the movies singing with Doris Day."

Luca turned to Carl and asked if he would sing *that* song for us. Then he took my hand and walked me slowly to the dance floor. Carl walked up onto the stage, accepted the microphone, and said, "Ladies and gentlemen. Please clear the dance floor—this one is for Luca and Maria." He nodded to Caesar, who coaxed his saxophone to play softly behind Carlo's baby-skin-smooth voice. A hush came over the crowd that encircled the empty dance floor. Luca gently pulled me toward him, clasped my right hand softly in his left, and placed his right hand firmly on the small of my back. I wrapped my right arm over his shoulder and closed whatever gap was left between us. I looked up at him, feeling the feather-soft kiss he put on my ear and the heat of our profound love. He whispered, "I love you so much," as Carlo began to sing Al Jolson's Anniversary song.

Oh how we danced—on the night we were wed
We vowed our true love though a word wasn't said.

No words could possibly describe my feelings at that moment. I wanted to be wrapped in Luca's arms forever.

The world was in bloom. There were stars in the skies
Except for the few that were there in your eyes.

I could always see the sky in Luca's deep blue eyes from the moment I saw them. But then, hearing those words sung so soft and lovely, I saw the stars in them too.

Dear, as I held you so close in my arms
Angels were singing a hymn to your charms
Two hearts gently beating were murmuring low
My darling, I love you so.

Luca and I danced cheek to cheek. Slowly. Silently. Then Luca stopped. Looked into my eyes and whispered, "Maria. My darling. I love you so."

I took a long deep breath and let it pass slowly through my pursed lips, trying to keep myself from fainting from emotional overload. Then, with my eyes closed and air seeping through my still puckered lips, Luca bent me slightly at the waist and kissed me. The crowd clapped, raised their glasses, and cheered. I could hear the sounds of metal and glass on glass and shouts of more more more. I didn't faint. Instead, I smiled big and waved at the crowd with both arms. There was no place in the world I'd rather be than among this noisy group of happy people celebrating and welcoming me into their lives.

Luca took me into a dressing room in the Club's basement to change into our street clothes. Then we went back upstairs, thanked our guests, and said our goodbyes before leaving for our overnight stay in Manhattan, then off to Rome the following afternoon.

"Tomorrow will be a long day, sweetbread."

"How long?"

"Well, two hours getting to and from airports on both ends plus ten hours in the air. So that `means we leave our hotel at 2 p.m. Sunday, we should arrive at the hotel in Rome at 6 a.m. on Monday, but it will be 11 a.m. local time. We'll be tired from the long flight, but we have to force ourselves to stay awake until 8 p.m. at least."

All my worrying about needing more time to plan and execute a proper wedding and honeymoon was wasted—everything worked out far better than I ever imagined.

We arrived at the Plaza Hotel in the wee hours of Sunday morning. Even the grass was quietly resting in Central Park when we got there. We checked into our room, threw open the curtains, held hands, and gazed out the window at the city that never sleeps.

"We've come a long way from La Valle, Maria, haven't we?"

"Did you ever wonder how we got here? Together? Married and all?"

"I've thought a lot about that on my long train ride from Florida. How about you?"

"Same. Especially when we were apart, and I was alone and felt so lonely."

"You know what? I fell in love with you the moment you turned your back and threw your phone number over your shoulder."

"Really? What took you so long finding me after that."

"It wasn't easy with you kept safer than the gold in Fort Knox."

"I suppose. And yet, here we are. Thousands of miles from where we started, and still not sure how we got here or where we're going next."

"We talked about this before—it's life, and that's what happens, I guess, and the best we can do is to keep learning as we go along."

"Right! Sister Verona always preached about that—learning a little something from everyone."

"I agree with that completely. My pop used to say if we just mirror the best qualities of others and learn from our experiences—good and bad—we have to strive, always, to reach the best that's in us."

"That's true. I learned the dos and don'ts from Sister Verona, the Marinelli, Sonya, people I met at school, the Club—even you."

"Me too. I think I'm tiny pieces of my family, neighborhood, schoolmates, people I worked for—nice people, and not-so-nice people, like the guy at the golf course, the guy with the Dog sign, and Billy. And their opposites, who are Junkyard Jimmy, Wally Ding-Ding, and the Chocolate Bud Man, the Egg Man, the guy who came around selling bibles, Mike, the Baker, and Mr. Russo, who is still handing out the same free popsicle stick he gave me ten years ago."

"You're lucky you had so many people in your life to help shape you. And most of them are still around. I hope to see Sister Verona again someday."

"When the time is right, we will."

When he said that, I had a fleeting thought that he arranged to see her when we got to Italy. I didn't want to ask because everything he planned and did was perfect from our engagement to this moment. It would be a lot to expect that he, somehow, was in touch with Sister Verona, so I didn't want him to think he disappointed me in any way by asking if we could try to find her. And I didn't.

We had a big day ahead, so we ended our philosophical chat, laid out our travel clothes, showered, and climbed into bed. This was a first for me, so I was a little awkward and embarrassed at first, but it was a fairy tale finish of my storybook wedding to my Charming Prince. I fell asleep wrapped in Luca's arms and woke the same way when Luca whispered, "Good morning, I love you, it's time to get up."

Over our continental breakfast, consisting of a hard roll, boiled egg, slices of meat, cheese, and apple slices, we recounted the events of our wedding, our reception, last night, and how happy we felt about ourselves and our future together. Then, finally, we checked out, took a cab to the airport, waited, boarded our plane, and talked, read, ate, slept, and talked some more on our long trip from New York to Rome.

Luca was right about being tired after our long trip, and when we stepped into the cab taking us to our hotel, I wondered how I could stay awake until evening. As we approached the heart of Rome, the sights smell the noise and chaos of bicycles and scooters squeezing through narrow tunnels created by too many vehicles driving too close to each other startled my senses awake and commanded my complete attention.

"Look, Maria—over there—the Colosseum."

We passed Circus Maximus Vatican City and many other famous streets and points of interest—that our cab driver called to our attention while taking the longest possible route to our hotel. It didn't matter. All of it gripping, breathtaking, and intoxicating. With my eyes open big as pie plates and my manhole-size gaping mouth, I wondered how many days it might take for me to fall asleep.

We spent three days in Rome enjoying everything in front of us—the art and architecture, the culture and cuisine. Then we boarded a train to Florence and stayed three more days where we tasted the clean mountain air that carried earthy fragrances of grapes, figs, almonds, and olives. We walked the streets of Cittevechio, before we left to tour the walled cities of Gubbio, Orvieto and Assisi pausing in restaurants, trattorias, pasticcerias, and street vendors for Linguini con Frutti di mare, Margherita Pizza, Sfogliatella and Gelato.

Monday, we stayed the night in Rome on our way south to Naples. It made me sad to see remnants of the war in Naples—rubble and bullet-pocked buildings brought about by the Greater German Reich. Yet, despite all the hard times past, the city was alive with the same energy we found everywhere else. There were loud conversations across distances, hands waving, men with hands folded behind themselves strolling, women dressed in black hanging out second-floor windows scanning the streets for the vegetable vendor. Smells of garlic, onion, carrots, celery, and tomato sizzling then riding on the warm breeze of a late Spring afternoon in Southern Italy.

Luca signed us up for tours of the area that would take three days to see just the highlights. I was happy he spoon-fed me the itinerary—I would have been overwhelmed if he had told me beforehand the details of all he had planned. Every place Sister Verona took me on imaginary trips was coming alive. To experience them with Luca fulfilled hopes and dreams I only imagined would ever become a reality. I was beyond grateful to Luca for all his thoughtfulness, kindness, and, most of all, for his love.

I was torn between asking him if we could try to find Sister Verona and just continue to enjoy Luca's itinerary being grateful for such a wonderful honeymoon he planned for us. I knew it took a lot for him to put everything into place, and I appreciated every second of being with him in Italy. Still, I felt her presence at every turn and suspected I may never get this close to her again. In the end, I decided to follow Luca's lead.

Our bus took us to Pompeii, Herculaneum, and an assortment of villas buried under the ash of an erupting Mount Vesuvius less than one hundred years after Jesus walked the earth. People, animals, chariots, vegetation, buildings- all buried under molten silica rock. Our excursions through ancient cities kept me excited and yearning to learn more about the history of my birth country. The displayed artifacts verified many of the stories Sister Verona told me about riches, royalty, poverty, peasantry, and the hundreds of people buried under ash—all of it informative and exciting, but it left me kind of sad especially. thinking of the broken-hearted people searching for loved ones safe in the aftermath and finding none.

I didn't know what to expect when Luca and our tour guide told us our trip would take us along the Amalfi Coast for the next few days. But, I was pleasantly surprised to meander the streets of Sorrento and watch the activity of all who lived their days in the quaint and lovely fishing villages. There was fish in the market places on vendor tables in restaurants and menus—more varieties than I recognized prepared cooked and served in more ways than I can count, and tasted far more delicious than I can describe.

The bus took close to an hour to cross the peninsula east and south to San Pietro, then east again to Positano, where we arrived at 7 p.m. That evening we dined in a restaurant featuring homemade pasta and hundred-year-old recipes combining local fish and meats blended with home-grown vegetables and aromatic herbs growing in window boxes everywhere. It was past 11 p.m. when we turned the lights out in our bedroom facing the Bay of Naples.

Chapter Twenty-Seven
Maria
Waiting for Signore Lucci

What a magnificent sight to see the sun inch up through sparkles of light dancing on top and hear sounds of crystal clear blue-green water lapping the shores of the Amalfi Drive, twisting and turning its way up and down the hills through lemon groves and between homes chiseled into the mountains. Breathtaking. We were on the go from the moment we stepped off the plane in Rome. I was still feeling euphoric about my wedding, the reception, and being married to Luca—it seemed to me that soon, there would be no space left in my being to hold any more joy.

We yawned, stretched, and sipped cappuccino on our balcony, quietly overlooking the indescribable beauty of the southern Italian coastline.

"Thank you, Luca. In my best dreams, I have never imagined feeling as I do now. To be in the most beautiful place I have ever seen. To smell the salt air and taste fragrances of tomatoes simmering in sizzled garlic, fresh from the oven-baked crusty bread, crispy coconut almond macaroons, Italian Crème Cake, Espresso, and Limoncello—all of that riding on the air under my nose and me next to the man I will love forever."

"I don't think I can top that, Cannoli. But I'll see what I've got. But, first, we've got to make our way down to the beach. We have tickets for the 11 o'clock Ferry to take us to a small island for the day. There were two to choose from: Ischia and Capri; I chose Capri.

The ferry ride to Capri was spectacular, especially for allowing a view of the mountains, homes, and greenery from the seaside. Capri was yet another charming town with all the beauty and every culinary delicacy that seemed to follow us throughout our trip. I was trying to absorb it all when Luca pulled me toward the funicular that would take us to Anacapri at the top. As we rode up the hill, looking down at the town and across the blue-green water, I looked at Luca and smiled. I was thinking of Sister Verona's favorite saying, "Relax, Principessa. See the beauty all around you. Let your life unfold as it will."

We spent a few hours sightseeing, sipping, tasting, and eating our whole way through Capri. Then Luca told me he hired a small boat and a man to take us around the island to the Blue Grotto, a sea cave not too far from the coastline. Once again, I was curious to learn what could be more fascinating than the three massive rocks we passed on the way to the grotto. As the boat slowed and we entered the cave, I sat mesmerized by the early evening light reflecting from the clear azure blue water. For a moment, I imagined heaven to be exactly like this—what could possibly be better? Finally, I snuggled close to Luca and rested my head on his shoulder. I was warmed by his hands gently pushing my hair aside when he put his lips close to my ear and whispered,

"Maria, honey. I have a surprise for you."

"Haha. You're funny. Every part of this fantastic trip you planned has been one big surprise after another. Whatever it is—I'm sure I will be happy about it."

"I hope so. This one can go either way, and you're the only one who can decide whether you even want it."

"That's an interesting comment—have I ever been disappointed in any of the many surprises you handed me since we met?"

"Well, this one is a little different."

"I was willing to wait and see but, now, I'm curious. What's going on?"

"Let's wait until we get back to shore. Then, we'll stop somewhere for a bite to eat and a cappuccino—I'll explain."

"How about finding a quiet spot along the beach where we can be alone under the stars with only the sound of splashing water to distract us."

"Perfect."

We found a small path that started on the main road, where the bus dropped us off earlier, leading to a cluster of rocks at the shore's edge. Luca took my hand in his, and we walked silently to the flattest rock and sat on it. Luca took a deep breath and let it slap at his lips on the way out."

"Maybe it wasn't my place to get involved in your business but, before I left Europe, I located a phone number for Signore Lucci. So I called and tried to talk with him about Sister Verona. Please forgive me if I overstepped my bounds."

"Heavens, no! I asked my parents to try and find them. Even with help from their professional friends, we had no luck in tracking them down. I gave up hope of ever seeing either of them again. What did he say? How is she? Where are they? Will we have a chance to see her? Why didn't you tell me until now?"

"I knew you'd have lots of questions. So I'll answer as many as I can, starting with why I didn't say anything until now. The first time I spoke with Signore Lucci, he remembered my family and me when I went into his fields with my father and brothers. So when I told him I was inquiring about Sister Verona for you, he got upset and told me he wasn't interested in helping me make a path for you to see her."

"Why? He seemed to like me when he drove me to the pier in Naples. We even stayed at his brother's family's house the night before we left for America."

"I know, you told me that but, he said you disrespected him and Sister Verona when you failed to let her know when you arrived."

"And that was a mistake I've regretted ever since."

"I'm sorry, Hon. I didn't intend to open old wounds or dampen the fantastic time we've had these past eleven days, but I thought neither of us would be happy if we didn't try to find her while we were this close."

"Are you saying we can't?"

"I'm saying our only hope is with Signore Lucci's help, and I'm still unsure if he is willing to provide that."

"What do we have to do to find out?"

"Signore Lucci has agreed to meet us tomorrow morning if you feel up to it. He gave me the name of a hotel in Naples where we could talk and have breakfast with him. Depending upon how the conversation goes, he may be willing to help you meet with Sister Verona. However, he prefers to speak with you alone."

I had to let that settle in my mind before I addressed Luca's comments. But first, I needed to understand the reason for Signore Lucci's request to meet me alone. I could think of no reason to exclude Luca.

"No! I'm not doing that."

"Maria, I gave him my word that you'd be there."

"And I will—with you by my side. We promised each other there would be no secrets between us. This meeting with Sister Verona—if it happens—

may cause changes in me that may affect both of us. So if Signore Lucci refuses to grant my request to have you there, then he can eat his breakfast by himself."

"Don't be stubborn, Creme cake. You'll be the loser unless you're willing to turn your back on Sister Verona forever."

"I don't believe that Signore Lucci is that heartless. If he agreed to meet me and lead me to Sister Verona, I'm sure he spoke to her about it first. By failing to arrange a visit with her, Signore Lucci would be crushing my hopes and hers. He talks about getting respect. Let's see if he's willing to give me some."

"OK. Let's go for it."

We arrived at the hotel in the outskirts of Naples at 8 a.m. on Friday morning. It was smaller than I expected—sandwiched between two taller buildings with the front door opening into a small reception area. A lone clerk stood behind the desk, and a wooden board hanging on the sidewall with eight metal skeleton keys hung loosely on hooks. Next to the hanging hooks, a closed door opened to a medium-sized area where breakfast was available for hotel guests. The smell of strong coffee seeped into the reception room and invited us in but not before the clerk on duty checked our credentials.

"May I see your passports please? Do you have reservations?"

We presented our passports and told the clerk we had no reservations but expected to meet Signore Lucci this morning.

"Ah. Yes, of course. Signore Lucci is inside. I will show you to the table."

Luca turned to me and said he should go in first. I disagreed and said we'd go in together or I would go alone as Signore Lucci requested. I went in alone.

"Buongiorno, Signore Lucci. I am Maria Romano."

"Yes, I was expecting you. Please be seated."

"Signore Lucci. With all due respect, I'd like my husband to join us—he's waiting in the lobby."

"As you are aware, life sometimes denies us the things we'd like most to have. Please sit so we can talk about it."

I stood face to face with him, each of our eyes searching for something in the others. Neither of us sat. I intended to neither offend him nor appear defiant, but I wanted to know what Signore Lucci had to say to me that he wished to keep from my husband. I decided to ask.

"Signore Lucci. I am most grateful for your willingness to meet with us this morning, just as I am for your care in taking me to the pier in Naples. You and your family were gracious and kind."

"Please, Signora. I did not come here looking for thanks from you. However, there are more important things to discuss than a car ride and some courtesies extended to you. So I'd like to get on with that if you would kindly be seated."

"Yes. I must apologize and make amends for some poor behavior on my part—and I intend to do that. But I want my husband with me when I do. There's nothing about this that he doesn't already know."

"Perhaps so. My intent is only to spare you the embarrassment if our conversation becomes difficult."

"If embarrassment is my penalty for having my husband at my side, then I accept that."

"I will allow Signore Romano to join us if he remains silent, but if we should come to agree that a visit with Sister Verona would benefit her, you must agree to visit her alone."

"What if Sister Verona wishes to meet my husband?"

"I doubt that, but of course, if that is *her* wish, it will be granted."

Signore Lucci walked to the door to wave Luca inside while I sat down in the seat he suggested. They walked across the hall to our table without sharing a word. The men sat, and Signore Lucci spoke first.

"You destroyed Sister Verona's spirit, broke her heart, and left her alone and lonely."

"She did the same to me."

"Your insolence will dictate the length of time I am willing to spend with you."

"I'm sorry, Signore Lucci, but she turned her back on me when she sent me to America. I was bitter."

"What was most bitter for you—trading life in an orphanage for a stable home with loving parents? Exchanging a maximum of six grades elementary schooling for a university degree? Two degrees, I understand."

Everything he said was right, and I knew it. Judging by his questions and the way he looked at me, I felt that he, or someone, had been watching over me the whole time—even though no one came forward or provided me with a link back to him, Sister Verona, or my roots. I *was* embarrassed by my selfish attitude. I wanted to interrupt and scream my regrets and apologies, but he wouldn't let up.

"Replacing a life of poverty with one of possibility and wealth? Did she send you to an orphanage? Was a good home arranged for you, or did she ask you to fend for yourself? Tell me, Signora. What was so bitter to swallow that you couldn't do the one thing she asked from you?"

"I was ten years old. I was scared. I didn't know what was going to happen to me."

"What did you think would happen to you if you dropped a stamped, self-addressed envelope in a mailbox? That's all Sister Verona asked of you."

"I didn't have it when I arrived at Philadelphia. In my anger, I tore it up on the boat and lived to regret that ever since."

"So you went to America and lived in a fine home. You enjoyed the benefits that came with successful, well-paid professionals—you were well educated, found meaningful work, fell in love, and got married. Is that right?"

"Yes."

"While you were away doing all that, Sister Verona experienced the ravages of war and the loss of her family and friends in two devastating earthquakes—even Mother Superior died in the second earthquake. Two days after she died, rescuers found Sister Verona buried under piles of rubble, whispering prayers pleading for the well-being of others. I visited her several times a week—more whenever possible. Very often, she doesn't speak—she sits and stares at the rosary beads she keeps wrapped around her hands. She prays—primarily for you, your safety and well-being."

I wanted to stand and shout STOP! But I couldn't swallow—tears were streaming down my face—I clutched my folded hands and placed them between my knees and squeezed them tight. My body trembled, my shoulders moved up and down as I sobbed uncontrollably. Luca put his arms over my shoulders without uttering a word.

"Please," I sobbed. "I'm so so sorry. Please, Signore Lucci, lead me to Sister Verona—wherever she is."

"She's where you left her. Unfortunately, the orphanage was destroyed during the war. My family rebuilt the structure after the second earthquake—it now serves as a sanitarium."

"We have only today and tomorrow before we must return to America. Will it be possible to see her before we leave?"

"You may want to reconsider your quest to reunite with her."

"Why would you say that?"

"It's hard to know how she will react. She may or may not speak or even recognize you after all this time."

"But I believe it will be a good reunion. If Sister Verona prays for me as you say, then why wouldn't she be happy for my visit?"

"I can't speak for her, but I can assure you—if I were her and in the same situation, I would damn you to hell before I gave you one second of my time."

I bit my tongue and suppressed my urge to lash out, arguing my defense. I would have regretted whatever anger spewed from my loose lips. "Words can be hurtful, Principessa. Choose them carefully—you can never unsay them. Like feathers in a pillow…"

To my surprise, Signore Lucci handed Luca a piece of paper with a telephone number scribbled on it.

"Call me at this number. It will ring in my office, which is near the sanitarium. I'll stop in on Sister Verona and tell her that you are both in Italy and request her permission to visit with you. I'll be in my office at 3 p.m. I'll let you know either way what I find—call me then."

With that, Signore Lucci left us to wait and wonder what would happen next.

Chapter Twenty-Eight
Maria
Stories and Rocks

Luca and I left the small hotel and for hours, walked the streets and back alleys of the little town stopping in the small boutiques and coffee shops to help unburden our thoughts of a failed endeavor. But hard as we tried to avoid it, our conversation constantly looped back to our meeting with Signore Lucci.

"I was so selfish and wrong. I should have mailed that envelope."

"I know, creampuff. You said that at least a hundred times since we met."

"But it's true. So Signore Lucci was right in scolding me."

"I thought he was harder on you than he should have been. He didn't have to keep at you. There was no need for him to bring you to tears. I felt so bad for you."

"You didn't have to. I was feeling pretty bad for myself until I accepted the fact I was totally wrong."

"You were only ten years old, for crying out loud."

"That's just an excuse."

"It seems to me that they could have found you if they wanted."

"Right! Somewhere between helping orphans and staying alive through war and two earthquakes, they could have set up a search party for some spoiled Italian-American kid too spiteful and lazy to drop an envelope into a mailbox. Who knows, maybe they did?"

"Are you going to be a martyr the rest of your life and carry that passionate feeling of guilt over a mistake you made fourteen years ago?"

"No. I already apologized to Signore Lucci. I know he's a kind and compassionate man despite all the barking you heard this morning. I would be surprised if he does less than his best to reunite us."

"I hope you're right."

"Trust me. I am right on this one."

"Then how about this? If, as Lucci said, Sister Verona is where you left her, then we know she's in La Valle. So let's go there now—to La Valle. We'll call Signore Lucci from there at 3 p.m. So, if the way for you to see Sister has been cleared, maybe, you can see her today *and* tomorrow."

"Let's do it."

"What if he says no?"

"No harm done. We tried our best. I will accept whatever happens and move on from here."

We arrived in La Valle at 2 p.m. We looked down at the valley from a streetside hilltop, scanning the entire area from west to east. We assumed the approximate locations of Luca's boyhood home and the orphanage. What we saw only vaguely resembled what we remembered from our childhood. We saw a few vineyards here and there, and the smell of grapes from last year's harvest lingered in the air. But the vast area of plowed fields and patches of orchards were missing. Instead, creases in the earth, rock formations, and broken homes littered large spaces—all reminders of the damage wrought by war and earthquakes. We stood staring for a while—silent and saddened by the difference between what we remembered and what was.

"I guess we were the lucky ones, Luca."

"I'll say. We got to the land of opportunity on the sweat, determination, hopes, and dreams of the people who loved us. It's getting time to make the call, Cannoli."

We walked back to the hotel we had seen earlier that had a telephone. Luca dialed the number, and Signore Lucci picked it up after the third ring.

"Pronto."

"Giorno. Sono Luca."

"I sat with Sister Verona for several hours today. I told her about our meeting and how sad and sorry Maria felt that she had failed to notify on her arrival in America. I also mentioned that I reprimanded Maria for that. She let me go on for an hour and never spoke until I made Maria's request to visit. 'Yes,' she said. 'The poor girl has been through so much. It will be my privilege to offer her some comfort.'"

"Thank you, Signore Lucci. That's great news. When?"

"Tomorrow morning—if you can make it."

"We can make it right now. We're here in La Valle—at the Centro Storico."

"I'll pick you up from there in fifteen minutes."

When Luca finished the phone call and told me every detail, I melted into his arms—my favorite place, in good times and bad, better or worse, forever.

It was less than a fifteen-minute drive to the Sanitarium. Along the way, Signore Lucci reiterated that he wanted me to see Sister Verona alone—at least at first, and told me I should move slowly with Sister Verona, that she may not speak and that I shouldn't try to force her. He didn't want to upset her for any reason. I wouldn't do that—never again, not after the last time.

I saw the building first as we approached the Sanitarium—it looked vaguely similar to the one I remembered. But, as we moved closer, I noticed the surroundings were different, too—nothing was the same as I remembered. "Nothing lasts forever, Principessa. Things change and, when it becomes necessary, we must change accordingly."

Signore Lucci drove to the far end of the building to a path leading to the front gate and an open area. In the field, young fruit trees scattered about—planted to replace the ones that stood for decades and were swallowed twice by earthquakes. Then, off in the distance, I saw a silhouette—the only image remaining in my mind that I remembered that was real, that I could touch, and that stood waiting for me less than twenty yards away. It was the side profile of a nun wearing a black habit with a white bib. She was sitting on the edge of a large gray stone near a small cluster of young apple trees. Her head was bent slightly. Rosary beads encircled her clasped hands.

"Go ahead, Maria. She's waiting for you," Signore Lucci assured me.

I strolled slowly toward the waiting image, not wanting to startle her. Yet, I wanted to shout, just as I had when I was a kid, excited and anxious to see her, "Sono qui—sono qui" and to hear her reply, "Benvenuto!" I strayed to my left off the path, so I would become more visible as I approached her. I was less than ten feet away from her when she looked up. She stood up, and I kept walking softly toward her.

"Sono qui—sono qui. I'm here—I'm here," I said.

She replied, "Benvenuto a casa!—Welcome home."

All my worries, fears, concerns, and doubts I had about losing my place in Sister Verona's heart disappeared when she cradled my face in her hands, looked straight into my eyes, and whispered feather-soft, "I'm so happy to see you here, safe, well, and beautiful. You have grown to be a Queen, Principessa."

"I'm so sorry, Sister—for the mean things I said to you and for not mailing the envelope you gave me. That was so wrong. Will you forgive me?"

"Shh. There's nothing to forgive. You were a child behaving like a child."

"Maybe so, but it makes me sad to think of all you did for me and to know of all you have suffered since we were last together."

"All of that has passed, Principessa. We can't change any of it. Neither the past nor the future is ours to live. We have only now to live, to love, and to appreciate all the beauty that surrounds us."

I lost all track of time and the sense that Luca and Signore Lucci were waiting for me. I had fourteen years of my life to cram into my conversation with Sister Verona, and I tried hard to apologize more, explain, show, and tell more. But Sister Verona was having none of that.

"Sister. Soon it will be time for me to leave. Would it be ok for me to come back tomorrow to continue our conversation?"

"I'm sorry, Principessa, but that will be most difficult for me. Besides, before you leave today, I'm sure both our needs for this meeting will be satisfied."

"Would you mind if I asked Signore Lucci for a little more patience in waiting for me? Also, I'd like to introduce my husband to you—he's with Signore Lucci."

"Please do, Principessa. I will be here."

I raced back to the car and hurriedly explained the unexpected turn of events in my reunion with Sister Verona. Signore Lucci said they would "of course" wait. He suggested that Luca walk back with me but make his stay short, leaving me with more time alone with Sister. Then he turned to me and said, "Please don't say I told you, but our friend has been diagnosed with terminal cancer. All her caring physicians anticipated her life to end a month ago. Perhaps it's silly to say, but I believe she has been waiting for this day. Go on."

"Sister. This is my husband, Luca Romano. Luca? Please greet Sister Verona."

"It's my great pleasure and honor to meet you, Sister. Maria has told me so much about you—I feel I know you."

"Likewise—Signore Lucci has spoken many times of your loving, hard-working family. I was pleased to learn that Maria has found a warm heart to beat next to hers."

Sister asked, and Luca told her about meeting me on the boat to America and how we met again years later. I filled her in briefly about circumstances that separated again then put us back together—I gave her the highlights that led to our marriage. Forty-five minutes later, Luca expressed his thanks, bid farewell to Sister Verona, and left us alone to finish our conversation.

"I wish I could stay here with you forever, Sister."

"That's nice to say, Principessa, but that was never meant to be. When I left my parents, my father gave me wings to find my place in the world and anchored me to his home that always welcomed me. This is the same, Principessa."

"But I never had a home where I was anchored."

"It's life, Principessa, and this is how ours have unfolded. You were anchored to my heart. This is why you're here today. "

Sister Verona's voice was calm, soothing, and confident as she continued to indulge me with her love and worldly wisdom. Down deep, I knew how much she cared for me, and in her presence, I felt the inseparable bond she had created for us the moment she held my infant self close to her heart. I had never left her, and she had never left me.

I told her a little about my work with seniors facing the end of their lives.

"It's good that they had you to touch them with your kindness in their last days."

"Whatever comfort I have given them, they have returned tenfold."

…and about my new job teaching ten-year-old children.

"Ten-year-olds. You must remember how precious and fragile they can be. Yet, I know their lives will be enriched having you to mentor them."

Wrapped up in our conversation, hanging on to her every word, I didn't notice she had gotten frail and that her once smooth face was creased—it looked strained with worry over troubles her life had presented, but her heart and soul and spirit remained intact. She was getting tired and needed rest. Our meeting, no doubt our last, was coming to a close. I showed her a picture of All Saints Elementary School and pointed to the second-floor window in the room where I was teaching. Then I showed her the landscape, the rock Luca had placed, and the inscription on the face. A tight smile and a single teardrop suggested she was pleased.

"You can see that now each of us has a Story Rock," I said, waiting for her to express some feeling of accomplishment. I thought, perhaps, she would say she was pleased to know I planned to carry her storytelling to American children and that she was responsible for a tradition I hoped would be long-standing in her memory. I should have known she would use our time together as her final teaching moment.

"I see that we have a symbol, Maria—a touchstone, a reminder of all the things we've learned or have yet to learn there. But the real *story* is our lives—it has joined us, nurtured us, taught us, made us realize the importance and strength of honest, open, trusting relationships. It provided us with experience. Our experiences enabled us to appreciate delicious food and beautiful art and culture, the gifts of birds and flowers, the sea and sky, the sun and moon, the seasons, and all our senses that allow us to know such magnificence.

"Our story has taught each of us about acceptance, appreciation, kindness, compassion, and understanding. These are qualities that form our character and allow us to get along in the world. And, most importantly, we learned about love—the love we have for ourselves and the love we share with those around us. That, Principessa, is what we learned, and *that* is: The Rock in our Story."

Afterword

Signore Lucci had alluded to it—Sister Verona couldn't hide it, but I knew she was breathing for *me only* from my days working with hospice patients. Several times as I held her hand and rubbed her arm gently, I whispered softly that it may be time for me to summon a nurse.

"No, Principessa. I promise. I'll let you know when it's time for you to go."

I tried once more to apologize for acting as I had when I left the orphanage, but she wouldn't hear of it. So instead, she turned the conversation to the many other beautiful times we shared—the times we giggled and laughed and twirled and danced on stars, picked flowers, and slid down rainbows. She was happy to listen to me talk about Luca, his big family, and their love for each other that helped draw me to him. Her eyes twinkled hearing about my growing out of school uniforms and into my graduation and wedding gowns, and I was content revisiting the scores of imaginary trips she planned for me and planted in my mind.

I told her I was grateful for having her guidance which ultimately led me to meet and fall in love with Luca. She said she believed I was well suited to be an exceptional wife, teacher, and mother—if I were blessed with our own children. I pray she was right.

"Before you go, Principessa, I'd like you to have this. It's a poem that my father bought and framed for me when you were just four years old. I intended to put it in your suitcase, but in all the confusion, I forgot. I'm so happy about your visit. Thank you, Principessa. I love you. I think it's time for you to go."

We embraced, and I held on until I felt her arms loosening. "Spread your wings, Maria, and fly. Let your keen mind and loving heart take you where they will. Arrivederci, Principessa."

That was the last time I saw Sister Verona. A telegram from Signore Lucci was waiting for me when I got home. He was with her when she died peacefully in her sleep. She wanted me to know that I had lived in her heart my entire life.

The framed poem she gave me hangs on the wall next to our bed. I picture her at night and in the morning when I wake. I hear her voice and wisdom in the exact words she has spoken to me since I was a child. "Arrivederci, Sister Verona, Un milione di grazie."

Desiderata

Max Ehrmann 1927

Go placidly amid the noise and the haste, and remember what peace there may be in silence.

As far as possible, without surrender, be on good terms with all persons.

Speak your truth quietly and clearly; listen to others, even the dull and ignorant; they too have their story.

Avoid loud and aggressive persons; they are vexatious to the spirit.

If you compare yourself with others, you may become vain or bitter, for always there will be greater and lesser persons than yourself.

Enjoy your achievements as well as your plans.

Keep interested in your own career, however humble; it is a real possession in the changing fortunes of time.

Exercise caution in your business affairs, for the world is full of trickery. But let this not blind you to what virtue there is; many persons strive for high ideals, and everywhere life is full of heroism.

Be yourself. Especially do not feign affection. Neither be cynical about love; for in the face of all aridity and disenchantment, it is as perennial as the grass.

Take kindly the counsel of the years, gracefully surrendering the things of youth.

Nurture strength of spirit to shield you in sudden misfortune. But do not distress yourself with dark imaginings. Many fears are born of fatigue and loneliness. Beyond a wholesome discipline, be gentle with yourself.

You are a child of the universe no less than the trees and the stars; you have a right to be here. And whether or not it is clear to you, no doubt the universe is unfolding as it should.

Therefore be at peace with God, whatever you conceive Him to be.

And whatever your labors and aspirations, in the noisy confusion of life, keep peace in your soul. With all its sham, drudgery, and broken dreams, it is still a beautiful world. Be cheerful. Strive to be happy.

Printed in the USA
CPSIA information can be obtained
at www.ICGtesting.com
LVHW020321080923
757248LV00007B/110